A  M A N  and  a  W O M A N  and  a  M A N

# A MAN and a

 O M A N

## and a M A N

*a novel by*

# SAVYON LIEBRECHT

**Translated from the Hebrew by Marsha Pomerantz**

**A Karen and Michael Braziller Book**
PERSEA BOOKS / NEW YORK

First published in the original Hebrew in 1998 by Keter (Jerusalem).
Published in the English language in 2001 by Persea Books (New York).

Copyright © 1998 by Savyon Liebrecht

English translation copyright © 2001 by Persea Books, Inc.

Worldwide translation copyright © 1998 by
The Institute for the Translation of Hebrew Literature

Persea Books, Inc.
171 Madison Avenue
New York, New York 10016

Library of Congress Caaloging-in-Publication Data

Liebrecht, Savyon, 1948-
   [Ish ve-ishah ve-ish. English]
   A man and a woman and a man : a novel / by Savyon Liebrecht ;
translated from the Hebrew by Marsha Pomerantz.
     p. cm.
   ISBN 0-89255-266-2 (alk. paper)
    I. Pomerantz, Marsha.

   PJ5054.L444 I7513 2001
   892.4'36—dc21                       00-069226

Designed by Rita Lascaro. Typeset in Fairfield.
Printed on acid-free, recycled paper.
Manufactured in the United States of America.

First Printing

# A MAN and a WOMAN and a MAN

# CHAPTER ONE

"It's me, Mother—Hamutal."

She was standing by the glass door, pulling her scarf tight before venturing into the wind, when the nurse's aide shouted after her: "Excuse me, Shifra's daughter, do me a big favor if you're going now. You see that man in the green jacket? Get a hold of him and tell him his father's diapers are all used up." She added: "Thanks such a million."

Hamutal, suddenly recalling the days when she was "Shifra's daughter," turned her head and peered past the edge of her scarf at the aide.

"Size Maxi, tell him to bring some today, if you don't mind, otherwise first thing tomorrow. He got so thin and all, with the Super Maxi everything leaks out."

And that's how it began.

In the parking lot outside the nursing home, beside his car with the newspapers tossed onto the back seat, in front of the building whose windows watched them like dozens of pairs of eyes, with wind whipping the edges of her scarf to her right, his collar to his left. There they stood, face to face. She'd seen him opening the car door and rushed to call him before he got away: "Excuse me, please," and then when he looked up and saw her running toward him, waving her arms, he straightened up and waited, like someone expecting a bearer of bad news.

At that moment she couldn't find the words.

"I . . . the aide asked me to tell you about . . . uh, your father . . . "

Only then did she take in the full meaning of what she'd been asked to relay. And she saw him standing there, waiting, very serious, inclining his head like a tolerant doctor toward an annoying patient, regarding her with indulgent curiosity, as if to say, "What was that stupid running all about, and now this stuttering?" She said, embarrassed, feeling her color rise, feeling a glimmer of anger over this mission she'd been asked to carry out, intruding on a stranger, bringing this mortifying moment on herself. "The diapers . . . that is, she asked, the aide asked if you could do it today . . . he's running out of diapers . . . and you have to . . . bring him Maxi . . . because with the Super Maxi everything . . . the Super Maxi no longer fits."

They stood for a moment on either side of the sentence, two people dressed with a certain elegance, one clutching the collar of his jacket, the other the ends of her scarf, witnesses to the absurdity and the terror, the futility and the despair in the sentence suspended between them, as if for one moment a screen had dropped and revealed to them with rare clarity the world as it was and themselves as they were: two strangers in an accidental place at an unexpected time, exposed together to something that inexplicably breached their anonymity, so that the pretense with which they daily adorned themselves was suddenly uncalled for. It was as if, in the game everyone played according to familiar rules, they were starting in new positions.

He said, "Thank you very much," his look free of arrogance, and she, glad that she had washed her hair after all before coming to visit her mother, said in a mild voice, "You're welcome," and turned to her car, with its toys scattered on the back seat and its stickers on both bumpers that read LET ANIMALS LIVE.

They got into their cars and went their separate ways.

"What's with the philosophical look?" Her husband aimed a wedge of pear at her and she opened her mouth, fishlike. Then she remembered the nursing home and took the wedge from his hand.

"I went to see my mother today." She dodged his hand, which was moving another wedge toward her mouth.

"The pears are too hard." He ignored what she said and raised the wedge level with his eyes.

"She recognized me immediately and kept pleading with me to take her home," she continued, ignoring his attempt to move the conversation away from the nursing home. "But there was someone there in worse shape. A man with blue eyes. In diapers. Imagine, a man in diapers. He was lying there staring at the doorway without blinking. His son was there—"

"Before I forget, our daughter left a note saying she was going to Semadar's after dance class."

"He was a good-looking man, if the son is any indication. Must have had lovers"—she didn't know why she said what she said—"and to think that this man is lying there now with strange women changing his diapers—" She was silent.

"So?"

"Can you picture anything more horrible than that?"

"Yes."

"No you can't."

"Actually it could be quite enjoyable." He dropped onto his back, flailing his arms and legs like an infant on a changing table.

"You are so warped." But she was amazed at the way he'd managed to extract a laugh from her.

"That reminds me of the nurse we had in high school. Have I ever told you about the school nurse?"

"I don't remember."

"They said she was from Finland. A real beauty, like on the cover of those noir novels, looking as if she just that second got out of a warm bed, you know the type? Kind of rosy. We used to wait for her between periods and follow her down the hall. I spent whole classes daydreaming that a snake bit me and they took me to the nurse's office and she had to take off all my clothes to find the wound. Why this mysterious smile?"

"You should have brought the snake to school yourself." She'd forgotten about the nursing home.

"Now that's an idea."

"Since statistically speaking, the probability that a snake would turn up at your particular school and bite you in particular—"

"Too bad I didn't know you then. You've got such a practical approach."

"To make fantasies come true you have to be practical."

"This is a rule?"

"Yes. Otherwise you'd never succeed in deluding yourself."

"That means," he said carefully, "am I to understand from this—"

He was crossing a line that had blurred between them in the last few months. With light banter they still sometimes managed to imitate the old, familiar ease, but this was an attempt to inject something they knew for its simplicity into what had now become complicated. Unsure where he was aiming the sentence, she did her best to keep the game going and maintain the blithe tone: "Why, certainly."

"If so," he said, "might I hope that you won't fall asleep on me tonight before—"

Now she had no doubt where he was headed, and to overcome her awkwardness she surrendered to the wave of gaiety: "Might I remind you that the carpenter was here today and walked off with the door because of the hinge problem?"

"We won't let hinges get in our way."

"And where will we find a snake?" There was a momentum to affected merriment.

"I'm willing to stand in for now."

"And the Finnish nurse?"

"She must be in the nursing home herself. You can take her place."

They kept their voices low that night, conscious of the girls across the hall, and pretended that everything was as usual, the way they had during the evening's amusing conversation, which recalled but did not revive something of substance that they had shared until about three months ago. Even if they could both sense other, subterranean currents revealing themselves in their bodies' involuntary movements—inept liars that bodies are—they could still pin the blame on the missing door.

And all that time—even as, with eyes half-shut, she murmured the usual nothings in Arnon's ear—the wraith-like old man in diapers was with them, a pale presence lying at the foot of the double bed, fixing stricken eyes on the doorway that gaped through the darkness toward the hall, as a foul liquid trickled slowly from the gap between his chalky, withered thigh and the gathered plastic edge of the diaper into a sticky pool around his haunches, staining the elegant irises outlined on the sheet.

Once, she was certain, beautiful women had lain beside him; now he was shrinking day by day, lying motionless in the room opposite her mother's, and soon would need an even smaller size. She dived under the blanket, pulling the irises up to her eyes, suddenly aware that the man in the green jacket had also been in the room with them the whole time, never taking his eyes off her, somberly observing her every move while considering where he might find his father size Maxi that night.

The next day, still disturbed by the awkwardness that had accompanied the sex with Arnon, by the memory of a body obeying like a bored but assiduous student, she sat in her office confronting the images that Noa, the graphic designer, was stacking on her desk, saying: "Let's go with Dalí, Max Ernst, and Frida Kahlo—and maybe van Gogh. Those seem most suited to the subject. I'd love to put in Magritte, but they warned me not to go near him—his work is handled by hysterical agents who charge a fortune for rights. So I'll do without those, much as it hurts. Look at this one: it would be terrific with the dream about the woman and two men in Noah's ark. A Dalí landscape."

Hamutal looked carefully at the picture, her eyes sweeping past the black islands that floated up in the distance out of pale water, past the figures and the angel standing at the edge of a cliff, to concentrate on one stone in the wall, focusing on the marginal detail as if a camera had been mounted in her pupils and was zooming in for a close-up.

"What is it, Hamutal?"

Hamutal grasped the print with both hands, understanding suddenly why her eyes were drawn to the stone:

it was the same green as the jacket of the man who was sent to get diapers for his father.

She put the picture down slowly, aware of an urgent, certain, clamorous excitement stirring in her, aware also of the insistent tone in Noa's voice, asking again:

"What's going on with you, Hamutal?"

"Nothing's going on." Hamutal caught Noa's inquiring glance, remembered the nursing home, and shook herself.

At that moment the secretary's metallic voice came over the intercom: "Sorry to bother you, Hamutal, but your daughter's here."

"Who?" She realized she wasn't managing very well to conceal her turmoil.

"She wants to talk to you."

Hamutal hesitated a moment, wondering whether Noa, who was now looking over the reproductions, whose eyes observed and ears absorbed more than Hamutal intended to convey, had picked up the shock in her voice. She apologized, then worried that she was exposing herself by apologizing, then got up and left the office. In the waiting room she found Hila standing and hugging her book bag to her chest as if she were trying to hide something, her rigid posture taking the shape of a dare.

"Has something happened, Hila?"

"No disaster, if that's what you mean."

Hamutal stood facing Hila, calculating how to behave toward her daughter with her secretary watching and Noa listening—still in her office and undoubtedly straining to hear. Though they weren't in the habit of touching, she lifted her fingers to the elbow pressed against the book bag, knowing they were both aware the gesture was artificial.

"Am I disturbing you?" Hila asked in an accusatory tone, shaking off the fingers at her elbow.

"No, no." The fingers dropped, insulted.

"They told me you were in the middle of a meeting." The accusation was more overt.

"I've got the graphic designer in my office." Hamutal wondered what she was being accused of. "We can wind things up quickly, though. If you wait just—"

But Hila had already pivoted toward the exit, the book bag swinging with the momentum of the spin and sliding over her shoulder. Now it seemed to Hamutal that she was trying to conceal her back.

"I'll see you as soon as we finish," Hamutal called after her, as if with the force of her voice she could stop the hand reaching for the doorknob. She was aware of the attentive ears of the secretary, who was now carefully perusing the phone book.

"'As soon as' doesn't work for me. Bye-bye." The door slammed. Hamutal pulled herself up like a trained performer, camouflaging the pain and the anger, and strode toward her office and Noa, waiting there. She arranged a meeting for the next day and let her go.

After that she took a couple of aspirin, put her head between her hands, and pressed her fingertips against her eyelids in a relaxation gesture she had practiced since high-school exams.

At about age eight Hila had begun to withdraw from her for reasons that remained unclear: she sealed herself off more and more, said as little as possible, locked the bathroom door to keep her mother out, never asked anything of her, took care not to touch. During the same period she established a bond with her father, timed her return from friends' houses to his return from work, whispered confidences, volunteered to go with him to the garage and the bank and anywhere else he went after work. Sometimes

Hamutal would invite herself along on their outings with the dog, or waylay Hila when she got home early and try to engage her in conversation without Arnon around, but the girl would dodge her, give vague answers, and shut herself in her room, emerging only when she heard her father come home.

She had tried to talk to Arnon about this, but he shrugged it off with a joke. Hamutal told herself he was just pretending not to understand what she was trying to say and that maybe he was right and it was better that way, since things sometimes had a way of setting themselves straight through some intelligence of their own, something inherent. She recalled a Chinese saying, that the path is wiser than those who walk it. If she left Hila alone and ignored her capricious behavior, maybe things would go back to normal on their own.

Today—she pressed harder with her fingers to stop the tremor in her eyelids—a golden opportunity had happened along and she had failed to take it. Today Hila had tried in her confrontational way to invite her across the boundary she had drawn between them, and Hamutal had hesitated at the critical moment. Had Hila sensed the undercurrents between her parents and tried to offer herself as a bridge? A malicious voice inside her retorted: Hila wasn't offering herself for any lofty purpose; she had come to provoke and wasn't willing to wait two seconds for her mother to end the meeting her arrival had interrupted. She just stood there hugging her book bag— Hamutal's head shot up in alarm: had her daughter been announcing unconsciously that she was pregnant?

She packed up her things in a hurry and drove home, where she found Hila sitting alone in the living room, watching a movie.

"We can talk now if you want," Hamutal said, eyeing her daughter's belly.

"I'm in the middle of a movie." Hila showed no sign of surprise that her mother had come home early.

"I wanted to tell you I'm glad you came in today."

Hila hunched over toward the screen. "Could have fooled me."

"But that's the truth."

"It doesn't matter now." Hila pulled her lips taut and screwed up the corners of her mouth.

"I can wait till the movie's over," said Hamutal, resenting her own humility.

"I have to go out after this."

"If you want to come with me to see Grandma, she'd be delighted."

"I guess I'll pass on that."

"Just tell me, what did you want to talk about so urgently today?" Hamutal swallowed her pride.

"I got ninety in math. I wanted to brag."

"Is that all?" She knew immediately she'd made a mistake, and it was too late.

Hila took her eyes off the screen and gave her mother a piercing look.

"I mean, not 'Is that all?' about the grade. Ninety in math is really . . . I mean I thought you'd come about something else altogether." But it was too late to make amends.

"That was all," said Hila icily and moved her eyes back to the screen.

The impotence she felt at the sight of her daughter's impervious profile gave rise to violence, and Hamutal, terrified of the new urge gaining in her, felt a tingling in the hand that yearned to fly off and slam itself against the tranquil cheek, to smack and smack until the storm in her subsided.

By the time she reached her mother's room the memory of Arnon's touch had dimmed, and the unease she felt all morning had shifted to the fight with Hila, the resentment at her provocative behavior, the knowledge that their relationship was seriously ailing and that now, when she should be mobilizing all her energy to heal it, that energy was being diverted to the frightening developments in the nursing home. Try as she would to reassure herself, the thought of pregnancy persisted. Yet none of this stifled the shudder the man in the green jacket had sent through her, as if some electrical charge had flashed from him to her, igniting an extinguished thing, and now she was linked to him by an inexplicable force, waiting in suspense for some inevitable next step.

Immediately after the moment that stopped her breath every day—when she quickly assessed the signs and informed herself that her mother's condition was no worse than the day before—she dragged the chair that was at the head of the bed to the foot of the bed so she could see from where she was sitting anyone entering the room across the hall. Even as she went through the usual round of questions with her mother, her eyes were on the people passing by and she was waiting for the man in the green jacket.

"How did you sleep?" she asked, without pausing for an answer.

"Did you wake up in the middle of the night?"

"Did you get out of bed by yourself?"

"Did they give you a pill before you went to sleep?"

The new roommate was observing them from the next bed. She replaced the old woman who used to sing children's songs in a tremulous voice every night, then had suddenly fallen silent and, a week later, died. The roommate fastened her eyes on Hamutal wistfully, as if she knew something was about to happen and was getting herself ready, adjusting her head on the pillow so as not to miss the moment.

Her mother started talking. Her sentences seemed to begin in the middle, continuing aloud what had apparently been going on in her head, with no distinction between what was thought and what was said, her voice a listless monotone: " . . . and you have to finish the shopping for the Sabbath. First take the cheese back, you hear me? It's spoiled. Yesterday there weren't any decent tomatoes. He said he was getting some in today, so don't forget tomatoes. For the eggs you'll need the little basket—"

Hamutal remembered Hila, her defiant posture in the office and then the sneer with which she spat out the words "That was all," and thought of the convoluted relationships between mothers and daughters, the snare that bound them so tightly to one another that they needed some violent act to tear the connection and separate. Then one day, after they'd recovered from that act, they yearned for something vaguely remembered and wanted to go back. Wasn't there a danger that that day would be delayed, would come only when one of them was very feeble, so that it would be too late for real reconciliation, though still too early for understanding?

In the room across the hall, by the bed near the door, she saw the chair, but this evening there was no green jacket slung across its back. A little earlier, coming down the hall on the way to her mother's room, she had given in to temptation and lingered outside that room, pretending to have stopped to straighten her belt buckle, and meanwhile peeked in and saw the father of the man with the green jacket, lying in his bed, looking vacantly toward the door. She had the impression that some spark arose in his eye when he saw her and he blinked and fixed his gaze on her face. Maybe he recognized her from the few times they had passed each other in the hall, he led by a male aide and she walking her mother, two odd couples wobbling toward each other and passing by. Now it seemed to her that he was exerting himself to lift his head to see her better, as if expecting her to come over. But she remained in the hall, her hands on her belt, her eyes on the blanket rolled down to his belly. She had the urge to go over and cover him, as if he already played some part in her life and his health was precious to her, but she rebelled at the thought and turned in at the door of her mother's room, as reason played apologist for rebellion: What if the old man were to raise a hue and cry at the sight of a strange woman laying a hand on his blankets?

Now she allowed the stream of words spilling out of her mother's mouth to pass close to her ear—a constant and irritating hum—until she suddenly heard a new voice, agitated, diverging from the monotonous stream, bursting from her mother's throat: "You hear me?"

"What?"

"Get carp, too."

"Get what?"

"Carp!"

Hamutal wondered at the mechanism whose gears were now driving the urgent need to prepare the Sabbath meal, blocking out the sight of this room in which three very pale women lay in three white beds, with a clock hanging above the door indicating the time it must be elsewhere, since here there was no sign of the passage of days except for the Sabbath, when suddenly the visitors proliferated.

"Carp?"

"Carp, of course carp!" her mother said in a fresh voice, so vital and full of energy that the aide who came into the room holding a giant plastic bag regarded her with amazement.

What was the meaning of this carp-induced emotional upheaval? Hamutal examined the pursed mouth, the focused eyes, the purposeful expression. Until a moment ago her mother had been talking in a faint voice, going down the list of groceries to buy: pickles, a bag of yeast, three packets of baking powder. Now suddenly she was sitting up and, in a forceful, no-nonsense tone, demanding carp.

"Why carp all of a sudden?"

"Because that's what we need, you hear me?" She propped herself up on her elbows and leaned toward Hamutal like someone responding to a provocation with the suggestion of a threat. "You hear me?"

"Yes." Hamutal surrendered.

"Ask for the biggest one."

"All right."

"Last week he gave you such a small one that it was more bones than flesh. So remember to tell him big, okay? 'BIG'—say it like that."

"Yes, Mother."

"And you have to clean out the candlesticks, there's no room left for candles."

"Okay."

"And if he gives you a small one, tell him, 'Mommy says BIG.' The nerve, taking advantage of little kids. Will you remember?"

"Yes."

The stink of the fish store in her memory—seeping into the fabric of customers' clothing, creeping into their hair, taking over the air outside the store, even grazing the people waiting for the bus—was mixed now with the odor that had enveloped her mother these last three months, from the day she was moved into the nursing-care facility. In the old age home Hamutal hadn't encountered this particular smell. Only here, when she first came into the room, did she sense it: not hurrying to declare itself, sallying forth only intermittently, delivering a blow to the nostrils, overwhelming the pungent emanations of medicines and disinfectant. Then she identified it: the insistent smell of decay, of neglect, of bad teeth, like the smell from the public shelter that winter when neighbors had poisoned the kittens and days passed before the city sanitation workers cleared out the corpses.

"What's that smell?" she had asked the aide when she first discovered it.

The aide had looked at Hamutal's flaring nostrils and said flatly: "It's the smell of their bodies. Their insides are all rotten." Hamutal pictured the wooden block on which the butcher used to split chickens before tossing the hearts and gizzards into separate bowls and the intestines into a blue enamel basin speckled with white, where they slid like long, slimy noodles and gave off that same stench of body offal.

She had taken a little bottle of cologne out of her purse and sprayed lavender scent all around, the scent of freshly bathed infants.

"You can spray from today till doomsday," the aide had said, glancing at the nostrils now relaxed, "but you're better off in life getting used to things, believe me."

Her mother was saying—every least twitch releasing a gust of that odor from her blankets—"Tell him Shifra from the clinic wants BIG."

The aide, adept behind the mask of her face, managed to restrain her lips, which remained as tranquil as a sleeper's. Only the tiny lines gathering around her eyes attested to her effort to suppress a smile. The garbage bag was in her left hand, and her right raked leftover food and crumpled napkins off night tables into its gullet as she made her way among the beds.

The grandson of the religious woman near the window who always slept with her face toward heaven didn't turn his head. Silent as usual, he sat beside his grandmother, holding the hand that lay on the blanket.

Hamutal thought she detected movement in the room opposite, and she got up and crossed the hall to the doorway, glancing in. She saw only the old man's pajama top riding up, most of its buttons undone, exposing his chest, and returned immediately to her mother, sitting down on the chair and keeping the corridor in her range of vision.

"You went away?" Her mother's eyes were on Hamutal and one hand was protectively at her neck.

"I just got up for a minute."

"The nerve, taking advantage of children." Her mother's face had changed in a flash, her lips now sucked inward in sorrow. "What is it now, morning or evening?"

"It's three in the afternoon."

"How could it be three? Ten minutes ago it was three-thirty."

"Now it's exactly three. I've got a watch."

"So it's still closed. Go at four, then, so you can be first. And tell him: 'BIG.'"

The aide quickly turned her back on them and left the room. Hamutal looked at her mother and felt sad, wondering what exactly went on there on the other side of that forehead creased with exertion, and where the vast store of knowledge had gone, the names of diseases and medications in which she was so expert, the languages she spoke so impressively, the poems of Adam Mickiewicz that she knew by heart in Polish from the books she had brought with her and in Hebrew from the literary-supplement clippings that she saved between the pages of the books. Had the memory cells all collapsed and jiggled loose, wheeling around in her brain like millions of pieces of a puzzle that would never come together again? And wondrously, according to some law beyond logic that assigns new priorities to whatever thought remains, a concern arose for the size of a carp? If what remained was what was most important, as one expert had said on some late-night radio program, was this then not the most important thing to her mother? Why had her mother never mentioned Tzippie, whom she had loved like a daughter? And what place did her husband have, who had died amid much suffering twenty-two years earlier, and what about her grandchildren, and her friends? Against all that, what was the significance of the carp, which she had talked about three times now with such alacrity? Did it take her back to her childhood? Had Hamutal's grandmother, in that distant Polish city where they had lived among masses of gentiles, sent her mother as a child to buy carp and stressed: BIG? And yet, the store that opened at four couldn't be part of the Polish childhood. This confusion—Hamutal looked at her mother, who was dozing, her hand still protectively at her throat—this cruel confusion: as if someone were amusing himself with the shreds of memory whizzing around in the great reservoir that for seventy years had gulped in sights and sounds and smells, and now they were all devouring one another.

Usually she waited for this moment when her mother's

eyes shut and her breathing became regular, and then quickly left, saying to the aide: "When my mother wakes up, tell her I was here." But this time she continued to sit, her face turned toward her mother and the corner of her eye on the hallway. A male nurse went into the room across the hall and came right out, and Hamutal hoped he had covered the old man's chest. The aide returned, pushing a dolly on which there were cleaning agents, a pail of water, and a mop that looked like a huge ruffle.

"Your mother's sleeping," she said.

"I'll wait a little while. I've hardly talked to her." Hamutal glanced at the room across the hall.

"No problem."

There was a short, tense silence, and Hamutal, hearing her mother's wheezing breaths, was shaken. Now that her mother was sleeping, she looked at her carefully, surveying the face with an unforgiving eye, shocked by how much she had changed in the last three months, as if her features, following the lead of her memory cells, had also gone awry.

As a child Hamutal had spent a great deal of time in the clinic where her mother worked. At the white Formica table in the nurses' room, amid the acrid smell of alcohol and medicine—a smell she'd learned to love—she would do her homework, drawing flowers and fishes on sheets of paper with the clinic logo at the top. Sometimes she would help the nurses, sharpening the points of syringes, or follow the hands of the clock so she could remind her mother twenty minutes before closing that it was time to boil the instruments. Then, standing before the basin of bubbling water, she would watch the syringes and the tongue depressors getting ever more immaculate. But most of the time she would sit and watch the people coming in for treatment, adults or weepy children arriving with skinned knees or scratched arms or burns, all of them groaning in pain as their wounds were dressed, sometimes letting out a yell behind the curtain as a needle entered their flesh.

Her mother carried out her work with efficiency and pursed lips. Precise and purposeful, not given to small talk, addressing old people and children in a gentle voice, caressing the heads of infants, explaining pleasantly and patiently time after time, comforting them with the feeling that she was doing just the right thing and if they would only listen to her, their pain would be gone in a moment. She spoke Polish with the Polish-speakers and German with the German-speakers and Yiddish with the Yiddish-speakers, and all of them, grateful that in time of trouble they could speak their mother tongue and not grope after unfamiliar words, thanked her and wished her long life and blessed her and her household and her daughter, who was sitting and watching them all this time with a steady eye.

When the clinic's outside doors had been closed and the two of them were left alone in the white room, her mother would give it a final once-over, peering into drawers, pulling the metal instruments out of the boiling water with tongs—as the agitation Hamutal knew so well began to creep back and take over her mother's movements. Hamutal, already standing by the door, then braced herself for the moment when the magic would vanish: when the head nurse, so patient and polite, would hang up her smock, lock the white door of the nurses' room and turn back into her mother, constant complainer, with the habitual headache pounding at her temples by the time they reached home.

But before that, Hamutal had rehearsed to herself one day, she would tell about the composition.

"Did you buy bread?" Her mother preempted her.

"There was no brown. I got white."

"Maybe someday you'll get there in time."

"All right . . . " The matter of the composition was on the tip of her tongue.

"When there's still brown." Her mother preempted her again.

"All right," Hamutal said and hurried to add, breathless: "The teacher read my composition to the whole class."

"What composition?"

"I wrote about a poem by Adam Mickiewicz."

"What do you know about Adam Mickiewicz?" she asked without a pause and without amazement.

"I read about him in the encyclopedia."

"The teacher said that was okay?" The clear note of contempt contained the rest: "As if this Sabra could have any idea of the greatness of Adam Mickiewicz!"

"She said the writing showed a lot of talent."

"Whose? Mickiewicz's?"

"No. My composition."

"Yes, well . . . What was I going to ask? Did the laundry come back?"

"Yes."

"Did you put it out on the line?"

"Just the smaller things. I left the sheets."

"So now I'll have to do it, with the headache starting already."

Regarding Hamutal's cough, which set in every winter from the time she was three and lasted until spring, her mother was unimpressed. In the morning, before she went to work, she would sometimes tell Hamutal: "Drink tea. It's good for your throat. Cough syrup isn't any better."

Sometimes one of the teachers would notice that she came to school on cold winter days with flimsy shoes and no coat, and make some comment to her. Once, as she was walking down the hall with a group of friends, the school nurse had called her into her room and said in astonishment: "You're Shifra Baum's daughter, aren't you? The nurse at the clinic?"

"Yes."

"I see you in the schoolyard during breaks. You shouldn't go outside on days like this."

"I go out with my friends."

"But your friends don't come to school in open shoes. Your mother doesn't notice that you're wearing those shoes to school?"

"She leaves the house before I do."

"And are you taking something for that cough?"

"I drink tea."

"Maybe she can bring you something for it. That cough sounds pretty bad."

"She brings me cough syrup," Hamutal had lied without a blink.

Her mother let out a noisy snore and turned her head, exposing the cheek that had gotten burned many years ago and was finely lined with scars, like a delicate tattoo. The aide stopped beside her, flipped the overhanging edge of the blanket onto the bed, leaned down, and with an arc of her arm brushed the dust out from under the bed.

"She talked all night, your mother. The whole week she hasn't shut her mouth, if you'll excuse the expression."

Hamutal got up quickly, went to the door of the room across the hall, looked in, and came back to her chair.

"What did she talk about?"

"What didn't she talk about? If you heard the way they talk at night, you wouldn't know where you were. There's one nurse that makes a joke of it. It's not nice to laugh, but the truth is it's funny. In the next room here there's a woman, I just came from her, who drives everyone crazy: she wants cherries. I told her: 'Lady, maybe where you came from in Poland there were cherries. This is the Land of Israel, here there's cactus. You have to like what there is.' And there was another woman, this was before your mother—fine woman, you never saw anything so fine. I was sure she grew up in the President's House, at least—manicure, pedicure, the whole works. You should have heard the curses she came out with in her sleep, Arabic, Russian, you name it. I never in my life heard a man curse like that. And your mother, what did she talk about? She talked in Yiddish, how would I know? Maybe about carp again. With them everything in the head turns into one big salad."

"Tell me, I wanted to ask you, the old man with the diapers yesterday—"

"Thanks for telling his son." The aide straightened up, leaned on the broom handle and looked her in the eye.

"I hope . . . did it help?"

"Of course. Thanks so much. He was back with the diapers in an hour. What a terrific son. There are children who don't care about their father, he could lay there and leak. Them, what do they care. They go out and have a good time, what do they have to think about their father leaking. Him, no. He went out and he looked—what a guy. He didn't even know where to get diapers at night. But he came back with Maxi, just like I asked. Really, what a guy."

"How come he didn't know where? This couldn't be the first time he had to buy diapers."

"He's not from around here. He doesn't know what's open at night, that's what he told me."

"Ah," said Hamutal and saw the aide's hand pause for a moment, then continue vigorously wiping the high metal rod around the bed.

"What's wrong with his father?"

"What's wrong with them all here? Old age is wrong with him."

"But not all old people end up in a nursing home." Hamutal was fascinated by the aide, whose words tumbled out in a steady stream, whose hands never came to rest, who kept her sober mask on the whole time, as if she'd learned to wear it over her mirthful face as part of the uniform, an expression suited to the workplace.

"Everybody ends up here. Today you see them talking on TV, this one's a government minister and that one's some V.I.P., all that fancy talk. Six months later you come in— and here they are. Like clockwork. He scratches and he leaks just like the guy who can't read. Here there's no difference. Here's it's, how do you say, a real democracy."

Hamutal glanced at her watch and peered again toward the room across the hall.

"And his son—"

"What a guy. A good boy."

"When does he usually come?"

The aide straightened the mop handle as if she intended to rest, and a tangle of cotton strands flopped out on the floor between her feet like a white octopus. She fixed her gaze on Hamutal. Her face had long since learned to take everything in and give nothing away.

"Sometimes I see him in the middle of the night— comes, pulls up his father's covers, and leaves. Sometimes he comes early in the morning, at six or seven, even, but every day, every day he comes at dinner time to feed him. Dinner here is at six, you know that."

"Thank you," said Hamutal, and immediately regretted it.

"You're welcome." The voice remained neutral.

"If my mother wakes up—"

"Of course, of course." The cloth octopus had already been rolled up and wrung out. "I'll tell her you were here."

When she got home she found the house empty and was glad Arnon hadn't come back yet. She collapsed into the armchair, her handbag in her lap, her body drained of energy, her head a commotion of thoughts. She closed her eyes, hoping to be drawn into the calm and the clean smell of the house. Something new was happening in her life— for some reason she recalled the burning passion to smack Hila as well as the sense of responsibility that had seized her at the sight of his father lying exposed in bed—and now she had to sit quietly, gather the thoughts that came and went in tumult, and sort things out for herself. Before falling asleep the previous night she had been too upset, and in the morning too busy, to attend to her thoughts. Hila's visit to the office had diverted her attention even from work. But as the hours passed she had consciously repressed the idea that Hila was pregnant, until now it seemed untenable. Then came the visit to the nursing home—beginning with the moment she parked her car in the lot next to the building and her eyes scanned for his car—and again confirmed the sense of urgency she had been feeling since the previous night and not yet named. She also had to remember the moments after sex with Arnon, the insult felt by a body detecting the pretense of the neighboring body—for some reason that moment, too, was related to the son of the man in diapers.

Now she got up, cleared the weekend papers and the last few days' mail off the table, and smoothed out the tablecloth. Then she made herself a cup of coffee and sat down to drink it amid order.

The man in the green jacket, she forced herself to admit, had not left her for a moment. The trembling that set in at their first meeting had not vanished, only come and gone from time to time and been damped by annoyances of the day-to-day; and whenever she thought of him again, even for a second, something erupted in her with a rackety pounding of the heart. Have I fallen in love? she asked herself now, aware of the absurdity of the idea but not allowing herself to dodge it, posing the question in all its folly. The coffee cup, as if trying to make a statement, tipped and spilled, and she hurried to get a dishrag and contain the liquid that was already spreading to the middle of the table and seeping into the cloth's embroidery. Was it possible to fall in love in such a blinding storm of emotion like this, after one meeting, when one was well past adolescence? She pulled off the tablecloth and closed in on the coffee drips trying to escape the rag. What had there been between them, after all? A look, two or three sentences, "thank you" and "you're welcome." She finally conquered the coffee spill and went to pour herself another cup.

But beyond any self-deception, she had a clear image of the somber man in the green jacket. She thought of the pact established between them yesterday and had no doubt of its reality, recalled the gaze that was troubling, serious, without a hint of mischief, a gaze that studied her even at night. Suddenly she remembered Arnon the previous evening, saw him turning over on the rug, flailing his arms and legs like a baby wanting his diaper changed. How could she describe to that man rolling on the rug what her mother was like—hollow-eyed, stunned as a little lost girl, clutching Hamutal's fingers so hard she left marks on them, her gaze meandering as she said, three days ago: "Where am I?"

"You're in the nursing home. Everything is okay."

"I want to go home."

"You are home."

"This is not my home."

"Yes it is. Now this is your home."

"Who are you?"

"I'm Hamutal, Mother."

Sometimes when she was about to tell her husband about a visit to her mother, she would take a deep breath, clear her throat, and indicate in a colorless voice whether or not her mother had recognized her on that particular visit, straining to assume an offhand tone, with none of the skipped beats triggered by that "I'm Hamutal, Mother." How could she ever entrust Arnon with "I'm Hamutal, Mother"? What amusement would he invent for himself out of that nightmare phrase? Would he dress up like a woman on Purim, with a curly wig, jump out from behind the door and shout, "I'm Hamutal, Mother"? The man in the green jacket, she was certain, would recognize the terror and the sorrow of "I'm Hamutal, Mother."

She glanced at the clock on the wall and saw that it was five to six. Without considering whether she was doing the right thing, without any accounting whatsoever, she got up, put on her coat, shouldered her bag, and hurried out of the house. On a side road on the way to the nursing home she checked her face in the mirror, then stopped the car, rummaged for her cosmetic bag, and took time to apply mascara.

His car wasn't in the parking lot, and she felt a mounting suspense that surprised her, as if some hunting instinct she was unaware of had been aroused. She glanced at her watch: six-twenty. He must be feeding his father now. Perhaps he had parked somewhere else; maybe he'd decided to walk today.

In the dining room she saw his father even before she saw her mother, sitting at the end of the table and staring at his bowl. Next to him sat a short old man whose chin touched the tabletop as he lifted an empty spoon from an empty bowl to his mouth, sipping air. Then he carefully returned the spoon to the bowl, tipped it slightly to refill it, and lifted it again to his lips.

"Tasty?" One of the visitors had stopped at his side. The old man nodded.

At the next table sat her mother, bound to her chair by a rubber strap, a long dribble of soup wending its way from her mouth to her neck as she regarded the spoon in her hand with wonder, trying hard, it seemed, to guess what one did with this peculiar implement they had stuck between her fingers.

"How are you feeling, Mother?" Hamutal sat down, pulled a paper napkin out of her bag, and wiped her mother's mouth.

Her mother's eyes, tired of blinking, were fastened on her with what seemed like reproach but was more likely vacancy. Hamutal touched her mother's listless hand, pressing her fingertips against the dry skin, saw her lips begin to curl and was afraid that next would come the sentence "I want to go home," whimpered or whispered beseechingly or shouted in outrage, but always sending a shudder through her like the very first time.

"How are you feeling, Mother?"

"Bad."

"Why bad?"

Her eyes were open wide. "I haven't had anything to eat," she said tonelessly.

"Looks to me like you ate."

"That wasn't food."

"What was it?"

"Straw. The food tastes like straw."

"It actually looks pretty tasty."

Her mouth clamped shut and the outline of her lips disappeared. "I have no taste in my mouth anymore. Everything is like mortar. Mortar and straw."

"That's too bad."

Until not too many months ago, each time Hamutal came to visit, her mother's first question would be: "Have you eaten?" But for the last two weeks she hadn't shown any interest in other people, had not mentioned even her granddaughters.

Across from her mother sat a large-boned, light-complexioned nurse who was feeding an old woman out of a porcelain dish decorated with plump red cherries, a dish that was different from all the others on the table. The old woman kept stretching a shaky finger toward the dish, pointing out the painted cherries, and the nurse would say in a foreign accent, "There you go, now another one," and put a teaspoon of cereal into the woman's mouth.

A new nurse, girlish-looking, went over to the father of the man with the green jacket and raised her voice next to his ear: "Your son isn't coming today, Ya'akov. He called and said to tell you he can't come because of work. Do you understand? He can't come today." The old man, if he heard and understood, received the news with equanimity.

"Do you hear me, Ya'akov? He has to stay at work."

Hamutal got up suddenly and said to her mother, "I have to go now. I'll bring you pears tomorrow," and in a split second was at the elevator. Usually as she waited she would take a last look at her mother, but this time she stood with her back to the dining room, refusing to see the old man's impassive face, her mother's empty eyes; her entire being was focused on the thought that she had to find the man in the green jacket.

It was raining out. She fled to her car, started the engine, and took off as if in some action-movie chase scene, speeding to the light, signaling left as if she knew where she was going, forgetting that she didn't even know the man's profession and that most offices were already closed at this hour. At the light near the Arlosoroff Street train station she tensed up and squinted to see through the heavy rain, her foot trembling above the gas pedal as she wondered for a second how she had gotten through all the lights on Namir Street without remembering a single one. The instant the light changed she had to stop thinking as the car lurched forward, passing the others and now whizzing along the winding road toward the museum. At that moment she had no doubt: he was at the museum. Not in the least astounded by the news that had come to her just like that, she slowed down and looked for a parking space.

Cars were parked in a tight line opposite the plaza in front of the museum, and she double-parked without hesitation, blocking another car and one traffic lane. Stepping briskly, she headed toward the museum. She had a feeling she'd left the door ajar and so the inside light was on, but she couldn't stop and look back: the story of Lot's wife flashed through her mind as her fleet feet, seeming to

devour the distance without touching down, reached the
threshold of the museum. The guard tried to stop her, but
she was insistent as she passed him: "I'm just looking for
someone. It's very urgent." She gestured absently to the
right, the direction in which, across the main road, the city
hospital stood.

Looking perplexed, without another word, he watched
her pass—and in any case she was far beyond him now,
loping into the Impressionist gallery. There she stood for a
second in the doorway and clearly saw the green jacket—
there was no mistaking it—standing among other jackets
clustered in front of one of the paintings. She strode over
decisively and stood behind the man. Urgency was apparently evident in her face, and the docent who was at that
moment saying something about the effect of light in a
work by Monet paused for a moment and looked at her,
and the head above the green collar rotated in her direction, puzzled and unfamiliar, and from behind her someone breathing heavily said, "Lady, you're blocking my car."
She said "Excuse me" to all the heads that were turned
toward her and pivoted around to the man behind her and
said "Excuse me" to him as well. He said, "I saw you from
the library, parking your car and blocking me," and again
she said, "Excuse me," and he said, "You're lucky I saw you,
you know, you left the door open," and turned to the group
of heads and said, "People these days have the most
incredible nerve," but she was already making her way
down the ramp to the museum foyer, her thigh muscles
hurting from the effort to brake the momentum and a
voice inside her saying: This is apparently a nightmare.

It was still raining when she walked past the sculptures
on the plaza between the museum and the road. From a
distance she could see the line of cars stuck behind hers,

waiting for a chance to merge into the traffic snaking through the other lanes, and by the time she reached her car, ignoring the angry glare from the woman in the first car behind it, her hair and shoulders were soaked, and she said to herself out loud, "Maybe I'm starting to go crazy."

When she got home, shivering from the cold, fully aware that the dreamlike event was indeed reality, worried about her loss of control, she found Michal standing at the door.

"Where have you been?"

"I went to see my mother." Hamutal restrained her voice, unaccustomed to attacks from Michal, and waited for the girl to come up and kiss her.

"Is she more important than me?" Michal bristled, and Hamutal knew she would have to forgo the kiss.

"What kind of question is that, Michal?"

"Well, you were supposed to meet with my teacher today."

"Today?"

"Today—yes, today!"

"Are you sure it was today?" Hamutal looked at her watch.

"You forgot!" Michal flung at her.

"I can still make it," Hamutal said, her heart sinking.

"You completely forgot about it." Now there was astonishment in Michal's voice, as if the realization had just dawned on her.

"I'm going right now."

"Thanks a lot. The teacher called, so I phoned Dad, and he went there straight from work." Michal turned to go to her room. "And if you're planning to forget to pick me up after dance class tomorrow, just let me know ahead of time."

That evening she felt the way she had on a class trip to Eilat years ago, when her friends froze her out after she complained to the guide that they'd painted her face with shoe polish. Her daughters ignored her and she put a lot of time and effort into making sandwiches, garnishing them with special care, knowing that the next day she'd find them untouched. Arnon came home late, looking grave. He sat down at the dining-room table and Michal sat next to him, putting her hand on his arm as they conferred in low tones like comrades in the underground. From the kitchen, where she stood slicing cucumbers, Hamutal could see them huddling, and felt insulted that she hadn't been invited to join. For a moment she wondered if it wasn't better to absorb the growing humiliation, swallow her pride, go out there with the platter of sandwiches and sit down with them naturally and ask what the teacher had said. But she knew they'd only give her a sidelong glance, like the looks Hila had been throwing her way lately, and when she finished garnishing the sandwiches she left the kitchen for the bedroom, burning with mortification.

"What did Michal's teacher say?" she asked Arnon that night.

"That she was surprised you didn't show up and didn't call to say you weren't coming."

"I was at my mother's." She ignored his anger, suddenly remembering the blazing sky above the Parliament building in the Monet at the museum.

"She failed physics and English. They'll give her a chance to redo the exams after the Passover break, and if she doesn't pass, the failing grade will go down on her record."

"That physics business isn't new."

"So you're well informed," he said acidly. "Too bad you didn't think of doing something with your privileged information."

"I told Michal to find out about tutors."

"That's really nice of you. In any case, the teacher asked if there had been problems at home recently, whether Michal should be given a referral to the guidance counselor or sent for some sessions during the summer."

"What did you say?"

"I'm careful to hide the dirty laundry, the way they did in your family. I said her grandmother had been transferred to a nursing-care facility and that was affecting everyone at home."

At other times she would have targeted his sore spot, put the full force of her venom into a few nasty words about dirty washing and the laundry at the kibbutz, but now she just tugged the blanket up to her neck and said: "It's true," and thought: What do I know about the truth?

The next day, sitting at her mother's bedside, Hamutal couldn't shake off thoughts of the frenzy that had seized her the previous evening; she kept reviewing in amazement how she'd gotten into the car and sped through a driving rain without knowing where to, how she'd abandoned the car in the middle of the road, dashed up the stairs in the direction of the Monet.

There was a shrill, insistent sound nearby, and Hamutal realized it had come from her mother's mouth. Her mother had a strange expression on her face, screwing up her eyes at her suddenly, sucking in her lips, biting them, her whole face straining as if she were trying desperately to remember something.

"What is it, Mother?"

"No one comes to see me!" The mouth ruptured in a shout, the lips stretched until they blanched, then tired and retreated back to place.

"I was here twice yesterday."

"They're all liars. No one ever comes to see me."

"You wanted me to buy groceries for the Sabbath, you wanted carp."

"Everyone else gets visitors, but not me."

"That's not true, Mother."

"Only the male nurse comes. Touches me."

"What male nurse?"

"The one with the hair."

"Touches you where?"

"Where he shouldn't. Down there."

"What does he do?" Hamutal restrained her voice to conceal the shock.

"Yes, yes. Comes over and touches me."

"What?" Her voice gave in to astonishment.

"Touches me there." The old woman jerked her head and threw back the corner of the blanket. She thrust both hands into her pajama bottoms, toward her crotch, exposing a bald pubis that stunned Hamutal, and started to rub the insides of her thighs with both hands as if scraping at some filth she alone could see. Hamutal hurried to cover her mother with the blanket, to conceal the pitiable state of a body that no longer knew how to contain its fire, but her mother tore off the blanket, lifted one hand and cupped her breast: "Here, too. Just touching and touching. All night long."

During the second month of seventh grade, right after the Rosh Hashanah holidays, the school nurse had come into the room, her expression pregnant with meaning, and asked the boys to leave and the girls to move up into the empty seats. The boys had gotten up and gone toward the door, gesticulating on their way, exchanging glances and snickering. The girls waited, expectant. Everyone knew what the nurse was going to talk about: menstrual periods, which two of the girls were suspected to have had already during the summer. In the silence that filled the room the nurse went to the blackboard, wrote REPRODUCTIVE SYSTEM, sketched a peculiar shape and started to describe, in a voice that strained loudly to overcome her own embarrassment, the structure of the uterus and fallopian tubes, tracing the life path of the egg, which resided in its secret place and waited for a girl to err and perform the forbidden act so that it could link up with a sperm cell and result in pregnancy. But usually—here the nurse's tone was full of foreboding—the egg smashed on a particular date each month with the result being blood on your underpants, and as the girls' eyes widened at the sound of "blood on your underpants," she paused, spun around, erased the board quickly, and fled from the room.

Frightened by the big drawing, with its obstacle course traveled by the cunning egg whose sole desire was to betray the body that carried it, Hamutal ran all the way home. Her mother, in the throes of one of her headaches since that morning, had stayed in bed and been reading, and when Hamutal arrived was still pressing the fingers of her right hand to her temple. Hamutal, obeying the rule that one did not interrupt Mother's reading before she finished the page, waited, puffing noisily, until the thumb touched the edge of the page to turn it.

"Today the girls had a class with the nurse," Hamutal burst out, her school bag still strapped to her back and her lunch bag swinging beneath her elbow.

"She was checking for lice?"

"No. She talked to us. The boys went out and only the girls stayed."

"That's nice. There's food for you on the stove. Help yourself and don't make a mess."

"She explained to us about the egg and about blood on your underpants," Hamutal said urgently.

Her mother let the book slide a bit, until it rested on her belly.

"What did she explain?"

"She said that every month either you're pregnant or you have blood on your underpants." She was terrified by both alternatives.

"That's what she said?" The hand fell away from the temple.

"Yes." A crushed sound came out of her throat. "Either pregnancy or blood."

"Well, now you know everything, then. Get yourself some food." The book rose up and came between them.

Everything she knew about the act performed to bring the egg to its desired goal she had learned elsewhere. She did not speak to her mother again on the subject until just before her wedding, when her mother said to her half-heartedly, choosing the moment when guests had started to arrive and there would hardly be time to answer her question: "So you know whatever you need to know about the husband-and-wife business, right?" and Hamutal said: "Everything is okay, Mother." Her lungs hurt under the tight lace of the wedding dress as she recalled the elegant, almost seductive hands of the woman doctor slipping into transparent gloves in preparation for the abortion.

All these years the subject had never come up between

them until this moment when one of her mother's hands was feeling her genitals and the other was squeezing her breast and her mouth was saying, amid the contortions of her face. "He comes and touches me at night. In the dark, rapes and rapes and no one sees."

A few weeks earlier, on one of her first visits, Hamutal had come into the ward when one of the patients was raising a ruckus, spreading her legs and accusing the male aide on duty of stealing up to her at night when she was sleeping and trying to take off her clothes and put his head between her legs. The woman had pulled her nightgown up above her thighs, as people stood around and looked embarrassed. The aide, unperturbed, had pushed her legs together, pulled her nightgown back down and said: "Time to sleep now. Good night. Enough nonsense for today."

Before leaving for home she looked for the aide so he could explain to her what had happened with her mother, hoping that such a conversation would make it clear to him that he was dealing with a patient whose children would ensure she was not abused.

"Ask the doctor," he said, lowering his glance and looking awkward in a way that seemed to betray guilt. "He's better at explaining. Their heads invent stories. They have fantasies at this age, a lot of fantasies about . . . how should I say . . . about sex . . . "

Hamutal looked into her mother's widening eyes, remembering that day when she had run all the way home without stopping, a girl at the beginning of seventh grade, in shock over what the nurse had said, praying that she'd find her mother home to comfort her. Now she saw the terrified eyes looking to her, saw the snowy roots exposed under the dyed hair, and took pity on the woman whose body was aroused so wildly only after she had lost control of her mind. She was suddenly saddened by the missed opportunities, the waste, saddened to see what was most magical and pleasurable made shameful here.

Someone came up behind her and said, "Excuse me," and she turned her head and saw the man from the parking lot.

If she hadn't been in the grip of the current trauma, her heart would have leapt from its place now and thudded against the wall of her chest. But as it was, still agitated by her mother's words and by the memories suddenly rousted from their safe lair, she only stared into his somber eyes, which looked as if they were indeed begging her pardon.

"I wanted to thank you for...for your mission yesterday. Can I buy you a cup of coffee?"

The first sentence she said to him, even before he asked her what she wanted to drink and went to get two cups of coffee on a tray patterned with huge watermelon slices, was: "My mother claims that the male nurse on the ward touches her genitals."

He said, as if her statement were the usual formula for beginning a conversation with a stranger: "She's having erotic hallucinations. That's common in these situations. What would you like to drink?"

While waiting for him to come back with the watermelon tray, she thought how relaxed she felt in his presence, as if some promise had been given in advance that nothing would embarrass her or shock her, that everything was understood and permitted, and she knew that the sentence she had spoken to the man whose name she didn't know she would have withheld from Arnon.

"Who says it's common in these situations?" she asked when he came back and put the tray down between them.

"The professional literature says."

"Does your father also have erotic hallucinations?"

"My father hasn't said a word for several weeks."

"Because of his vocal cords?"

"No. Because he's depressed."

"I have to tell you, the business about the diapers really threw me."

"Yes. I had that impression."

"In the parking lot."

"I remember. Your mother doesn't use them, I gather."

"No."

"Most of the people here are in diapers."

"It's no surprise that he's depressed."

"True."

"He looks like a proud man."

"And he's lucid, relatively. In his situation, maybe it's better to be less lucid."

This conversation, like a very dim, distant recollection, had already taken place in her lifetime. She remembered the intonation as a kind of familiar but elusive melody, and this special atmosphere of strangeness and closeness. Had she dreamt it? She studied the packets of sugar and artificial sweetener lined up in a small wooden holder and tried hard to recall when the conversation had taken place that now flickered at the threshold of memory, determined to evade her.

"It's a horrible thing, old age," she mused aloud without stopping her investigation of the memory.

"Yes." He put the cup of coffee in front of her. "They moved her here because of the confusion?"

"Yes. She was in assisted living for three years. A few

months ago she started leaving the gas burner on, and once she got violent with one of her neighbors. The worst was one night when she tried to go out the main gate in her nightgown. But now she's also limited physically. She spends most of the day in bed. They brought her here three months ago. She's deteriorating so quickly that every time I come near this place I'm afraid of what state I'll find her in. Yesterday I saw they tied her to a chair."

Hamutal picked up a paper packet, tore off a corner, dumped the contents into the cup and stirred absent-mindedly.

"So that isn't new to me, her confusion, she's been confused for a while, but today suddenly it was what she said, that subject. She had never talked about it. It was taboo at home from the time I was a little girl."

"The subjects they repressed come up because of their weakened defenses. The whole unconscious floats up."

"Yes, I know the theory, but that doesn't make it any easier when it happens in reality." She thought another moment about the floating unconscious and in her mind's eye pictured the interior of her mother's skull, a big lake inside with slimy reptiles rising higher and higher off the bottom till they covered the surface of the water.

His eyes, she suddenly saw, were the brown of soft sand-stone, and at the sight of them she noted to herself that the feeling of immediate connection between them had skewed the usual procedures for a first meeting between a man and a woman, when the eyes, as if on automatic, keep scanning the new features, learning them one after the other. Eye color had always been the first thing she noticed.

"More milk?" The sandstone eyes were looking at her as if she'd been familiar for a long time.

"Yes, thanks. Is your mother still alive?

"No." He touched her cup with the lip of the stainless-steel creamer.

"My father died when I was seventeen." She knew he was about to ask. "What exactly is wrong with your father?"

"All his systems are impaired, but the big problem was prostate cancer. He had surgery that didn't quite succeed."

"You resemble him, as you've probably heard before."

"Yes."

They drank in silence for a moment, then she suddenly said, as if confessing: "My mother has Alzheimer's."

"So I understood."

"Are you a psychologist?"

"No. I work with computers."

"You talked about the floating unconscious, so I thought—"

"I've read a lot on the subject. I thought information could help."

"It can't."

"No."

"What can?"

"Nothing."

She lowered her eyes to the tray and said, "I feel like having watermelon."

She recalled the waiting room in the mother-and-child clinic, a row of look-alike mothers sitting there on the bench with look-alike infants on their laps; the babies asleep or fidgety, the mothers carefully studying the other children, sometimes with a look of envy, sometimes with contempt, constantly comparing. A conversation that took place there echoed just now in her conversation with him.

"He turns over by himself?"

"Yes. From belly to back since he was five months."

"Mine's been turning over from back to belly, too, from four months."

"My neighbor's son started turning over at three months."

And now:

"That threw me, the business about your father's diapers."

"Yes, I noticed. Your mother doesn't use them, I gather."

"No."

"Most of the people here are in diapers."

He said, "You'll have to wait until summer."

She said, "Excuse me?"

He said, "For watermelon."

She said, "Aah."

He said, "What were you thinking about?"

She said, "That this is the most inhuman environment anyone could imagine."

He said, "Are you a psychologist yourself?"

"No. But I edit a psychology journal."

"Interesting?"

"Usually. The issue I'm working on now is devoted to dreams."

"Did you say dreams?"

"Yes, nightmares to be exact."

"A whole issue on nightmares?"

"Yes. It's actually the summary of an international seminar that was held a couple of months ago at Tel Aviv University."

"An international seminar on that?"

"Yes, it does sound strange. Psychologists and psychiatrists presented case studies based on a method developed by someone at Columbia University. The principle behind the therapy is that the dreamer repairs what upset him in the dream, without having any analysis or interpretation of the dream beforehand. Simply a correction at the level of narrative, on the assumption that the person knows, sub-consciously, what problem the dream was dealing with—and that's what he fixes. It works along the lines of guided imagery without the guidance, if that's any explanation—" and she burst out laughing.

"It's funny?"

"No, but all of a sudden I felt as if I were launching into a lecture myself. In any case, afterward, according to the correction, they try to understand the meaning of the dream consciously, and at that point the work actually starts—that's the method, more or less."

"For instance—"

"For instance." She opened her briefcase and took out a sheaf of papers, perused them, and held out one page:

*[Page 5. Fonts: all text in David light (12 pt), first two words of each piece in 14 pt bold. Leave quarter page for detail of Picasso (Guernica).]*

**The dream of a man who suspected his wife had betrayed him, as presented to the international seminar by Dr. Margaret Longley of Trinity College, Dublin.**

The man was forty-six years old, a devout Catholic with consider-able means, father of ten-year-old twin boys, who had lost his much-loved wife after thirteen years of marriage. A year after his wife died, at the urging of his father, he married her younger sister, who had been single, a kindergarten teacher by profession, and who once had a long affair with a married man. Though the man was still pained by the death of his first wife, the new wife managed to win his affection through her love for his children and the bold and innovative bedroom pleasures she proposed to him, which excited his imagination even in broad daylight.

About three months after their wedding, the man had to go away for several days on business. That was when he had the first nightmare, following thoughts about the lover his wife had had before their marriage and fears that the lover was having sex with her now in his (the dreamer's) own bed. On returning home, he hired a private detective to determine if there was any basis for his suspicions and even gave the detective the man's name and address. After a month of surveillance the detective found nothing suspicious except for the fact that the wife frequently went to extravagant shoe stores and tried on shoes without buying anything. Still, the man's nightmares were unrelenting.

The dream: The man is sitting and reading a newspaper when God appears to him and says that soon there will be a flood and that he must take a pair of every kind of creature and put them in a cave he is to prepare in a high mountain. He understands that he is the biblical Noah, and he hastens to carry out God's command. He prepares a huge loudspeaker, puts it on the mountaintop, and invites a pair of every kind of creature. Animals begin to arrive, but in threes, and he is very frightened because the place can't accommodate them all. At the end of the line he sees two apes approaching, walking upright, arm in arm. Something in the female's gait is familiar to him and, looking at her face, he recognizes his wife, but the male's face is unfamiliar. He blocks the opening to let in only one pair of each kind, but the extra individuals refuse to leave and try to force their way into the cave with the rest. He explains to his wife that the ape she came with has to go back because he himself is her mate, but the male ape bursts out laughing. Meanwhile a riot is developing, and he can't seem to keep the extra animals out. He even tries to use force, but they overcome him and stream in. His ape-wife and the unfamiliar ape come in, embracing. He calls out to God, but He is nowhere to be found.

In the correction of the dream the man decides to arm himself with a hunting rifle. He sits in the cave and shoots every extra mate that tries to break into the cave by force. Most of the animals are scared and leave on their own. Those that insist on entry he shoots, and he drags their bodies aside. As the rain begins the apes arrive: his wife and the unfamiliar male. His wife tries to escape the other's embrace, but he won't release her. The husband shoots him, and he falls at the mouth of the cave. His wife runs in, and the door of the cave is locked behind her immediately. The rain intensifies and washes the body of the male ape down the mountainside.

The whole time he was reading Hamutal was looking out the window into the back garden, watching an old man no taller than a boy straining tenaciously behind a large wheelchair occupied by the woman who must have been his childhood sweetheart many years ago, a woman with her tongue poking out of a slack mouth, her eyes fixed vacantly ahead, as her body flopped back and forth between the strap across her chest and the back of the chair, and her head jerked toward her shoulder now and then as though her neck were broken.

He looked up from the page, his sandstone eyes large.

"This is what you do?"

"All the time." She didn't take her eyes off the couple outside.

"Doesn't it affect your everyday life?"

"It is my everyday life." She watched the old man take a paper napkin out of his pocket and gently wipe the woman's mouth.

And so it went on.

It was as if that beginning in the parking lot had dictated what was to follow; as if they had known each other well in a previous life and now had only to dip into memory to retrieve the sights and sounds; as if this conversation were the continuation of a distant one, and all the right conjunctions came easily; as if they had always known that when they met again some day, even in a large crowd, they would spot each other immediately, and that, in fact, had happened. She began to wonder how she had lived all these years, many of them with a sense of completeness, without this man in her life—this man whose name she still didn't know, but whose presence was now as natural as if he'd always been with her. She found herself appalled by the madness that had gripped her the previous day, since she no longer doubted that this conversation, which had had a prologue, would go on. There was also something sad in the encounter. In this place, with its prospect of a tiny old man tottering down a gravel path, the fragility of life and the fleeting nature of what was coming into being between her and the man across the table were suddenly clarified. He hadn't smiled once, had not gone out of his way to impress her as people do in a first meeting, knowing that there was no need to dissemble, particularly in this place. His eyes, sunken in their orbits, were constantly perturbed, as if he had just received news of some disaster.

"I have to go." She glanced at her watch, jumped up from her seat, started gathering the tissues and keys she'd scattered on the table and stuffing them into her bag. "I have to pick up my daughter from her dance class."

"Ballet?"

"Jazz."

"She's the one with the Rubik's cube?"

"No." She understood that driving behind her the previous day as far as the traffic light, he had surveyed the rear window of her car. "It's her sister with the Rubik's cube and the chess. This one is a space cadet."

"Thank you for agreeing to have coffee with me." He wasn't talking about the brew.

"Thank you for inviting me to have coffee with you." She was confirming that she knew.

In the car, outside the dance school, trying to quell the new storm, Hamutal pulled out her binder and started going over the material, knowing full well that she wasn't focused enough to make proper decisions, but determined to read anyway:

**The dream of a woman who was hospitalized after a suicide attempt, presented at the international seminar at Tel Aviv University by Dr. Emilio Morera of the University of Padua.**

This was a twenty six-year-old woman, single parent of a four-and-a-half-year-old girl, whose parents were religious and had broken off all contact when they learned of her pregnancy. The child's father, a married man, supported the woman emotionally and financially, and promised that sometime in the future, when his children were grown, he would leave his wife and marry her. They even planned to have another child.

The man was critically injured in a car accident and hospitalized in a coma, and his financial support to her was cut off. The man's brother visited the woman and threatened that if she bothered the family or dared to speak to the man's wife (who knew nothing of her existence or the girl's), she would be endangering herself and her daughter.

She waited several months for some improvement in the condition of her daughter's father, and even secretly visited him a few times. After about six months, when no improvement had occurred, her situation started to decline. The electricity and telephone service in her apartment were suspended for non-payment, the lease was about to run out, the bank refused her credit, the girl fell ill and needed expensive medical treatment, and she herself sank into a depression. For the girl's fifth birthday she prepared a present: a letter in which she requested that her daughter be put up for adoption so that she could grow up in a stable home with two parents. That night the woman tried to kill herself with an overdose of sleeping pills. She was saved by her daughter's resourcefulness; the girl alerted neighbors when she heard her mother gurgling.

The woman dreams that she is at home with a female infant and has to do many things at once. The baby is hungry and crying in her crib, the milk heating on the stove boils over, and as she hurries to turn off the burner, the phone rings. The caller says, "Just a moment, please" and puts her on hold with classical music. At the same time she hears a thud, the baby screams and is silent, and the doorbell rings. As she runs to the baby, the music on the phone changes and someone on the line says her name in a threatening tone. Outside a siren sounds and a voice on a loudspeaker says something about evacuation because the buildings are in danger of collapse. She picks up the unconscious infant and runs to the window, leaning out to see what is happening in the street. There's a tremendous storm, lots of policemen running around, and people beginning to stream out of their apartment houses. Someone bangs wildly on her door and suddenly a strong gust of wind whips the child out of her arms. The baby flies like a large bird, and the woman races down the stairs and into the street, where the baby floats above her. The wind continues to thrash her, knocking off, in succession, her watch, her ring, her hair clip, and every article of clothing, until she is left completely naked. Suddenly she also loses her hair, her breasts, her fingernails; then her internal organs are removed—heart, lungs, stomach, intestines, bladder, ovaries, and all the other organs, some of which she cannot identify—until all that remains of her is a skeleton.

A teacher and a group of students are passing by. The teacher stands her next to a tree, and the students sit down all around, open their briefcases, and take out notebooks and pencils. The teacher gives them a lesson in human anatomy, piercing her with a pointer as he says, "This is where the heart was, and this was the site of the brain." She tries to tell him that her heart and brain still exist, but she is incapable of moving her mouth; she has no teeth or tongue. She can't move her legs either, and, as she discovers that, she notices her baby drifting farther and farther away, until she turns into a white speck and disappears.

Correction of the dream: In the first session the woman tried to correct the dream through aggressive action. She seized the teacher's pointer, turned it into an iron bar, and started beating the teacher and the students. Then she tried to catch the baby in a huge butterfly net, but failed and only hurt the child. In the second session she suggests that she first lie down to rest. She uses a relaxation technique she's familiar with to get back her internal organs, her hair, and her skin, and turns the skeleton into a woman's body. Then she gets dressed and goes out to sit on a bench near the entrance to her apartment house. The wind dies down and a white speck appears, distant, in the sky: her baby, sleeping peacefully on a cloud. The cloud moves closer, until it comes to rest on her lap and then disperses, leaving the sleeping baby.

*[Page 19. Fonts: David, all but first two words of each piece in light, like previous pages. Justified and framed, no word breaks, no extra leading. Leave quarter-page for paid obit, Prof. Ben-Yitzhak.]*

**The dream of a woman with bipolar disorder, presented at the inter-**

**national seminar by Dr. Ora Sirkin of Ben-Gurion University,
Beersheba.**

A sixty-year-old widow is suffering from depression, Her son was
killed in the Lebanon War

The girls had started streaming out of the building, and
Hamutal stopped reading in mid-sentence and put the
papers back in the binder, her eyes scanning for Michal.
Even after the last girl had come out, Michal was nowhere
to be seen. Hamutal waited another moment, then got out
of the car to look for the teacher. She found her slipping
off her dance shoes, exchanging them for boots, and
explaining as she did so that Michal had sent a message
with a friend that her dog had been hurt and she'd taken
him to the vet.

"But I'm glad I have this chance to speak to you," the
teacher said, her eyes still on the complicated buckles.
"Has anything happened at home recently?"

"Like what?" said Hamutal, frightened.

"I don't know. She just hasn't been concentrating lately."
The teacher gave Hamutal a searching look.

Hamutal, almost happy to have an explanation again,
said in a even voice, "Her grandmother has been transferred to a nursing home."

"And that has such an effect on her?"

"It affects all of us," she said, aware of the inflation of
that statement, aware of its precision as well.

What had seemed to her in the nursing-home cafeteria to
be right and simple, flowing in its inevitable course,
demonstrated the full force of its menace as soon as she
got home.

Even from the gate she could hear the girls' whooping

shouts. Before opening the door to find Hila and four of her friends in the living room, she paused a moment and tried to orient herself toward home, like a traveler returning from distant parts, careful to turn her watch back to local time.

"We needed space to rehearse, so we came downstairs," Hila told her in a voice that Hamutal imagined was free of hostility. "But in a little while they'll all say bye-bye very nicely and be out of here, because I'm dying of hunger and I saw lots of goodies in that delivery from the supermarket."

Apparently she hadn't done a good job of orienting herself. In the kitchen she couldn't control the sensation of floating, as if a part of herself had torn itself off and gone soaring, no longer belonged, and from its safe haven was calling to the other parts of her, hinting at the danger and the shelter to be found in that other place, enticing her to come, proclaiming the possibilities and blocking her return, here in the kitchen, to her old persona, to the usual pre-dinner frenzy. She unpacked the delivery box, jolting back and forth between the routine her hands performed on their own and the thought of this new thing that had invaded her life, flooding her with a sense of unreality. She contemplated the container of raspberry yogurt at length, her eyes fixed on the picture of the peculiar lumpy fruit, which resembled an earring she once wore.

From a distance, muffled, as though they were not a mere seven paces away, she heard Hila and her friends rehearsing a scene from some play, teasing each other endlessly, and Michal dodging among the chairs after the dog so she could clean his wounds, and the evening news reporting on skeletons of children discovered in a cellar in a remote Irish village.

Still eyeing the raspberry as she pondered Hila's surprising affability, Hamutal resolved to pull herself together,
shake off the strange state of longing and agitation that
had come over her these last two days and get herself back
home once and for all. Her gestures now precise and ener-
getic, she continued to empty the delivery box, talking to
herself all the while, admonishing and persuading, reconstructing everything that had occurred since the previous
night and finding it had all been an error. What exactly had
happened in her life? She had been asked to approach a
man she didn't know, someone not particularly receptive,
and there was some unpleasantness in what she'd been
asked to tell him. In a sensitive situation like that, mildly
distressed, she had given in to feelings that were inappro-
priate, a sense of closeness that was all in her mind and
that he registered with a hunter's instinct, discerning her
vulnerability to the sadness he broadcast so expertly and
asking her to join him for a cup of coffee. And beyond that,
what? She didn't even know his name, and when he started
telling her about his father's prostate cancer, she recoiled
and asked a neutral question to change the subject. What
did they have to do with each other? What significance did
he have in her world? Why did she imagine he was a threat
to the stability of her life? She heard Hila applauding her
friends triumphantly, and Michal lovingly whispering
unfounded encouragement to the puppy whimpering in
pain—how could she have thought that some incidental
someone, a man off the street, of no importance, with no
name, could undermine all this? She lifted out the egg carton and found it dripping wet, with yolk and white pooling
in the cupped bottom. And the walnuts were crushed.

Hila came into the kitchen suddenly to get her friends
some juice, and paused in front of her mother.

"Are you okay?"

Hamutal immediately set the egg carton down, closed the door, and, taking advantage of the moment and of the new resolve that had possessed her, said, "Hila, I wanted to ask you something about your coming to the office yesterday."

"Forget it, I said you should forget it." Her voice was more weary than sharp.

"I have to know if it was really the math," Hamutal said to the back of Hila's neck as the girl stood in front of the open refrigerator.

Hila turned around and regarded her mother with curiosity, and Hamutal recalled the fury yesterday that made her want to slap that face.

"What's the big deal?" she said, using the English phrase. "Math or physics or whatever." Hamutal heard the genuine incredulity and felt tremendous relief.

Until Arnon came home she went about her work energetically and efficiently, reconstructing, as she would a play she'd just seen, the way she'd allowed her imagination to carry her off on an adventure with a strange man, wondering at herself, at the fact that a person could surprise herself in this way, and muttering ironically, "It's me, Hamutal—Hamutal!"

When Arnon was out of the shower and Hila's friends had left and the dog had calmed down and the news was over, the four of them gathered around the table under the radiant dome of the Murano glass light fixture, eating and once more trotting out their plan for a trip to the Large Crater in the Negev—a trip they'd postponed many times. And Hamutal, listening contentedly, taking a slice of bread from the basket Hila handed her with a flourish of generosity, knew that the hovering presence of the man in the green jacket had vaporized completely. Michal was relating the antics of the neighbor's dumb cat. "However you drop it, it lands on its head," she said, roaring with laughter at her own joke, and Hila talked about another neighbor, whose car had been such a target for kids' pranks that he'd started parking it next to the police station on Dizengoff Street. Then Michal told them about the visit to the vet, imitating the various dogs there and their masters, in particular one dog that specialized in swallowing the nipples from pacifiers and had to be brought in every two months for surgery to remove the stash from his stomach.

"Nipples . . . who said dogs are stupid?" mused Arnon, as if to himself, without lifting his eyes from the bread he was buttering. Hila grew quiet, looking at him like a secret agent who'd just heard a password uttered in public, and asked cautiously, "What do you mean, Dad?"

"Why are you sounding like a Supreme Court justice?"

"Because I think I know what you mean."

"What do you think you know I mean?"

"Something gross."

"Don't be silly," said Michal. "He's using antiphrasis."

"Using what?"

"Well, what's so clever about having surgery every two months?"

"What's *antiphrasis*?" said Arnon.

"You don't know what *antiphrasis* is?"

"No. I went to a kibbutz school. There even the teachers don't know what *antiphrasis* is."

"*Antiphrasis* is the opposite, when you say the opposite of what you mean."

"Very nice. I've learned something. Now what was the context for this antiphrasis?"

Hamutal, quietly being won over, her internal organs

slowly relenting, remembered how she'd imagined this very morning that her life was threatened with wrack and ruin, and thought about that miracle of complications seeking their own resolution.

She leaned back in her chair, listening to her loved ones, the pleasant murmur that rose with their voices, and thought that if ever—maybe when tossing in her bed in some nursing home—she wanted to remember a perfect moment, one of those moments that contained the essence of life, she would summon this one from the depths of memory: the light above casting a glow on their heads, the girls' laughter, the breadbasket moving from hand to hand, the jam jar Michal passes to her father so he can tackle the stubborn lid, the ease with which he lifts it off, the dog lying satisfied and appeased at their feet, the commanding fragrance of clementine wafting in from the neighbor's garden.

Was this alienation from home and family the past few weeks all because of the nursing home? Is that what was sucking the energy out of her, leaving her indifferent to everything else? Was she distorting her perception of her own life out of identification with her mother, who had no idea now what was real?

"Our mother is in la-la-land today," said Hila with disapproval, poking her hand into the salad bowl and fishing out a whole small cucumber, grasping it by the bit of stem at its tip the way a child would dangle a dead mouse. "Look what a lovely diced salad she made."

Hamutal sat bolt upright, confused by the brutality with which she'd been jarred from her musings.

"What's with our mother that she's such a dreamer today?" Hila drew out the words in a storytime-for-toddlers sort of tone.

"Hila," Michal scolded. "That's not nice."

"Neither is the salad," said Hila, swinging the cucumber.

"Stop that this minute," snapped Hamutal, and was surprised by the violence of the sound from her throat.

It must have been violent indeed and most bizarre, from the way all three faces turned toward her in astonishment, like friends in the midst of an intimate chat discovering a stranger among them.

"Stop what?" asked Hila, the cucumber swaying to and fro.

"That." Hamutal slapped at Hila's fingers and the cucumber fell back into the bowl.

Arnon leaned over toward her and she recoiled, feeling she'd become transparent and he could now look inside her and read her thoughts, see the wheels turning feverishly in her brain as she struggled to put some restraint in her voice: "I can't stand it when people touch food, that's all. I simply can't stand it when food is touched, can't stand it."

There was silence around the table, and Hamutal heard herself say, as if she didn't realize how ridiculous it sounded, "I just don't know what happened to them today. They brought the order from the supermarket. Out of the dozen eggs eight were broken, and the nuts were crushed."

The silence was heavy, and Hamutal thought they were now regretting that the exquisite family tranquillity had been broken, that Hila had put her on the spot like this, until she heard Arnon's low, measured voice: "What does Her Supreme Judicial Honor have to say about that?"— and shrank back in her seat.

"She actually has something important to say in the matter of the nuts, but hesitates out of respect for the Court," said Hila, choking back the giggles, and Arnon burst out laughing. Michal managed to control herself for one more moment, out of allegiance to her mother, but then gave in and joined her sister and her father in peals of laughter.

Hamutal tried to rise from the table in a movement that suddenly turned clumsy as she struggled with limbs that now rebelled, pulling her like an anchor back into her chair. Extricating herself with difficulty, she passed between the chair and the table, heading for the bathroom like a blind person who knows the way but can't see it, her heart sinking at the sound of their merriment. Behind the locked door she lowered the cover of the toilet seat and sat down, feeling small and fragile and very alone. Then she stuck her head into the sink, under the faucet, letting the water soak her hair. When she lifted her head and looked in the mirror she saw a face that was grave and gray, with wet hair plastered to her skull and cheeks, and remembered the man who'd suffered a head injury and dreamed about water bursting out of the faucet and flooding his apartment, and she was overcome by a yearning whose meaning and force went beyond anything she'd imagined—for the man in the green jacket, for whom there was now room in her life.

# CHAPTER TWO

"Look hard and you'll remember: This is your mother,
this is your father, this is you at fifteen."

*[Page 34. Fonts: David (light and bold as before, but the light in italics). Leave space for ad from the School of Alternative Medicine (size to be determined) or condolence ad for Prof. Yohanan Gartine.]*

**The dream of a man left paralyzed from the waist down by a car accident, as presented at the international seminar by Prof. Henry Wasserman of Duke University, North Carolina.**

The man dreams that he is running in the mountains. As he runs he looks around and spots his parents' house, where he sees his mother standing in the yard and hanging his underwear out to dry. An animal he can't identify is running alongside him but not threatening him; it moves with him like a shadow, and he knows it is a male. Other animals slowly begin to join them: lions, tigers, deer. Now there is noise and tumult, and he can't see the landscape. Suddenly he understands that they're having a race, and he is one of the contestants. He runs very fast, almost beating out the animals beside him. Suddenly he looks into their eyes and now realizes that they are the eyes of beasts of prey and somehow understands that they are all female. It is clear to him that if he outruns them he will be devoured, and he starts to slow down, until he stops altogether and sees them off in the distance. Even the male animal that was his shadow disappears with the others. Now he feels safer, but very much alone without his shadow. He looks around and sees his mother still hanging laundry. She puts her hand into the laundry basket and takes out the dreamer himself, all crumpled and wrung out, and shakes him out as she would a shirt. He screams in pain but she doesn't hear him, just hangs him on the line and secures him with metal clothespins that she clamps on his testicles.

As a correction, the dreamer suggested the following ending: After the animals fade into the distance, he faints and falls down. His mother raises a hue and cry and the animals stop. They turn around and see him stretched out on the ground. They all come back and start to nuzzle and lick him. He sits on the back of a lioness, who takes him to his mother's house.

Hamutal read the description of the dream over and over. What struck her most was the mother hanging the son's underpants out to dry. In her parents' house it had been her job to hang the laundry, and she remembered the resistance in her fingers when they came upon her parents' underwear amid the wet things—her mother's bras and panties and her father's briefs, which she would fish out with two fingers and try to hide from the neighbors' eyes behind a row of towels or sheets, on the line closest to the house.

She banished that image from her mind and forced herself to go through the pile of papers in front of her: the dreams of a girl, an only child, whose parents are divorced and who remains in the custody of her mother. She always has these dreams when she returns from a visit to her father, who has married again, a young, amiable woman with whom he has twins. The dreams are always about a disaster that befalls the twins, usually plunging into a deep pit. The dreams of a Holocaust survivor after a trip to Poland during which she visited the house she'd lived in until the age of twelve and the front yard where she was parted from her father. The dreams usually begin with some pleasant experience, which is violently interrupted. The dreams of a boy who lost his stamp collection in a fire that broke out in his room because of his fifteen-year-old brother, who had fallen asleep in bed with a lighted cigarette; the dreams of a taxi driver who ran over a disabled woman crossing the street in the crosswalk; the dreams of

a young woman teacher after the father of one of her students, a known criminal, threatened to hurt her baby; the
dreams of a blind woman who worked as a switchboard
operator and overheard by chance that—

At exactly five-thirty she stopped in mid-sentence, put a
paperweight on top of the stack, called home to make sure
Michal was back, announced that she would be late, and
hurried outside.

From her parked car outside the nursing home she saw
him getting out of his car. Though she had prepared herself for the moment of encounter, all the way there drum-
ming into herself the need for rational behavior, the sight
of him made her heart stand still, and her eyes fastened on
him, followed every move, watching him from behind for
the first time as he stepped quickly into the distance,
toward the door of the building. There was already something familiar in his movements, the gestures of an ever-
busy man, the impatience with which he thrust his left
hand into the pocket of his blazer, the way he tilted his
head slightly toward his left shoulder, as if about to scold
someone. At the same time, he was a complete stranger,
maybe because of that navy-blue blazer he was wearing,
and for a split second she found herself wondering if this
was in fact the man.

She sat there and watched him, riveted by this mixture
of familiarity and strangeness, restraining the fingers
inclined to reach for the horn. But as if he'd heard the
horn that never sounded, he glanced back as he stepped
onto the sidewalk and, when he saw her, stopped and
raised his hand, palm toward her as if swearing an oath, his
other hand still deep in the blazer pocket. He stood like
that and waited for her.

She hesitated another moment in the car, knowing it

was too late now for makeup but still glancing quickly in the mirror to discover that the eye makeup had faded and that at the corners of her mouth, where the end of the blue pencil always pressed, the lipstick had worn off. Since he was watching, she had to get out of the car, and noticed as she did so that the Rubik's cube was still in the back, near the rear window.

As she approached him, he took one step toward her as if in some ceremony, and then came the outstretched hand that in her view was too formal, as if he were following rules unknown to her, and again she was struck by the feeling of closeness and strangeness.

"I was thinking after you left that it was very impolite of me not to introduce myself: Saul Inlander."

Between his fingers and his upright thumb was a gap, and her hand was dispatched there like an animal into a trap. He closed on it, and warmth immediately joined their palms.

"Seems I should be allowed to know your name at this point."

"Hamutal." She gave herself away.

"Isn't Hamutal from the Bible?"

"Like Saul." She stepped onto the sidewalk, her hand still captive in his.

"I had the feeling we'd already met." He released her hand without a smile, and her heart jumped.

In the elevator they found themselves among strangers and stood facing each other, very close, her right shoulder and his left shoulder touching the mirror, their glances averted as if the closeness inspired guilt. If they'd been alone, and if she'd forgotten what she had tried to drum into herself all the way there, and if she'd been bold and determined enough to realize her desires, she would have pressed her temple against his shoulder without a word and buried her face in his neck, precisely in that gap between the collar of his navy-blue blazer and the edge of his ear, a place that must have been warm to the touch, giving off a scent reminiscent of eucalyptus. But she continued standing with her head lifted toward the flashing numbers of the floors, and when they reached the fifth, she preceded him out of the elevator. In the hall they had to file carefully past the wheelchairs lined up along the wall, and they couldn't talk until they reached the doorways of their parents' rooms, when he said, "At seven may I invite you—"

"Today it's my turn to invite you."

Her mother was sleeping. Apparently the condition of the woman named Rivka, who just yesterday had lain next to the window and been caressed by her grandson and her daughters, had worsened during the night and she had been transferred elsewhere, or maybe was already dead and buried. In the bed that had become available a tiny, startled old woman now sat, engulfed by pillows. On the edge of the bed, pressing the startled old woman toward the wall, sat a pale woman of about forty, dressed in black. Photographs lay in her black lap and one was in her hand in front of the sick woman's face.

"Who's this, Mama?"

The old woman turned frightened eyes toward the glossy square.

"Who is this?" The woman in black was relentless, her fingertip gliding over the surface of the photo. "And this, who's this?"

The old woman looked helplessly at the photo in front of her, her features assembling on the verge of tears, and shook her head in despair.

The woman in black suddenly shifted her glance toward Hamutal and said, "Her whole memory got blotted out. I don't understand how that can be. She was fine a week ago, I go to Munich for five days, come back—all of a sudden she has no memory." She turned back to the tiny old woman, whose face was now completely contorted even as she continued her efforts to look at the picture, like a diligent student.

"And two months ago they found cancer on the optic nerve," the woman said, turning again to Hamutal. "She had bypass surgery three and a half years ago, so because of her heart condition they can't operate under anesthesia and the professor said she could go blind at any moment—and then of course it'll be impossible to jog her memory at all."

Apparently alarmed by her own words and recalling the huge task ahead of her, the woman in black turned back to the old woman, who had shrunk into the corner.

"Look hard and you'll remember," she said, picking up momentum. "This is you. About thirty years ago. When we still lived on Habakuk Street. You remember the kitchen balcony, where you used to keep the laundry basket with the straw cover? Here, you can even see the braid of garlic you used to hang on the wall there. This is your brother Dudik, who used to tell funny stories, like yours. He came from America for Shoshana's wedding, and here we're sitting in the dining area next to the kitchen. This is me, and this is Shoshana. This is Haimke, with his broken arm in a cast, from when he fell off his bike. We're drinking tea from the fancy set of Rosenthal china, with the red flowers, you see?"

The old woman looked at the picture and tried, no doubt, to make some connection between the verbiage pouring from the mouth of the woman in black and what met her eye in the photo. Her daughter sat patiently, allowing her to investigate the picture that she held by the edge with one hand while stroking the crook of her mother's withered arm with the other.

"Look hard and you'll remember," she said in a tone neither severe nor indulgent, like a teacher guiding a slow child, "this is your mother, this is your father, and this is you at fifteen. Now look carefully at this: this is the dog we had, Ricky. He used to come into our beds and you would get mad, and in the end he was hit by a car because he was old and couldn't run anymore. This is Shoshana, your daughter, with Moran, your first granddaughter. She was born in Jerusalem, and we went there in the snow to see her, and you said she was as beautiful as Snow White, remember? And this, look at this picture: You remember the trip we took to France? The way half the plane was singing 'Jerusalem of Gold' and the noise was driving the French stewardess crazy? You remember we bought a jacket for Papa and it was small on him and in the end Shoshana's husband got it? And the necklace of green beads you bought that fell apart in the middle of a play at Habima and scattered all over the floor and made a racket and the actor gave you a look? And this is Haimke in basic training when he got an award and they sent him to the President's House. And here's the ceremony, where you cried so hard you got an eye inflammation, remember?"

Hamutal sat beside her sleeping mother, hearing the life story of the tiny old woman whose memory had suddenly gone dead, wondering about the inert memory cells, which maybe hadn't died but only blacked out for a while and were slowly coming to, in the depths of the silent woman's brain, linking the sounds being made to the sights being shown, so that her life could be resurrected before her eyes. Or maybe when she heard the names of the streets she had lived on and the names of her children and grandchildren, she found them completely foreign, asked herself where on earth this woman in black had come from and why she was sitting on the edge of her bed like that, trapping her where the walls met, and what was the meaning of these colored squares she was putting in front of her? Hamutal couldn't help being impressed by the patience of the black-clad woman who held up picture after picture, reconstructing her mother's history year by year, trying to breathe life into recollections now erased, evoking detail after detail, even the smallest of them, for which she used a magnifying glass to bend this resistant memory to her will.

"Look at these pictures I found in the drawer in the linen cupboard: the renovations in the Gluck Street apartment before we moved in. Here's the living room. Here's the balcony. And facing it you can see the living room of that young couple that used to fight all the time, you remember all the yelling? This is where the table stood, and over here was the painting of a mother holding a child. Next to it was Shoshana's certificate, saying she was born at the same moment as the State of Israel, with a picture of her sitting there eating ice cream. This is the bedroom, yours and Papa's. Here, over here is that armoire that had a section with drawers. This is where you kept your jewelry, remember? You remember the ring Papa bought you for your thirtieth anniversary? Look through the magnifying glass, you'll see it clearer. Over here on the wall was that tapestry of blue flowers that Rivka gave you, you remember Rivka, Papa's cousin from the kibbutz, how Haimke said there's no such thing as a blue flower and she dragged him out to the field and showed him thistles with blue flowers? She sang in a choir and once we were invited to a concert hall in Tel Aviv to hear them, and she waved to us from the stage, remember?"

It got to be oppressive, overhearing the great and small events of decades of the woman's life that had all been wiped out of her mind in a single week. What was the point of an existence in which only the body was awake, persisting like a skeleton in motion, empty of memory? And what was the riddle of this emptying, like erasing an extra copy of a document and, along with it, the smells and colors and tastes of dozens of years that had been lived, some quietly, some happily, hopefully, pleasurably, in eager anticipation, some in despair, in suffering, in terror, in disappointment, in regret, and in longing? How was it possible to leave the world that way, empty as a shell, as if nothing had happened and nothing had been learned?

The woman closed her eyes. Her daughter gathered up the stack of photos from her black lap and put them into a black velvet bag. Then she gently stroked her mother's forehead, stood up, said goodbye to Hamutal, and left the room.

Hamutal remained in her chair, her gaze resting on the forehead that had just been stroked, re-creating in her mind the happier days of the woman in black: sitting with her mother and sister on the kitchen balcony on Habakuk Street, under the braided garlic hanging on the wall, the three of them laughing at one of the amusing stories, and the dog Ricky standing by the table waiting for scraps. The hand that had stroked the old forehead must certainly remember, Hamutal thought with a pang of envy; otherwise it would never have found the love required to move the fingers so gently.

Her mother's eyes rolled open like a china doll's, look-ing lost, her expression confused. She propped herself up on her elbows with some effort and directed her gaze to Hamutal's face.

"It's me, Mother—Hamutal."

The lost look meandered toward the door.

"So they don't come at all anymore?" she complained with a fierceness that boded ill.

"Who?"

"The swindlers."

"What swindlers?"

"Your swindlers."

"If you mean Arnon and the children—"

"You know who I mean. The swindlers."

"I won't allow you to call them that."

"They're swindlers, and even worse. They're murderers."

"You can't call them that!"

"That's what they are: murderers!"

"And who exactly did they kill?"

"They haven't killed yet. They will kill." Her eyes were blinking faster.

"Who are they going to kill?"

"You."

"Me?"

"Yes. They want to murder you. I dreamed it. I saw everything."

"You dreamed?" Hamutal froze.

"Yes. I saw everything in the dream."

"I didn't know you dream."

"Why shouldn't I dream?"

"You've never talked about it."

"It wasn't important." The racing eyes belonged to the sick woman, but there was something firm and purposeful in the voice that recalled the person she had been in her previous incarnation, Shifra the Head Nurse, and Hamutal found herself addressing her words to that woman, speaking to her with the same logic she used to use then.

"What did you dream?"

"I dreamed their whole plan. They've got everything worked out now. They'll do it when they're not home. You'll be home alone, and they'll make out that they've gone away."

"I always go with them. I don't stay home alone."

"You will be alone, and they'll arrange it so the windows won't open and the door won't open and the gas will come out and come out until it fills you up. That's what they're planning."

Hamutal remembered how lonely she'd felt, sitting with her family the previous day. Is that what was in the air, the plot her husband and children had concocted, shunting her aside as if she didn't belong? She recalled with a start how last fall Arnon had looked into heating stoves and come back all enthusiastic about gas.

One of the articles she'd published in the previous issue, on the unconscious, was by an Australian psychologist who described how people who are mentally ill absorb information they are unable to decipher consciously, and it goes directly into their dreams. Had her mother absorbed things that she herself was unaware of?

"And after they finish you off, they'll come and get me. First he took my money, but that's not enough for them. Now they want to kill."

Two weeks earlier, on a routine visit with Arnon and Michal, when the four of them were sitting around a table in the dining room, her mother had complained that the rice being served was riddled with orange worms, and had suddenly pointed to Arnon and whispered, "It's him."

"Who?"

Her mother shouted, "It's him! He stole all the money for the apartment."

Arnon blanched. The nurse's aide was there in a moment, and some of the old people sitting around other tables—a few who had been strapped to their chairs to keep them upright, a few who had slouched toward the tabletops, their heads audibly clunking on Formica—lifted their eyes in frightened stares, as if the fears bursting out of her mother had ignited their own hidden fears.

"Mother, it's Arnon," Hamutal whispered in her ear.

"I know very well who he is!"

"He never stole anything from you. He's been taking care of your bank account for years."

"He's a thief!" Her mother turned to the aide: "I want the police. I want a judge. Let them take him to jail!" She surveyed the circle of eyes fixed on her till she got to Hamutal and opened her mouth to shout, saliva spraying: "Liars and scum! Every one of them scum!"

Michal suddenly burst out crying, and all the flickering gazes veered toward her. She quickly hid behind her father, pressing her face against his back and pulling the fabric of his shirt to cover her head, as if she wanted his body to swallow her up. Arnon reached behind protectively, cupping her head with his hand, and then, her face still buried in his shirt, led her outside.

"To jail!" her mother screeched after them, her hands pressing on the arms of the chair as though she were about to get up and run after them and drag them to prison herself. Her voice, surprisingly powerful, caught up with them in the corridor.

The aide alerted the head nurse, and the two of them moved the frantic woman from her wheelchair into bed. Shortly after she was given a tranquilizer shot, her features returned to normal and she fell asleep, her hand in Hamutal's hand, very soft, almost lovely in its laxity, with the fingers, so often covered with sores, now hanging limp. Hamutal looked then at their joined hands and chuckled to herself at the thought that until her mother entered the nursing home they had never touched each other with such ease, and another thought, troubling, came and displaced the first: Had this outburst been some cunning plan of her mother's? Had she purposely gotten rid of Arnon and the girls to force Hamutal to come and visit her without them?

She sat for some time like that by her mother's side, trying to put her thoughts in order. From the day her mother was moved into the nursing home, two and a half months earlier, Hamutal had never come to visit her alone. Arnon or one of the girls was always with her for protection, and once every two weeks her cousin Tzippie would come down from the Galilee. From now on she would have to come here alone every day. There was no point in exposing the girls to their grandmother in this state, with her condition changing rapidly and her responses unpredictable, and Arnon, to judge from the rare expression of injury on his face, would certainly refuse to come again.

Hamutal suddenly felt betrayed, as if, on a hike with her friends, she had fallen into a trap and they hadn't even noticed her absence, just kept on going, the sound of their laughter fading in the distance.

When she got home that day she found Michal grumbling and Arnon still pale. She reached out her hand to Michal, but the girl ducked her, and Hamutal said, "It was nothing against you, Michalie. That happens to people in her condition."

"I hate her."

"Remember how she was before she got sick. You have to remember people at their best."

"I always hated her."

"I'm sure she's sorry now."

"Couldn't care less. I'm not going there ever again."

"She didn't mean what she said."

"Never in a million years."

Arnon remained tight-lipped, which was unlike him, then asked, "Am I to be deprived of this pleasure as well?"

She didn't answer him with the girl there, just marveled at how easily he projected onto her mother all the anger he'd built up elsewhere. In their bedroom she said later, "Do I have to explain to you, too, that she's sick?"

"If she's so sick then it won't matter to her whether we come or not."

"You just stumbled on a good excuse for getting out of it, that's all," she said, and he didn't bother answering.

Later, as they lay frozen in the darkness, taking care not to touch each other accidentally, she said something whose meaning she wasn't aware of at the time, like a prophecy. She said it about the three of them, but meant only him: "If you make me go there alone, you're all abandoning me, and I don't know to what."

"We'll take that risk," he said without sympathy.

She searched for some malicious, hurtful phrase to hurl at him and, when she couldn't find one, gave up on Hebrew and said "Be my guest" in English, knowing that the English was too mild for all the bitterness accumulated in her mouth, that there wasn't enough defiance in those words, but they were the ones her tongue could reach. She tossed for a long time, enumerating to herself the suitable Hebrew words that now presented themselves and regretting that they hadn't turned up when needed.

The following day Hamutal had gone to the nursing home for the first time without Arnon and the girls, feeling as exposed and vulnerable as she had as a child. There was nothing now that would recall the girl she used to be and the woman her mother had been, but an old, fossil fear arose, of the sort she felt that night when her father had gone to Acre to pick up goods at the factory and stayed over in Nahariya with people from his town in Europe, and all evening and night and morning it was just she and her mother at home.

Although she'd walked across the gray floor of the lobby nearly every day for the last two and a half months, she was surprised to note just how gray it was and stood still for a moment, examining the tiles as if looking for something she'd lost. From then on she saw everything with fresh eyes: the white heads that lifted toward her when she walked into their dining room or activity room; the empty eyes lighting up with the sudden hope of an unexpected visit when she came down the hall; their disappointment when they realized she wasn't coming to them; the hint of envy that she could pass through, stepping so lightly, and soon conclude her visit and go back to her life outside this trap where they sat or lay in beds or dragged themselves down the hall and would continue to do so until one day they dropped and died in slow agony or, if luck was with them, suddenly.

From one of the wheelchairs a hand darted out, the gesture of a practiced hunter, and grabbed her skirt.

"Remember me?" An old woman with bad teeth lifted squinting eyes toward her, shading them as though looking at the sun.

"Who are you?"

"I'm Yochie's mother. I used to cook corn for you all in the summer."

"Don't pay any attention," said another old woman huffily: regal-looking, caged behind a walker, inching it along and thrusting herself forward as she spoke. "Anybody passes by on their own two feet, she grabs them and yammers about the corn."

Hamutal tried to free her skirt from the fingers that had become tangled in it, but the old woman only clutched more tightly and whispered, "She's jealous because I'm Yochie's mother."

"I saw this Yochie—there's nothing to be jealous of," said the huffy one with lofty indifference, and nudged the walker ahead. "Shows up once in five years."

"Every week!" The one with rotten teeth withdrew her hand from Hamutal's skirt and gripped the armrests of her wheelchair menacingly, her elbows flapping out to the sides like wings ready for takeoff. Old men started gathering around, emerging from their rooms up and down the corridor, shuffling along the railings on the walls.

"She comes, stays a minute, and runs," the woman with the walker went on complacently, channeling all her energy into the tiny shift forward.

Hamutal retreated from the cluster of people waiting for the outcome, turned her back on them, and, giving up on the visit, fled to the elevator, down to the lobby with its gray floor, and out to the safety of her car, where she sat unmoving until she could summon up the energy to turn on the ignition and escape.

Since they had stopped coming with her, her family had taken no interest in her daily visits to the nursing home, and no one asked about her mother, as if the

three of them had decided unanimously, with no com-
punction whatsoever, to wipe out her very existence.
Despite the indifference from Arnon, Hamutal, with a
kind of dogged nonchalance, repeatedly subjected him
to reports of her visits, refusing at least for now to let
him abandon her to her fate and interpreting any will-
ingness to listen on his part as a sign. The increasing distance between her and the girls, particularly Hila, was
no longer a secret. And Michal, who until six months
earlier had been begging for a baby brother, no longer
mentioned the subject. Gradually Hamutal and Arnon
had stopped trying to keep up appearances in front of
the girls and with each other in the bedroom. She was
grateful to him for being undemanding and for taking
care to preserve some vestige of normal life, since her
reserves of strength were fast draining with her daily visits to the nursing home. For a few hours after each visit
she would feel some relief, but before she fell asleep
despondency would set in again in anticipation of the
next visit.

With the sentence she'd just heard, "Now they want to
kill you," still reverberating inside her, Hamutal found
her mother gaping at her, studying her face, lingering at
the eyebrows. The practical woman that Hamutal imagined had reappeared, the one who could decipher people's conspiracies with a penetrating glance, had by now
departed, leaving this one with the frightened, staring
eyes trying desperately to comprehend what they were
seeing.

   "It's me, Mother—Hamutal."

   "We have to kill them before they kill us." Her mother
was still in the grip of that story, linking their fates through

an instinct for survival that persisted in her with surprising strength.

Her gaze paused suddenly on Hamutal's earrings, then dropped and moved along the collar of her blouse, to the triangular metal tabs that caught its corners, to the transparent raindrop pendant she'd bought in Florence, to the heavy buckle on the strap of her shoulder bag, down the long sleeves with silver buttons fastening the cuffs, to her hands resting on the bed, where it hesitated, her eyes widening at the sight of the bracelet Arnon and the girls had bought her for Mother's Day, a gold bangle studded with green Eilat stones. Opening the elegant velvet box, Hamutal had been appalled by its ugliness and immediately said, "What a lovely bracelet!"

"What's that?"

"What?"

"Where did you get that from?"

"The bracelet?" Hamutal followed her mother's eyes. "Arnon and the girls gave me a present."

"You little thief," her mother whispered through lips pursed in disgust.

"Who?"

"You. You steal things from me. The ring with the diamond, too."

"I'm Hamutal, Mother."

"Lula stole from me, too."

"Lula didn't steal a thing from you."

"They steal and they steal. Scum."

Once her mother had dragged her to the sink and washed her mouth out with laundry soap after she referred to a teacher as "crazy." Pejoratives used to make her mother's blood boil, and at home Hamutal had never heard the word "scum," which now slipped so easily from her mother's lips.

"They come at night and steal from me." Her mother's gaze was still on the bracelet.

Hamutal raised her arm and brought the bracelet up to her mother's eyes. "This bracelet is yours?"

"Of course it's mine."

"Okay, here, I'm giving it back to you." Hamutal slid it off, took her mother's hand and poked the fingers through the gold hoop, feeling the fragility of the wrist and seeing from close up the brown age spots stamped in the light, translucent skin. Her mother looked at the bracelet with neither desire nor joy.

"Do you like it?" Hamutal asked, raising her mother's arm to show her the Eilat stones shimmering like tiny moving creatures. Her mother pulled her hand away with unexpected force and put it behind her back, hiding the bracelet.

"Thieves," she hissed at Hamutal with a malevolent glare. And Hamutal, still stuck on the word "scum," surprised by the aggressiveness, helpless before whatever obsessions were being played out behind the forehead in front of her, and desperate at that moment for the company of the man visiting his father in a nearby room, said, "I have to go now. Wear it well." With a firm step and no backward glance from the doorway, she strode across the hall to inform the man that she had concluded her visit earlier than anticipated.

Saul Inlander was sitting on a chair by his father's bed, his back to the door, his knees splayed so he could get as close as possible to the bed. He was holding an old-fashioned razor in his right hand, and his left seemed to caress his father's cheek as it carefully pulled the skin taut beneath the traveling razor. The old man, his eyes closed, was sitting up straight in his bed with a sense of occasion, yielding himself calmly, unconcerned, to the blade in his son's hand.

Hamutal stopped in the doorway, aware that the scene she was witnessing was not intended for the eyes of a stranger, that she should turn around right now and leave. But she continued to stand there as if mesmerized, in the grip of a voyeurism she couldn't resist, watching these two people immersed in the labor of shaving as if in an act of love, seeing the fingers touch the cheek with a softness reserved for the innermost of rooms, thrilling to the gentle contact between father and son. Suddenly she saw the resemblance clearly: one head in profile, the other from the back, one old, the other young, both from the same mold; the fingers guiding the razor were twins of the white fingers resting on the blanket. She stood there for some time, afraid the man would turn around and give her a reproachful look, then tore herself from the spot and retreated into the hall. There she hesitated for a moment before deciding to go down to the parking lot and wait in the car until seven, to try to review some of the material in the binder. But on her way to the car she saw a gravel path leading into the garden, and spent the next few minutes pacing back and forth on the path, which was flanked by low beds of pansies in colors she had never seen before. Finally she got tired and sat down on the bench.

That evening, she decided—and the decision lifted her spirits immediately—she would call her cousin Tzippie and ask her to visit the nursing home more often.

Tzippie had been coming to see her aunt once every two weeks, on Fridays, always laden with fruit from the trees in her yard, with jams she'd made herself and rolls she'd baked in her kitchen. Hamutal would take the jams and rolls home and they'd put the fruit in a drawer of her mother's cupboard. It would be gone by the next day. Tzippie always arrived with an entourage of children, hers and her friend's, who took advantage of the ride to visit their grandparents on the outskirts of Tel Aviv. On their first visit to the nursing home, one of the kids had gotten his toe smashed under a wheelchair, and another couldn't stop talking about how he'd seen an old woman being diapered like a baby. From then on the children would wait for Tzippie in the lobby, their voices rising to the fifth floor.

In childhood Hamutal and Tzippie had been like sisters, but as they got older they grew more distant, and their husbands seemed to feel a mutual hostility, so the women got together even less. Now they sometimes coordinated their visits so they could see each other in the nursing home. Tzippie would frankly survey Hamutal's fine suits, and Hamutal would take a quick glance at Tzippie's colorful cotton blouses and Indian skirts with narrow belts trailing bells that tinkled with every move. But still the old, surprising childhood warmth was rekindled, and the kind of camaraderie their parents had shared, which had linked the women since infancy. As soon as they emerged from their hug Hamutal would report the doctor's latest assessment and learn from the expression on Tzippie's face how much her mother's situation had worsened. Only then would the two of them go downstairs to sit on a bench in the garden and talk about family and work, with the flock of children scattering around them.

Hamutal's father and Tzippie's father had been first cousins born the same year, two months and seventeen days apart. As children they spent a great deal of time together, playing a little and fighting a lot, in the home of their grandfather, who owned the city's big bakery. Because their birthdays were close together, their grandfather decided to have a joint bar mitzvah for them. Ten years later, when the war broke out, the young men could still taste the pastries their grandfather had prepared for the occasion and still feel the blows they'd exchanged when one of them had a fit of jealousy over the magnificent speech the other had delivered without a single stammer. All evening long Hamutal's father had provoked Tzippie's father with words and pinches, until the celebration culminated in a punchout and a broken tooth.

For years afterward the cousins would not exchange a word, and when the Germans rounded everyone up in the market square and separated members of their family, they didn't exchange a glance. Even when their grandfather, about to be dispatched with their grandmother in the first truck, drew them both aside and embraced these two grandsons who now towered over him, they were careful not to touch.

After the war they met by coincidence in a displaced-persons camp in Germany: Hamutal's father, his lungs tattered by quarry dust at Mauthausen, and Tzippie's father, his big toe sliced off by the blade of a steel cutter at Auschwitz. Searches and inquiries made it clear that they were the only two remaining out of the entire family. For a whole night they sat and wept and reminisced and in the morning decided to share their lives as their parents had, to be neighbors, to celebrate the holidays together as they remembered them from their grandfather's house, and to raise their children together, as if trying to enlarge by force of will the family that had been decimated.

When they married they settled in the same city and together they moved three times, taking care to find apartments in the same building. Marek was born first, named, as his father had vowed, after the man who had saved his life at Auschwitz and later died there. Six years later Marek's sister was born, named after Grandma Tzipporah, and two months later Hamutal was born, named after Grandpa Mottel.

The wives, though very different—one busy outside the home, the other scrubbing her house down day and night—took to each other right away, but between the men there was latent tension until the end. Sometimes their tempers would get the better of them and they'd quarrel the way they had as kids, always about trivial things, usually excessive smoking on the part of Tzippie's father, who was inconsiderate of Hamutal's father's damaged lungs. But the friendship that had grown up between their wives, and a few days' silence, would result in a reconciliation, which was always marked with a good meal on the good china, after which they would listen to cantorial recitals on the radio. Since they spent every Sabbath eve and holiday together and jointly celebrated all the children's birthdays, Hamutal, Tzippie, and Marek saw a great deal of one another, usually with the two girls ganging up on the older boy.

A wheelchair appeared at the end of the path, and Hamutal recognized the couple she'd seen the previous day from the window of the cafeteria: she, tied to the back of the chair, her head flopping to one shoulder or the other, her tongue protruding from her open mouth, and he, his head rising only a bit above the back of the chair, his face exceedingly weary. When he reached the bench, he rotated the wheelchair, greeted Hamutal, and plunked himself down beside her. The old woman looked distractedly at Hamutal, and the sight of those shifting eyes triggered "It's me—Hamutal," which stuck in her throat. The woman leaned forward to survey Hamutal's face, and her tongue, like a lizard's, darted around in her open mouth.

"She thinks she knows you," the man said, breathing heavily.

The woman thrust her head out of her neck like a turtle poking out from its armor, intensifying her study of Hamutal's face.

"She doesn't know you," said the man, as if to reassure her.

At the sound of his words the woman jerked her head toward him, straining to examine his features, as if she recognized the voice but not the face.

"I'm Clara," he shouted to the woman, explaining apologetically to Hamutal: "When I tell her I'm Clara, she lets me be for a while. When she knows it's me, she makes me turn around."

"Who's Clara?" Hamutal asked.

"I don't have the strength to turn around," he said, almost in tears, then was silent, and Hamutal thought he was avoiding her question because it was too intrusive, so she, too, was silent.

"She had a caretaker named Clara," the old man said when he'd recovered his strength. "Clara was the only one she was afraid of. The rest of them she drove crazy, and that's why I had to put her here in the end. I didn't have the strength to lift her."

Something flashed in the eyes above the flitting tongue, and the man shrank backward into the bench, fearful that

the creature in the wheelchair was grasping at some fila-
ment of understanding and any moment now would know
who was Clara and who was not Clara.

"I have to go," Hamutal said, getting up, and imagined
she saw the tongue striking a new rhythm in the mouth.

At seven o'clock Saul Inlander was waiting for her in the
cafeteria. In front of him, on the tray decorated with
watermelons, were two cups of coffee, and she came and
sat down across from him like someone spotting a friend in
the midst of a mass emergency.

"Today it's my turn to buy."

"I'll give you another opportunity," he said, and she felt
relieved, as if, in a world where the rules kept changing all
around her, here was a relationship that promised some
regularity and order.

"How's your father?"

"A little better. Today I decided to shave him."

"I saw."

"You came into the room?"

"I stood in the doorway. You seemed immersed in yourselves and I didn't want to intrude."

"Really?" His eyes interrogated her face, as if he'd just
had a revelation about her.

"Yes. But I watched you for quite a while before deciding not to intrude." She didn't know why she was trying to
spoil the good impression.

"What did you see?"

"I saw just him. He looked calm."

"They changed his medication, and now he's sleeping
better."

"My mother apparently isn't sleeping very well. She was
acting very strangely." She suddenly recalled the idea of

murder by gas, and the bracelet, and asked, "Does it ever happen that he doesn't recognize you?"

"Once he looked confused and thought I was the doctor. Usually he recognizes me."

"She thought I was some woman who had come to steal her jewelry. She didn't know who I was." She spoke without difficulty, as if she were talking to herself. "She claimed I had stolen her bracelet, said everyone steals from her. She also blamed her best friend, who died five years ago. I gave her the bracelet and ran."

What she had told him just now, she knew, and the quaver in her voice, which she hadn't tried to control to disguise her depression and revulsion, was the kind of thing you didn't tell someone who wasn't really close. But in addition to the pact established between them from that first moment in the parking lot, there was now her memory of the pleasure with which he slid the razor along his father's jaw and how his father sat, relaxed, under the blade, and there were the eyes capable of understanding the annihilating pain inflicted by her mother's wicked eyes as she said, "You little thief." What did Arnon know—it was as if she had to apologize to herself—Arnon, whose parents still got up early every morning, summer and winter, and walked for an hour before breakfast, to the old gate of the kibbutz, the one next to the wadi, and then went to work in the kibbutz factory and in the evenings participated in a book group and discussion sessions on Israeli history and geography—what did he know about the heartbreak that went with "You little thief"?

"Do you have children?"

"Three."

"Can you conceive of the possibility that some day you

won't recognize them? That you'll think they're strangers come to rob you?"

"No."

"That's the thing that scares me most."

"I'm hoping my body will give out before my memory."

"You know, my mother was a very active woman. She was the head nurse at a neighborhood health clinic. I look at her, and nothing remains of that woman, not even her appearance. Maybe, once in a while, just a sort of brightening in her eyes, or aggressiveness in her voice. Today I had that impression for a minute, but just for a minute. . . . And there's a new patient, her daughter sitting there the whole time with photographs, trying to revive her memory. She says her mother's memory was wiped out in five days."

"She must have hit her head."

"How can the memory of an entire lifetime be erased in a few days?"

He suddenly leaned toward her, his chest touching the edge of the tray, his voice barely audible, intended for her ears only. "I have a request," he whispered.

"What?" Her knees snapped together of their own accord.

"I'm not sure if I can ask anything of you."

"Like what?"

"There's a movie playing at the theater near the beach. I read that it was filmed in Chicago and I'd like to see it. Have you seen *The Fugitive*?"

"No."

"Will you be my guest?"

"*The Fugitive*. Isn't that an action movie?"

"I believe it is."

Her sudden burst of laughter dispelled the tension in her knees.

"Why are you laughing?" He looked at her, puzzled.

"Because you're inviting me to an action flick."

"May I?"

"I thought who knows what you were going to ask." She couldn't stop laughing.

"And it won't be a problem . . . I mean . . . at home?

Afterward she would remember this as the moment when the first overture was made and the first obstacle examined: Here is a woman with a home, and someone is waiting for her in that home. Someone else is suggesting that she go with him to a movie. It still sounded innocent enough, but it bore all the earmarks of non-innocence. He was leaning on his elbows, his head bent toward her as if to observe from close up how she would deal with the problem that had now been placed before her.

"They're used to my getting home late. Sometimes I have to work in the evenings." She produced the lie without hesitation.

Later she would note to herself: at that moment the decision was made. The sentence she said, like an offhand comment about her daily schedule, could also be seen as groundwork for lies to come. And as soon as she said it she was startled that it came so naturally. She neither hesitated nor regretted nor blushed, as if she understood that she was about to do the right thing, conveniently believed that this was how things were fated to be and that she had no power to change them.

In the parking lot she directed him to her car: "No one living in Chicago would know the shortcuts to the movie theater."

"Guilty as charged." He meant living in Chicago.

Inside the little car, between the closed windows, they

were suddenly imprisoned together, very near each other. There was a closeness in the air, a murmur of heavy breathing consciously suppressed. And there was the tacit understanding that they were partners at the start of some thing forbidden, which for now could be dismissed with a message about being late. The smell of his blazer, including a hint of eucalyptus, gradually filled the whole space, and she found herself thinking about the order in which to move her hands and feet, movements that were always automatic. Her hand reaching for the gear shift got caught on the edge of his blazer, and she succeeded in starting the car only on the third try.

"You can play with the Rubik's cube meantime." She was trying to conceal her embarrassment.

"I'd rather watch you drive," he said, and she was repelled for a moment by the comment, which reminded her of Arnon's style. They hardly said a word all the way to the theater. The darkness produced something explosive in her lungs that pressed outward, overflowing into the air, until she imagined it would shatter the windows. There was no place here for talk of their parents, who had been the main subject of all their conversations so far. Hamutal said little, just a forced sentence here and there to break the silence, to ease the growing tension in the car. As she drove she suddenly realized she had no idea what street she had ended up on, and when she finally found her way out, she pointed to some buildings on the right that had been designated for preservation, saying like a tour guide, "This is the Great Synagogue," to which he said, "I know. The British found a Lehi arms cache there."

"So you know more about the place than I do," she said, embarrassed that he understood she'd gotten lost on the way to the theater.

"I lived in Israel until nine years ago, and my father's apartment is fairly close to our movie theater."

She fell silent, bewildered, letting the echo of "our" linger in the air, as if they already held property in common.

When they got out of the car it occurred to her that someone she knew might see her in the movie theater with a strange man. The last time she went to the movies with Arnon they'd run into her brother- and sister-in-law. How would she introduce him if they suddenly met friends or neighbors or colleagues from work? Had she been too hasty, deciding to go to a movie in the heart of the city?

Through the whole movie she wondered what she would tell Arnon when she got home, while out of the corner of her eye she kept glimpsing Saul Inlander's profile, unsmiling even when everyone around them burst out laughing. She could tell that in spite of herself she was surrendering to this man who didn't know how to laugh, who seemed to have something damaged in him, something that was willing to begin to show itself only to her because of the covert partnership that had sprung up between them, as if they were new recruits to intelligence and had just now been given the password. She sat all evening with her eyes on the screen, a shudder riffling through her when his shoulder touched her shoulder, when their fingers happened to meet in the huge container of popcorn they held between them, when he bent down to put the empty container on the floor and his hand brushed her skirt, and when he put his lips to her ear and whispered, "That's the Sears Tower" or "That's the John Hancock building," and then, "On the right you'll see the twin towers. They look like two ears of corn."

On the way back, too, they said little.

"Do you miss Chicago?" she asked when they were almost at the parking lot.

"Yes. I get attached to places."

"How long have you been in Israel now?"

"Two months, since my father started getting worse."

"And for two months you haven't been working?"

"My company's got a branch here. Sometimes I go to the offices in Jerusalem and Carmiel."

"And when will you go back to Chicago?"

"I don't have a return date. We'll see how my father's condition develops."

The word "develops" made her chuckle: something out of the vocabulary of a nurse at the baby clinic, and for some reason she recalled the woman in the wheelchair, with her quivering tongue. In what way was his condition going to develop? What he should have said was, "I don't have a return date. I'm waiting until my father dies."

In the parking lot of the nursing home she pulled up next to his car, and he put his hand over hers, which was resting on the knob of the gear shift, and said, as if everything had been agreed upon and the future was apparent to both of them and there was no hurry, "Thank you for the company. See you tomorrow." He removed his hand from her feverish hand and got out, taking with him the fragrance of eucalyptus, leaving her oddly winded, buzzing with a new tension that had been building up inside her from the moment he got into the car, and maybe even before that, when he had said, "I have a request."

She couldn't remember how she got to the walk in front of her house. At the door her feet and heart stopped together, and the question that had nagged at her earlier now presented itself head-on: What would she tell Arnon? Would she tell the truth? Would she say she'd been working at the office? And what if it turned out that he'd looked for her at the office?

She peered into the house and was surprised to find it just as it had been. Arnon was sitting in the living room, watching a television documentary about Japan in the Second World War, and there was music coming from Hila's room, and Hamutal knew she would not be able to tell the truth.

She came up behind him, and for fear that her voice would betray her, said nothing. He stretched his arms and happened to touch her hand, and both of them flinched, he in surprise and she out of fear that he'd discover the smell of popcorn on her fingers.

"Look at that bomb falling on Hiroshima," he said to no one in particular, and she said, straining to keep her voice steady, "I'm wiped out. I was busy with the new issue all day." She was astonished again at how easily the lie came out, noticing someone new and very different from the self she had known, someone emerging from inside her without the least difficulty, someone whose conscience was easy and whose tongue was slick, who had apparently been there inside all the time without announcing her existence, knowing for certain that one day she would be called upon and then would step forward and quite adeptly deliver her lines.

"Boom!" said Arnon. "That's one hell of a mushroom! If I didn't know what this was, I'd think it was a kids' movie."

When she arrived the next day around noon, Hamutal found her mother in the activity room, asleep in a wheelchair in the sun, snoring lightly, her fingers fidgeting at her neck as if tearing at the hands of a strangler. Hamutal went over and sat down beside her, looking at the knuckles turning white from the tension in the fingers and the face contorted with anguish.

Sitting on a chair against the wall was the daughter of the woman whose memory had been erased, leaning over her mother just as she had the previous day, showing photo after photo, insistent on describing each one down to the last detail, determined to win out over the lost memory and the tumor creeping along her mother's optic nerve: "Look hard. Here we're already in the apartment on Hame'asef Street, but we moved out because they put a bus stop right there and you couldn't stand the noise. Remember the bus? How you used to wait for the eleven-fifteen before you went to sleep because that was the last one? Remember the neighbor across the hall who used to make those spicy soups and bring them to us to taste, until one time Shoshana got an upset stomach and you asked her to stop bringing the soups and she got insulted? Here, look at this picture: Haimke's bar mitzvah. He didn't sleep the whole night before because he was so scared he'd forget his speech, and this was taken after he spoke, so he's all smiles. Look how Shoshana's holding her hand to her head. You remember how they cut her hair crooked and she made a scene and didn't even want to come to the party, and in the end she came and held her hand over the short side the whole evening? Look at this: Here's your brother, Dudik, with the rented car someone stole the mirror from, and there was a whole mess with the rental agency, remember?

"Here, look at this one: the picnic with your friends, Miri's parents. Her mother used to bring a big sesame bagel to picnics, and her father used to argue with Papa all the time. Here you're all playing cards. You see the cards in Miri's father's hands? And there's a plate. Must be for the bagel. Here's Miri's little brother—Benny, I think his name was. Remember how he got lost and Miri's mother had a fit and in the end two boys brought him back and he didn't want them to go because they played soccer with him? Here's Shoshana in her army uniform. You know who Shoshana is, right? Your daughter. The older daughter. I'm the younger one. Here's she's fat, she only went on the diet afterward."

On the other side of the table, watching them with curiosity, was an old woman Hamutal had often seen in the halls, going from room to room and looking in, once in a while sitting in her wheelchair, but usually walking with a walker or a cane, trying to make conversation with people, coming back the next day to visit them as if they were old acquaintances, introducing herself to their children and visitors. Once Hamutal had seen her downstairs in the lobby, sitting and watching the people coming in, and once she'd gone as far as the front gate and peered out at the passing cars. In her wanderings she often stopped by old Inlander's bed, straightening his blanket, rummaging in the drawer of the bedside cupboard, taking out a comb and gently combing his hair. She didn't try to engage him in conversation, as if she was respecting his preference for silence, but she would come back loyally every few hours. If she found his son there she would back off, and if Saul arrived while she was standing by his father's bed she would disappear without a word.

The aide asked Hamutal to wake her mother and take her back to bed, and Hamutal did so. The curious woman got up quickly, shuffled to her wheelchair, sat down in it

and hurried to catch up with Hamutal as she walked down
the hall.

"I can get around without this chair. I walk fine. Are you
her daughter?"

"Yes."

"She's your mother?"

"Yes."

"Today I moved into your mother's room."

"In the middle bed?"

"Yes."

"What happened to the woman who was there?" She
remembered the woman who used to watch her wistfully.

"She used to yell at night. Maybe she's dead by now."
The old woman squeezed into the room behind her and
watched her move her mother from the chair into the bed.

"We're friends." She waved to Hamutal's mother.

"You and my mother?"

"Yes. We're friends. My name is Bertha."

"Nice to meet you. I'm Hamutal."

"I know."

"How do you know?" She was hoping to hear that her
mother, in one of her lucid moments, had talked about her.

"Because you're always saying to her: 'I'm Hamutal. I'm
Hamutal.' Once I had a neighbor with a cat named
Hamutal."

"That's nice." She didn't know what to say.

"Ruined all the wicker in her chairs."

"That's too bad."

"She bought new ones. I'll watch over her."

"Over who?"

"Your mother."

"Good."

"Her name is Shifra."

"That's right."

"Once I had a neighbor named Shifra."

"Really?"

"Yes. She used to get packages of sourball candies from America."

"That's nice."

"But not for very long."

"What?"

"What what?"

"What not for very long?"

"I can't watch over your mother for very long."

"Why not?"

"Because I have to leave soon."

"Leave?" She remembered Arnon calling this place "the last stop."

"Yes. I have to go to Canada."

"To Canada?" Hamutal eyed the wheelchair.

"Canada, yes. My parents are coming soon to take me to Canada."

"Excuse me?" Hamutal was taken aback.

"Yes, yes. Why do you say 'Excuse me' like that?" The woman rolled herself to the other end of the bed.

"Your parents are taking you to Canada?" Hamutal tucked the blanket around her mother.

"They got a visa."

"Ah, that's nice," said Hamutal softly, her heart going out to her.

"Yes." The woman wriggled out of her wheelchair, shuffled to her bed, laboriously hoisted her legs up after her, and tunneled under the covers.

If Arnon and the girls had been there, Arnon would most certainly have said to Bertha, "Have a good trip," and drawn the girls into gales of laughter. She was glad they hadn't come with her, hadn't imposed their jokes on the airlessness in her throat. Her eyes were still on Bertha, who was turning under the mountain of blankets, undoubtedly dreaming the dreams of a girl whose parents have promised her another country. But Bertha wasn't asleep. She lifted her head and said, "I can walk fine. I don't need the wheels."

Her mother, who had shown no sign that she was awake, now lifted her head and gave Bertha a piercing look. Bertha sat up as if challenged to a duel.

"I can walk fine," Bertha said loudly, thrusting her head forward.

"So why are you here?" Mother asked weakly.

"Am I bothering you?" Bertha drew her shoulders up.

"You look pretty healthy to me." Hamutal heard a distant echo of Shifra the Nurse.

"What are you, a doctor?" Bertha, insulted, wrapped her head in her blankets.

Her mother closed her eyes—her energy spent in the brief fray—and didn't open them again, and Hamutal was relieved that the visit had ended without major mishap, as if she'd gotten away with something.

Though she knew this wasn't Saul Inlander's usual visiting time, she remained seated there, her eyes on the corridor, watchful, waiting. She had the feeling she'd sat like this before, casting sidelong glances, and remembered the physics teacher.

When Hamutal was in ninth grade, quite suddenly, with no advance notice, no warning whatsoever, she fell in love with the physics teacher. At the moment this occurred he was standing at the blackboard, looking at a drawing of a green pulley lifting a red crate, pointing to the end of the rope, under which he had written FORCE 50 KG, and to the crate, in which he had written LOAD 50 KG, and explaining again what is gained in force and what is lost through increased distance. Something touched her in the juxtaposition of the words *force* and *loss,* and in the moving way he tried to explain the complicated process, saying good-naturedly, "With complex pulleys it's different, there you save on force but pay for it in distance. But here we have a single pulley with a fixed axle, so we don't gain in force and don't lose on distance." He looked desperately into the eyes of his students, and she felt a whacking contraction of the heart and a pleasurable chill descending her spine like a rubber ball skimming down stairs, and a sharp, addictive sweetness seeped through her entire body and she knew without a doubt that now the thing had happened to her, though this was the first time in her life, and she was amazed at the way it had happened. Maybe she was influenced by a movie she had recently seen, about a love affair between a teacher and a student, or maybe her heart had ripened and was simply ready for love at that very moment when the physics teacher stood in front of the class—mainly girls who found his formulas incomprehensible—and made such a hopeless and heart-rending effort to penetrate their minds with this wheel and its fixed axle and the force and what is gained and what is lost along the way.

Every Sunday for weeks after that, during the two hours he taught her class, she would sit and gaze at him, hungrily taking in every detail: his sinuous earlobe, the back tooth that was lower than its neighbors, the part in his hair that was straight near the forehead and went awry at the crown, and she would try to blink less so as not to waste precious spectating time. But her hunger for the sight of him and the sweet heartthrob she felt at the very thought of him disturbed her peace at other times as well. At night before falling asleep she would press her hand to where her heart was hurting, as though to assuage the injured organ, and she imagined how she would hide in the entryway of the apartment building across from his and watch him standing at the window, and then steal around his house into the yard and wait there under cover of darkness until she could see him through the back window, sitting at his desk, wearing his at-home clothes, maybe even shorts—her cheeks flushed at the audacious thought—reading his thick and complex physics books. She tried to find out his address, surprising herself with her deviousness, and once even tried to follow him on the bus but had to give up when he was the only one getting off at a stop downtown. She remained seated like a prisoner by the window, gazing forlornly after him as the doors slammed shut, knowing she could never discover where he lived without revealing her secret.

One morning, on the way to school, she overheard someone saying to a friend that he'd run into the physics teacher at the public library. She stood stock still, breathless: this was an encouraging omen. That whole winter she hung around the two public libraries in town, on the prowl in the stacks, peering between the tops of books and the bottoms of shelves, hoping to meet him in one of the aisles, disappointed each time and full of hope for the next.

By the end of winter she was desperate. Her love was so strong she could barely answer his questions in class. He apparently understood, and stopped calling on her, which for her was another sign. From the beginning of spring until the end of the year she spent every long break on Sundays and Mondays outside the door of the teachers' room, exactly opposite his accustomed chair, absorbing his image in flashes as the door opened and closed, committing his appearance to memory so she could mull it over all day: bending over his notebook; taking a sip of tea; looking for something in his briefcase; speaking to the English teacher; reading a newspaper. So as not to arouse the suspicion of the secretary in the room across the hall, she developed a special talent for casting a lightning glance to snare his likeness the moment the door opened and looking away, thoroughly bored, as soon as it closed.

Sitting now next to her mother's bed, she felt her muscles tighten in that old anticipation, and the corner of her eye, like some state-of-the-art sensor, detected every movement in the corridor. There was a rustling of sheets nearby and, turning to her mother, she found her leaning forward, her arm gliding over the blankets, slow and snake-like, toward Hamutal's hand, which rested, limp and hidden, under a fold in the top blanket. There was something hypnotic in that limb whose advance was almost imperceptible but persistent, the fingers spread, their tips combing the blanket like sophisticated antennae, estimating the location of the daughter's hand by the weight on the mother's hip. The hand ducked under the blanket fold without for a moment suspending its forward motion. Suddenly the two hands met, nails to nails, like enemies face to face, and her mother's hand stopped for a moment as if assessing the situation, then immediately resumed its movement, its fingers climbing onto Hamutal's, sliding over the nails, meandering along, feeling their way over the knuckles, moving inexorably on until they rested over the whole hand, fingertips on wrist, wrist under fingertips, and stopped. Their eyes, too, met, and as Hamutal tried to guess whether her mother understood the meaning of the

dance of war and courtship their hands had carried on,
she felt the slight, steady warmth seeping into her from
this fragile hand, and was astonished by the direct gaze
meeting hers, astonished that there was nothing embar-
rassing in this new, rare contact between her mother's
skin and her own.

Beyond the window, like an illustration out of Genesis, a
ray of light flashed as if from a neon strip drawn across the
width of the sky, widening, brightening slowly till it
blinded, illuminating the room in all its detail.

Saul Inlander came into the room, and she was surprised: "I didn't know you come here at this hour."

"I canceled a trip to Carmiel. What do you say we take
them downstairs for a walk?"

"Them?"

"My father and your mother. The sun came out all of a
sudden. They'll enjoy being outside."

When she got to the garden with her mother, the two
were already waiting for them. Saul was sitting on a bench,
his hands in his pants pockets and his jacket flared out to
the sides, looking at the flowers planted on either side of
the gravel path; the elder Inlander, wrapped in a blanket
up to the neck, sat motionless as a statue, eyes front.
Hamutal rolled her mother's wheelchair up alongside his
father's and came and sat on the bench.

And so they sat and faced one another: one couple on
the bench looking at the other couple in wheelchairs. Her
mother fell asleep immediately. She blinked in the rich
light, closed her eyes, and her head dropped forward,
pulling the shoulders with it, until they were stopped by
the strap holding her to the chair. His father stared
absently into the air, his pupils glittering.

Hamutal looked at them and thought: Had they been ten years younger, maybe even less, his father would have gotten up and extended a gallant hand and invited her mother to a café. In summer, they might have eaten ice cream. If they had sat at a table near a dance floor, he might have asked her to dance. If she had worn her white summer outfit with the full skirt, the hem would have fluttered out about their legs. When the music stopped he would have bowed to her and led her back to their table. And if their conversation had been warm and the touch of their hands pleasant, he might have taken her back to his apartment, to his bed, and later they would have walked down the street arm in arm, telling each other about their children and about the people they'd loved and the countries they'd seen and the disasters that had befallen them and the good times they'd had and the many things they'd learned in their long lives.

Now they sat harnessed to their wheelchairs, each sunk in his own vague, shuttered world, without rule or reason, she with her eyelids trembling in sleep, he with his eyes wide open on nothing.

As if he'd read her thoughts, Saul Inlander put his hand over hers. His touch sent shivers through every inch of her body, and as the heat spread in her limbs she felt how, slowly and painlessly, her skin was being shed, like the snake's in its season, and a new creature was emerging from within, intriguing and bold and a bit dangerous.

Passing by on the path, walking slowly, were an elderly man and a woman whose beauty had long ago caught Hamutal's eye. She had even asked one of the nurses who the woman was and been told: Paula, the widow of a well-known diplomat. Now Hamutal observed this woman, who still bore the vestiges of a regal beauty: the high forehead, the perfect posture, the way her hand rested on the arm of her companion. In the past she must have fairly floated through the halls at diplomatic balls, and here she was, wobbling along the path, the diaper under her sweatpants flattening what was once a derriere that magnetized the eyes of diplomats.

"We shouldn't have come down. It's making you sad," said Saul Inlander, and she was amazed by the way he saw through her. She noticed Bertha watching them from the window on the fifth floor, her staunch eyes following them undeterred, and heard him say, "Let's take them back."

On the way to the elevator, as they walked side by side, pushing the wheelchairs before them, he suddenly said, "I dreamed about you last night."

She was speechless.

"That surprises you," he concluded.

"Yes."

"I'm telling you because you also happen to be an expert in dreams."

"I'm not."

"There was a man in it," he hurried to say before she refused to hear, "who dreams that his father sees a woman and pursues her in a wheelchair, and she disappears."

"A woman you know?"

"Not really, yet."

She said, aware that he knew that she knew that he knew, "And the man in the wheelchair was your father?"

"Yes."

Her heart was pounding. "That's a very simple dream. You don't need experts for that one. You resemble your father, after all."

He looked her straight in the eye and said, as if suggesting something that required grave consideration, "I invite you to come and see for yourself."

"Where?"

"In my father's apartment," he said naturally, as if this had already been agreed upon back then, in the parking lot. "Yesterday I took out an album of old pictures. I'd be happy to show it to you."

Here comes the moment, she said to herself after they'd put their parents in their beds and gone out to the parking lot, and she started her car and began to follow him in his, as they'd agreed, in the direction of his father's house on Avniyahu Street. Was this moment inevitable? Was she going to cast the responsibility on fate? Here, after all, at the next corner, she could turn right and go home. She suddenly remembered a sentence from the *Sayings of the Fathers* that had been posted above the blackboard during all of eighth grade: ALL IS FORESEEN, BUT FREEDOM OF CHOICE IS GIVEN. Freedom of choice is given—she thought of the girl who sat for a whole year facing the black embellishments of letters drawn on oak tag yellowing above the board—freedom of choice is given, and it's possible to stop and say: I got carried away. This far and no more.

And yet, with a giddiness accompanied by clear knowledge, there she was stopping her car next to his, walking toward him, putting her hand in his outstretched hand, gripping his fingers with more force than was necessary, the better to blot out the interior voice calling on her to stop. The warmth suffusing their hands was now familiar, as if they already had a common past. And so she followed him, knowing full well what was likely to happen, some part of her dissembling before the part that knew. She climbed the stairs like someone willingly led to a perilous place, stepping steadily toward the forbidden thing, determined to rid her-

self of the intrusive interior voice that was laughing now at
her pretense of innocence, for she knew precisely where she
was headed and could still have said, "Let's stop a minute
I'm not sure we should do this, that is, I think we're making
a mistake, that is, after all, we're both—" Now she was
standing at the door, facing a small copper plaque, adorned
with a serpentine border, that said YA'AKOV INLANDER. She
stifled the voice of restraint in mid-sentence to make way for
a thought about his father, who had mounted these stairs
himself thirty, twenty, ten, five years ago, with a step neither
heavy nor light, like that of his son, his soles echoing neither
loudly nor softly, like those of his son, leading his lovers just
as she was now being led, holding the railing just where her
fingers had touched it; with what eagerness he must have
mounted those stairs, he who was now lying there in diapers, staring vacantly toward the doorway.

"What are you thinking about?" He looked at her while
rummaging in his pocket for the key.

She chuckled. "You won't believe it. About your father."

"That's odd," he said, and paused a moment before
sticking the key in its hole. "For some reason I was thinking about your mother."

He went in without turning on the light, and she waited
a moment, then crossed the threshold. He closed the door
behind her, and in a second, in the darkness, they were
reaching toward each other, groping like blind people to
bring their faces together, as if from the very first day
they'd been waiting for the moment when the door would
close behind them and they'd find themselves alone. The
feel of his lips was different from anything she'd known,
different especially from Arnon's, rougher and more violent, like the feel of a man in distress. His hands, larger
and stronger than appearance would suggest, bit into her

back and her buttocks till they hurt, and the ardor his movements conveyed was surprising, given the ascetic air he managed to assume—like a gifted swindler. She gave herself up to the hands traveling all over her body, without ceasing to wonder if his father had been as demanding and passionate with his lovers as he was, if his hands, too, had been so skilled at undoing buttons, unzipping a skirt, unhooking a bra, if his lovers, too, had pulled his shirt off him the way she was doing. Then, when they met on the mattress hard as a board, there was that desperation in all his movements, as if he were about to devour her entire, and she was aroused and let him, still thinking about his father and wondering if he was thinking about her mother, and a memory flickered in her, of Arnon's first leave during the Lebanon War, after two months apart, how each had decided, without talking about it, that they would have a child. An act of insanity on their part amid the sounds of war, as the roster of the fallen scrolled up the black television screen, to give in to the storm that seized them, to a passion the likes of which they'd never known, and during that week of leave she conceived Hila. Even now the old urge arose in her to vanquish with this act something else entirely. Suddenly the storm intensified and he pounded inside her with such violence that she was crushed under him and seemed to hear herself scream in a strange voice, unrecognizable, moving quickly away like the call of a soaring bird, and she guessed it must have been the sound of his mother's scream or one of his father's lovers', trapped here for hundreds of nights until it could make itself heard, since she herself never lost control of her voice like that. She opened her eyes and from close up, her vision blurring, the man lost the outline of his face and body, which were anyway unfamiliar still, and stopped being this particular man and became all the men ever in her life and those perhaps to come.

He swung himself off her and relaxed, leaving her pulsing all over, then immediately reached out and stroked her face with his fingers, and she thought of his aggressiveness before and his gentle touch now, and remembered the tenderness with which he guided his hands as he shaved his father's face.

Then they lay quietly, adjusting to the new situation, no longer strangers, not yet close, his thigh resting on hers, his arm wrapped around her back, his hand resting protectively on her shoulder, her face nestled in the warmth of his neck, she riveted by the unfamiliar smell, trying to decipher it without success, her hands wandering on his ribs, the tips of her nails gently sketching little $x$'s like the ones in the Herzl motto she embroidered once in home-making class: IF YOU WILL IT, IT IS NO DREAM.

With Arnon, too, she remembered, she had lain like this the first time, at his parents' place, in their bed. His parents had gone off to a guesthouse on another kibbutz, and he had taken her into their apartment, found the key hanging on a nail in a small cupboard on the front balcony and invited her in. Later she discovered that he had a room of his own on the kibbutz, a cramped cell in a row with five others, separated by plywood walls, with ceilings sprouting mold. But he had earmarked his parents' bed for them—so he told her years afterward—from the moment he first saw her, wearing shorts.

When they arrived she was sweaty and dusty from walking down the cypress-lined road at the entrance to the kibbutz, and she threw her things down in a corner of the room and asked for the shower. He gave her a clean towel, slipped a new bar of soap out of its wrapper, explained how to direct the stream, wished her a pleasant shower, gave a mocking bow, and left the bathroom. She drew the shutter on the window, closed the door, hung the towel over the door handle to cover the keyhole, got undressed, stepped into the shower, drew the plastic curtain closed, adjusted the stream of water, poured some shampoo into her palm, closed her eyes and was swallowed up by the noise of the water.

When she opened her eyes she saw the curtain drawn aside and Arnon sitting cross-legged on the floor, leaning against the door, watching her.

"That's not fair," she yelled, insulted and angry, pulling the curtain around her.

"You're absolutely right." He sprang up and, with his clothes and shoes on, got into the shower, pushing her to the wet wall. "You're all wet and I'm all dry."

That was the first time she had experienced the sense of frustration she was to feel many times in the years to come: anger accumulating in her throat to the point of strangulation, then dispersed all at once by the surprise of a single word of his or some act that made her aware of her absurdity or stupidity and left her confused, laughing in spite of herself without having unpacked that anger entirely, an anger whose pieces returned and reassembled inside her throat. But that first time, having laughed, she had no chance of finding them an outlet and had to gulp them down, her throat constricted, the way it must feel to swallow poison. Under the spray of water he enveloped her in a fierce embrace, wiping her wet back with his still-dry sleeves until she was appeased and responded to his kisses and he whispered in her ear: "Can I make a request?"

"No," she said.

"What do you think I wanted to ask?"

"You know and I know and the answer is no."

"I wanted to ask if I could wear your shoes this evening, because mine are soaking wet," he laughed, dodging the fists pounding on his back and leading her to his parents' bed.

Now she thought, I've managed to haul all of them into bed with me: Arnon and Hila and Saul Inlander's father and mother and his father's lovers. Fatigue overtook her, her thinking grew foggy, and she sank into a doze. When she woke up, a sweet satiety filling every part of her, her back curved against Saul Inlander's chest, the two of them curled together like question marks, she let her eyes adjust to the shadowy darkness and wander over the objects dispersed around the room, like someone acquainting herself with a new country: photographs on the walls, mostly black-and-white, each in a different kind of frame; folded sheets and towels in an armoire with the door ajar, deposited in a clump by an unpracticed hand; house slippers resting prow to prow on a patch of floor between the wall and the closet; a dark suit hanging on a valet post that stood like a small man under the window; a rectangular briefcase resting upright on a chair, as if regarding its reflection in the mirror. On the dresser near the mirror were many items glinting in the beam of light that came through where a slat of the shutter was missing: a clothes-brush resting face-down, bristles bent under the weight of the thick wooden back; a fine-toothed comb for people with short hair; an unusually big bunch of keys; a small notebook with a pencil stuck between its pages. She trained her eyes around her: a room in which there was not a single article belonging to a woman, except for the puddle of clothing dropped on the narrow rug at the foot of the bed.

"Are you in any of those pictures on the wall?" she asked, knowing he was awake although he hadn't budged.

"In a lot of them, yes."

"So you were peeking when your father was here with his lovers."

"I'm sure I closed my eyes."

Her hand reached back to stroke his eyelids, an immediate gesture toward eyes that knew when to close, and he put his hand over her hand, leading it in the direction of his nose, over his lips, down the slope of his chin, the length of his neck, until he stopped over his heart and she could feel the blood vessels knocking on the palm of her hand.

"Nice of you to have closed your eyes."

"And I never even imagined a caress from you as a reward one day."

"The real reward was not knowing. . . . Kids don't really want to know what their parents do when they're not in the role of parents."

"Why not?"

"It's threatening." She remembered the strangeness she felt toward Shifra Baum, head nurse at the clinic, and observed in a questioning tone, "You said you have three children?"

"Yes. One daughter from my first wife, finishing high school, two young sons from my second wife."

"Your second wife is still your wife?"

"Yes."

"They're all in Chicago?"

"Yes."

"Is your wife Israeli?"

"My first wife was Israeli. The second is American."

"And do your children speak Hebrew?"

"My daughter does, of course. We spoke Hebrew at home. My sons don't."

"Are your wife's parents living?"

"Her mother was killed in a car accident. Her father is the principal of a school."

"So she doesn't know yet what a nursing-care facility is," she said, as if the woman's education were lacking.

"That's true, she doesn't know." He was practically apologizing.

She noted to herself that this was not the sort of dialogue one would expect between a man and woman on their first encounter in bed, yet there was something right about it, as if their relationship required definition. Here we have a man and a woman, and between them another man and other women, plus three girls and two boys, and they'd do well to keep that in mind now that they've set foot in territory where things worth remembering are easily forgotten. She noted to herself that the closeness she felt with him had not diminished; on the contrary, the conversation had expanded the horizon of their shared world to include all the people in their separate lives, and a kind of joy filled her, as if all at once the compass of her life had grown and she with it—and her thoughts immediately turned to her mother and his father and their shriveling worlds.

She asked, "Until when did your father sleep in this bed?"

"Until a year and a half ago."

"He's been in nursing care for a year and a half?"

"No, he was in assisted living before that."

"And since when—"

"Okay, I'll tell you the whole thing in order." Lying on his back, he slid his hands under his head in a way that suggested they had all the time in the world and he was planning to bring her into his life slowly but surely. "My mother died five years ago. I was already in Chicago by then. My father lived here alone for less than a year and then wanted to come live with me—"

"Did he love your mother?"

He was quiet. She seemed to have presented him with a question he had never bothered to ask himself. "I think that, on the whole, yes. Mainly he was used to her, so maybe a certain kind of habit is also love. But more and more I remember the fights. There was even a period when she went to her sister's for six months, and I stayed with him. I was in the sixth grade and I fell in love for the first time and I had no one to talk to about it, because he would leave early in the morning and come home late. Sixth grade was an awful year for me."

"Who did you fall in love with?"

"A girl named Rachel. She was the saddest girl in the class and she wanted to be a poet, and what worried her most was that there was already a famous Hebrew poet named Rachel."

What, she asked herself, was peculiar about his story?

"Suits you, falling in love with a poet."

"Right."

"And did she really become a poet?"

"I have no idea. The next year I was already in love with another girl."

"Another poet?"

"No. She liked gymnastics."

She knew what was peculiar about his story: even things

one would normally say with a smile he said with utter gravity. She noted, understanding that she had learned something about herself as well: he was the complete opposite of Arnon.

"Did your father bring women here when your mother was at her sister's?"

"Yes, apparently he did. Sometimes I thought I heard voices, but I never came out of my room. I used to pee into a potted plant on the balcony so I wouldn't have to come out. Kids, as you said, don't want to know."

"And then your mother came back?"

"Yes, she brought me a chessboard, and for a while things were quiet between them. But later they fought again."

"What did they fight about?"

"A lot of times things that had to do with me. For years I went around feeling something was my fault."

"Do you fight with your wife?"

"Sometimes."

"What do you fight about?"

"I don't fight. I usually keep quiet or defend myself. She picks fights for reasons that have nothing to do with us. I have no idea what the connection is, but I noticed it always happens at the beginning of the week."

Like Arnon, she thought to herself, you don't really want to understand. The boy who closed his eyes before his father's bed continues to keep them closed.

"Did your parents like being together?"

"I don't know."

"Did they laugh together?"

"My parents hardly ever laughed."

"You don't know how to laugh either."

"That's not true."

"Or how to get worked up about anything."

"On what are you basing your diagnosis?"

"At *The Fugitive* you weren't the least bit enthusiastic."

"That doesn't mean anything."

"You were more excited about the buildings of Chicago than the hero's troubles."

"I told you in advance that I wanted to see the movie because of Chicago."

"You really miss Chicago." She was surprised to discover she felt insulted on behalf of Tel Aviv.

"Yes, I guess you could say that."

"Is Chicago your home now?"

"Definitely. My sons were born there."

"You never think of coming back?"

"I don't know what the future holds, but I assume I won't come back."

"And if your daughter wants to come serve in the army, come back here to live?"

"I'll have a problem."

"And when your mother came back, did they fight a lot?" She returned to his parents.

"I don't know. He actually told me that their last years together were the best. Maybe they were just ground down by all the years of battling."

"Fatigue is sometimes mistaken for happiness," she said. "Their last years were the best because by then your father didn't have lovers."

"I'm not sure he had all that many lovers."

"He had, he had. I can tell."

He slipped his hands out from under his neck and turned toward her. "Should I continue with what happened to him in Chicago?"

"Yes."

"He spent two months roaming around town, amazed by the buildings and the sculptures and the gardens, and then it got cold and he started getting bored and wanted to come back here. He was corresponding with some woman and she was waiting for him. They lived together for a few months, but they didn't get along, and again he was alone. After that there were a few women here in succession, that part I heard from my aunt. He never talked to me about it. After that he decided to move into assisted living. A year later his cancer was discovered and he had surgery, and there were complications and they moved him from place to place until he got to the nursing home."

"Do you have any brothers or sisters?"

"No. I'm an only child."

"What time is it, can you see?"

"Six."

"So we have a little longer."

Arnon and the girls, for the few moments she remembered them during those hours, evoked no uneasiness in her, as if they had no relation to what she was doing in this place, and that realization was a kind of revelation; she hadn't imagined that's how she would feel. She continued to ask him about his parents even as she showered, and he stood and watched her as if this were not the first time he had seen her standing like that and shampooing her hair, with trickles of white foam winding down the length of her nakedness, and it seemed as if the two of them had resumed some old routine, to judge by the way his hand delivered a towel to her hand outstretched toward him. Then they got dressed and he made Turkish coffee the way he'd learned from a Bedouin during his army service, and she dried her hair in front of a space heater with a noisy fan in the little kitchen, which reminded her of the old kibbutz kitchens, something out of a museum: the kitchen of a conservative housewife who was comfortable with her old pots and pans and pitted countertop and scratched wooden cabinets, determined to keep her realm intact and fend off the latest in fashionable gadgetry.

"Your mother didn't like new things."

"Right. That was apparently one of the causes of fights. My father was a hedonist and my mother was an ascetic."

Hedonist, she thought, about the man lying in the nursing home.

It occurred to her suddenly that she now knew lots of details about his parents' lives and his aunt and his friends and his neighbors and even about the Bedouin who taught him to make coffee, but he hadn't asked about her at all, and that infuriated her more than she would have thought. As she continued to listen to him, she felt an aversion rising and growing and taking the place of the spell cast by that man in the parking lot. Now he seemed to her self-indulgent, grounded in memories whose parallels in her own life she couldn't even recall. Detail after detail about some neighbor who was a policeman and lived in the apartment above them and inspired a terrible fear in him when he was a kid, and she thought with distaste that anyone who invested so much energy in such detailed description must take himself a good deal more seriously than the first impression revealed, and the further he progressed in his story the greater her disappointment grew.

"After that, when I was about ten, I met him—" he said.

"I have to go." She withdrew her fingers from under his hand, got up, grabbed her coat and bag, and hurried to the door. He caught up with her there, exactly on the spot where they had been sucked into each other four hours earlier, and tried to bring his head toward hers, apparently to rekindle that moment, which now seemed distant and worth forgetting, and she dodged out, with a half-hearted "See you" in response to his, not returning his glance and knowing that he would continue standing in the doorway, totally bewildered, until she disappeared.

In the car, doing her best to forget the moments of pleasure and surrender and tranquillity she had known in the last few hours, and trying to inflame her anger, she began talking to herself with cold logic, as though addressing some woman she didn't know, who was deserving of neither respect nor affection: "You were attracted to a new experience—and now you've tried it out. You needed it, no point in going into why, it's also okay not to know. You don't have to torture yourself over it, it doesn't matter all that much. Fact: a minute after it started it was already over. There are some things you get over more quickly if you let yourself ride with them, because the things you fight tend to get blown out of all proportion, and that's what happened here. Now you just have to relax, get this nonsense out of your head, take a deep breath, and check what's happening at home."

But she didn't turn in the direction of home. Postponing the moment when she'd find herself face to face with Arnon and the girls, she stopped the car on a side street to calculate her moves and in the end decided to go to the office.

On her desk she found two dream summaries that had been faxed to her as promised:

**The dream of a woman serving five years in prison for the attempted murder of her husband's father, as presented at the**

**international seminar by Dr. Christoph Müller of the University of Freiburg.**

The woman dreams she's lying in bed with a terrible migraine. She rouses herself with great effort to get some painkiller out of the refrigerator.

She finds the house in tremendous disarray, with a terrible stench. In the middle of the living room is a huge mound of dirty laundry. The dog apparently hadn't been taken out for a walk and had done his business on the rugs and on the laundry.

Her husband, her three sons, her parents, and her husband's parents are sitting in the dining area around an empty table, all dressed up. It turns out they're expecting her to serve them a holiday meal. She doesn't remember inviting her parents and her husband's parents for a meal, and she doesn't know what holiday it is. She apologizes for her appearance and goes to the refrigerator to check whether there happen to be any prepared dishes in there. In the refrigerator she finds only her medicine. The freezer compartment is also empty.

She goes out to the guests in the dining area and explains the situation. Her husband's father gets up, grabs her, and drags her to the table. Everyone helps him lift her and lay her down on the empty table. They tie her head to one end of the table and her ankles to the other, and all eight of them sit down around the table, pick up forks and knives, cut into her flesh, and start to eat it. Her husband's father puts a pitcher under her wrist, slits a vein, and the blood streams into the pitcher.

She pleads with them to give her her painkillers, but they're busy comparing the flavor of the liver to that of her other organs; her husband has even gotten to the marrow and is trying to describe its taste. As they eat they talk about a trip and about the prices of computers.

In the correction of the dream the woman gets up in the morning, realizes she has a headache, and takes care of it immediately. She gets her husband to do the grocery shopping, her sons to clean the house, her mother to cook the meal, her mother-in-law to set the table, her father to take care of the dog, and her father-in-law to buy wine. She herself arranges the flowers.

In the evening they will all sit down and eat, enjoy themselves, and plan a trip together to Tuscany.

The storm in her that had subsided on the way to the office started up again as she read the nightmare of this anonymous woman, which seemed as familiar as if she had dreamed it herself. Her heart had clenched at the sight of her mother groping at her own genitals, her craving for touch overcoming any sense of modesty; at the sight of Bertha longing for her parents and their unfulfilled promise to take her some day to Canada; at the sight of the weary old man borrowing Clara the caretaker's identity to shield himself from persecution by his wife, who had lost any resemblance to the young woman he once loved—and that clenching was repeated now as she read this dream of terror: again she was peering into the dark pit where the stuff of horror is dredged up from a place without reason or order, only blind, haphazard impulse. Again she saw old Inlander and thought of his son, and her thoughts leapt to Arnon and the girls and she called home.

At the other end Hila picked up, and before she could ask why she was up so late, Hamutal heard her daughter's mocking tone: "Good morning, Ms. Mother!" and her shout, away from the receiver: "She's on the phone!"

Sobs gathered in her throat, and seemed to have been there all along, around the edges, ready to spring.

"Has something happened, Hila?"

"Something has happened, yes. Here's Dad."

"Listen to me," Arnon said. "We're going to the kibbutz for three weeks."

"Who's we?"

"The girls and I."

"Going when?"

"In another seven hours."

Her heart stopped, not knowing whether to sink or soar.

"But there's school tomorrow." She managed to compose the thought.

"We spoke to the teachers."

"Why is this so sudden?"

"For us, it's not so sudden. We've been talking about it for four days. You even promised Michal you'd get her sunscreen. Did you get it?"

She went mute, couldn't remember such a request or such a promise.

"You didn't get it," he answered for her.

"Because it's still early. We were talking about Passover vacation."

"Passover vacation is in another four days."

"Why do you have to leave in seven hours?"

There was a clicking sound.

"Who's that on the line? Michal?" Arnon asked.

"Yes. I want to hear what you decide."

"Hello, Michalie," said Hamutal.

"So is she coming with us?" Michal asked.

"She can't, she's busy," Arnon answered Michal.

"You said she'd come for the weekend."

"I said she'd find an excuse not to come for the weekend."

"Why are you leaving so early?"

"I have some urgent work in Beersheba," said Arnon, "and you're not home. In any case we were planning to go for Passover."

"What about Michal's physics?"

"I made arrangements for a tutor on the kibbutz. She'll take the test after the vacation. And Hila will work on two papers. The kibbutz librarian said she'd help her. Everything's taken care of. I also spoke to Shula. She's taking her vacation now, by the way, since there won't be anyone around to mess up the place."

"So are you coming for the weekend or not?" asked Michal.

"I can't get away now."

"Why can't you?" There was a new insistence in Michal's voice.

"Because of Grandma. I can't leave now."

"You can ask Tzippie to come."

"She can't come before Passover. And I'm also behind at the journal."

There was a short silence.

"Daddy said that's exactly what you would say and I bet him you wouldn't." There was amazement in Michal's voice, and Hamutal imagined she also heard disappointment, as if the girl had realized that all this time she'd been placing her trust in someone unworthy of it.

"Michal," said Arnon, "would you mind getting off the phone now?"

"At least come and say goodbye," challenged the new Michal.

"If she can spare the time for us," said Arnon, and Michal slammed down the receiver.

"What's this wise-guy juvenile bit in front of Michal?" Hamutal leapt on him, suddenly emboldened by the distance.

"We have an intelligent daughter. Give her a little credit."

"So why do you have to put a bug in her ear with 'If she can spare the time for us'?"

"Because that's exactly what's happening."

"That sounds like an accusation."

"That's exactly what it sounds like."

"Say it right out: accusation?"

"Yes." He, too, was taking advantage of the distance.

"What exactly are you accusing me of?"

"That since the business of the nursing home started, with those obsessive visits, or the excuses of visits—"

"I've been visiting my mother."

"—you have no time for any of us."

"What's wrong with my visiting my mother?"

"What's wrong is that you're not here. And even when you're here you're not here. Things happen. And you don't have a clue about them. Hila needs you, but you're not here. I'm not even mentioning myself, but—"

"How can you say—"

"And what's also wrong with this is there are too many things I don't understand lately."

"It's just that I'm—"

"And what's worse is that I don't particularly care any more—"

"—busy with my mother now."

"You don't have to tell me, of all people, about your fantastic relationship with your mother."

"I've been visiting my mother."

"I don't know what you're busy with, and I'm not sure you've been visiting your mother. When she was in assisted living, you didn't go for weeks at a time. If I didn't remind you to call her about all sorts of bank business, you wouldn't talk to her for months."

"She didn't need me then. Now she does."

"So now you'll have lots of time for her."

"When exactly are you leaving?"

"We'll sleep for six hours, get up at four and leave at five."

"I'm going to work here tonight. I'll be there at five."

"Like I give a damn," he said in English, and slammed the phone down. She was sorry for the heartache that drew phrases like that from him, things he didn't usually say, and then she thought: Thank you, Arnon. You're making it easier for me. And briefly panicked: Too easy.

She sat in the office for hours without managing to focus on her work, but she didn't dare go home to the bed in their room. At two in the morning, totally exhausted, she ordered a telephone wake-up call for four-thirty, folded her arms on her desk, put her head down, and fell asleep.

The gratitude she felt toward Arnon faded at five a.m. when she came to say goodbye to them. Arnon, purposeful and impatient, expressed no interest in her workload, nor did he ask what she'd been doing until she called at ten p.m., as if from now on it was each to his own. When they found themselves alone for a moment, she asked, "Am I allowed to know the real reason you're doing this?"

"I'm obeying you."

"What do you mean, 'obeying me'?"

"I always do my best to fulfill your desires, that's all." He went to the car, where he was immediately joined by the girls, and the riddle of his response remained unsolved.

He arranged the suitcases in the trunk with great efficiency, and she stood back awkwardly, like a stranger confronting a hostile clique, and heard herself tell the children, in an effort to preserve some semblance of a normal parting, "Take care of Daddy." Then she managed to exchange quick kisses on the cheek with Michal, as she glimpsed Hila sliding out of reach into the back seat. For another moment she stood peering into the car through the open window, and, finding nothing else to say, repeated, "Take care of Daddy."

"And who'll take care of Mommy?" He had straightened the rearview mirror and started moving before she managed to lift her hand from the car door. The dog ran after the car to the end of the block, and she stood in the middle of the street, rubbing her hands against the cold, hearing his barks of disappointment shatter the quiet, seeing the first signs that night was brightening toward its end. She waited another moment for the dog to give up and come home, thinking the girls must have wanted to take him along, but Arnon preferred to punish her, using the dog to tie her down to the house, and she felt the loneliness closing in on her from all directions, astonished that only a few hours earlier there had been two men in her life, and now both were gone. At the same time she knew she had the power to turn things around, and remembered the expression on Hila's face, as if she was trying to figure something out, remembered Michal's kiss, how she'd clung to her for a moment, her language matching her rebellious sister's but her body remaining loyal to her mother. She saw the dog zigzagging back up the empty street and turned to go into the house, suddenly recalling, unprompted, the smell of Saul Inlander's body. She was awed by the new possibilities that, without any real excuses now, only her willpower could curb.

Standing at the door, she peered into the empty house and let the dog in. She paused for a moment on the doormat that proclaimed WELCOME, and looked at the dog, who was watching her with curiosity and disappointment, apparently aware of what awaited him in the following days. Without budging from the spot she closed the door and locked it, hesitating only for a split second out of concern for the dog as she recalled her mother's crazy suspicion that Arnon would seal up the house and fill it with gas when they went away and left her alone.

At the all-night supermarket she bought a toothbrush, warm rolls, Syrian olives, and a bouquet of lilies with swelling buds, and at ten to six she knocked at Saul Inlander's door. A moment later she said into the neck still warm from bed, "Can't do without flowers in the house."

He wasn't surprised by her arrival, as if he knew she'd be coming back. But there was happiness in his movements, and recognition that they had passed the first test without excessive pain. Wordlessly he took the bouquet of lilies, the groceries, and the briefcase from her hands, put them down on the bookcase near the door and drew her after him to the bedroom, pulled her close, and laid her down on the bed in her clothes, wrapping her tightly in a blanket.

"This is the way they wrap women in India before they burn them," she said.

"Enough of your nightmares," he said. "In this bed only good things happen."

"I feel like a packed fish."

"Think of Cleopatra. That's how she felt rolled up in a carpet when they brought her to Julius Caesar."

"What's this about Cleopatra?"

"Once I was wild about the Cleopatra story. I read everything ever written."

"You do amaze me."

Two hours later, as they were eating the rolls and Syrian olives, she said, "You didn't ask why I came back so early in the morning."

He said, with what could be interpreted as evasion, "Because I know."

"You don't know."

He said, in what could be interpreted as jest, "Because

you wanted to hear the end of the story about my neighbor the cop."

When they arrived at the nursing home together that day, most of the old people were already in their beds, and a line of wheelchairs stretched down the corridor opposite the nurses' station.

The aide, spotting Hamutal from the end of the corridor, rushed up and said, "Your mother's an overnight miracle. You have to go and see—you won't recognize her! Sitting there reading a book like a whole person, one hundred percent. In another minute she'll be walking out of here looking for a husband and a dance class!"

Bertha was peering out of the doorway of Inlander's room, standing guard and surveying the corridor traffic. The moment she saw Saul she edged her way out and disappeared into one of the other rooms, without a word to him or a backward glance.

Her mother was sitting up in bed supported by a pillow, reading a book cradled in her hands.

Hamutal waited patiently until her mother's finger traced the last line of the page, and then, before she could turn it and read the first words on the next, hurried over to the bed and said breathlessly, "Hello, Mother."

The expression on her mother's face was one she had not seen in a long time: lucid and perceptive, as if she'd received a transplant of new eyes.

"What are you reading?"

"Adam Mickiewicz." She pronounced the name lovingly. "He has a ballad called 'Lilies,' about a woman who killed her husband, and her two brothers-in-law fall in love with her and want to marry her—their brother's murderer. Have I ever told you about this ballad?"

"No."

"But what I love most is a sonnet. It's in Polish, of course, but I remember it in Hebrew too. Listen." She lifted her head, closed her eyes, and recited in a rhythmic voice, full of moment:

> Laura! Do the lovely eons, our shared years
> still tinge your memory?
> When we were our only thought,
> when the world beyond was scarcely wrought . . .
>
> The moon, peering out from a cloud,
> illumined snow-white breasts and rings of gold,
> divine charm assisting beauty to unfold.

Hamutal sat and listened to the fluent, vital voice. She was tempted to get up and bring Saul Inlander in so he could see her mother like this.

"Everything okay with you?" Her mother had opened her eyes.

"Yes."

"Have you eaten?"

"Yes."

"The food here isn't very good." The old sentence had taken on a new tone.

"You know who I thought of all of a sudden?"

"Who?" She was afraid she'd say Arnon.

"I can't remember his name. Your cousin from Givatayim, Isaac's son."

"Zevik."

"That's it. He played musical combs, didn't he?"

"Yes!" Hamutal laughed, remembering.

"What a head full of nonsense! His dream was to do a

concert on combs. He had the ambitions of a lunatic and in the end turned out as normal as they come. He got a job in a bank."

"What made you think of him now?"

"Isn't that right, he became a bank teller?"

"Something like that."

"Today I got out of bed and I felt like dancing."

"What happened?"

"I don't know. I did a couple of waltz turns here."

"Maybe that's what made you think of Zevik."

"Did I tell you about Adam Mickiewicz's 'Lilies'?"

"Yes."

"Two brothers fall in love with the woman who murdered their brother and bring her flowers that they cut from his grave, but his ghost destroys them. . . . Everything okay with you?"

"Yes."

"Have you eaten?"

"Yes." Hamutal was scared the confusion had started all over again.

"So you can go then for today. I have something to occupy me," her mother said pleasantly, and went back to the book.

Hamutal got up to go, amazed at her mother, who was in a state of serenity she hadn't witnessed in a very long time. She stood and watched for another moment as her mother returned to the Mickiewicz ballad, unaware in her contentment that this was just a propitious interlude, a flash, as if the good memory cells had flickered among the masses of rogue cells, sparking a brief hope that would only intensify the despair to follow. She went to the room across the hall and beckoned Saul to the door, inviting him with a gesture of the hand to look at her mother, to remember her like that, sitting and reading a book, and to erase from his memory that other image, the empty husk of a woman who had sat in the sun, bound to a wheelchair.

In the elevator he said, "I want you to meet someone," and pressed the button for the second floor, the floor for those feeble of body but sound of mind. He led her through the corridors, glancing into private rooms and the common area, until he reached a balcony that had been closed in with windows and approached an old man in a colorful sweater who was sitting on a bench and looking outside.

"Hello, Master Eliahu," he said.

"Hello, Saul," the old man said, brightening.

"This is my teacher, Eliahu," Saul said to Hamutal, his voice full of warmth. "He was my Bible teacher and advisor in eleventh and twelfth grades."

The old man, like a gracious host, addressed himself to Hamutal. "His father is here, so he's been kind enough to visit me, too, a few times a week."

"How are you feeling today, Master Eliahu?" Saul asked, bending toward him.

Master Eliahu smiled. "In the Talmud tractate *Brachot* it says, 'Flesh-and-blood is here today and in the grave tomorrow.' I'm not here and not in the grave."

There was a wise look in his eyes that stood in marked contrast to his grin, made silly by missing front teeth.

"What happened to your teeth?" Saul asked, concerned.

"Somebody stole them." The insipid grin widened. "I said to the doctor, 'When Laban's household gods were stolen, there was a reason. When Joseph's coat of many colors was stolen, there was a reason. But what would be the reason for stealing my teeth?'"

"Somebody took them by mistake, and they'll return them," Saul said, trying to reassure him. Hamutal remembered the tenderness with which he had shaved his father and slipped her hand into his.

Master Eliahu looked at them and said, "Seas will not extinguish love, nor rivers wash it away," and Saul's fingers squeezed hers.

"Where's that from?" Master Eliahu wagged a finger, as he must have done with his students many years ago.

"Proverbs?" Saul guessed.

"The Song of Songs." The teacher corrected without admonishing. "Song of Songs chapter eight, verse seven— and your wife is very nice." Again the fingers closed around her fingers.

"Was he a good student, my husband?" Hamutal asked, amusing herself.

"In his generation they were all good," Master Eliahu said sadly. "It's written, 'A young man speaks in song; when he grows up, he explains; when he gets old, no brains.' You won't know where that one's from: *Yalkut Shimoni*."

"Do you need anything, Master Eliahu?"

Master Eliahu gave his eleventh-and-twelfth-grade student a sorrowful look. "What I need only the Holy One, blessed be He, can give me."

"Maybe there's something I can bring you?"

The old man's eyes lit up.

"There is something."

"What is it, Master Eliahu?"

"Are you sure it's not a problem?"

"No problem."

"In the tractate *Pesachim* it says, 'He who performs a good deed will not encounter trouble on the way.' So maybe I'll ask a favor of you after all."

"Please."

"A class picture," he said, lowering his voice as if the request were indecent. "So I can see all the teachers, and the students."

"If I can't find a class picture, there are some from class trips—"

"No, no," Master Eliahu protested with surprising vehemence. "It has to be a class picture."

"But we posed with the teachers on the trips—"

"I have to see the secretary, too . . . "

In the evening, when they had returned from their respective offices and showered and made love and eaten the Chinese takeout he brought home with him, Saul produced all the albums he had unearthed and slid out the secret leaves of the kitchen table, doubling its size. They sat down side by side to search for the high-school class picture.

"What did the secretary look like?" Hamutal asked.

"I don't remember . . . blonde, I think, fat, wore glasses maybe . . . "

"He was in love with her, your Master Eliahu."

"And seas will not extinguish love," he said without a trace of a smile.

They never did find the class picture, but Hamutal, whose parents had taken very few photographs, was fascinated by the abundance of these. One of them was from Saul's bar mitzvah. He was looking very serious, standing at the door of the synagogue, holding the velvet pouch containing his phylacteries.

"Isn't that the Great Synagogue on Allenby Road?" she asked.

"Yes."

"When we passed by, you said something about the Lehi arms cache that was uncovered there, but you didn't mention that that's where you had your bar mitzvah."

"It seemed too personal," he said, which she translated in her head into Arnon-speak, equally insulting: "At the time I still couldn't check my baggage at your counter."

In other photos she recognized places from her own childhood, which surprised and moved her. The two of them continued to examine the pictures together, amazed that they shared memories despite the eleven years that separated them: they remembered a military parade on Independence Day when she was nine and he was a soldier of twenty, the Whitman Ice Cream stand, the wooden shack where the scouts met, the beggar who used to sleep on the benches on Rothschild Boulevard, the huge lions in the zoo near City Hall, where neighbors kept complaining that the roaring kept them up at night, until the animals were transferred to another city. They went beyond the photos, remembering a summer when English schoolchildren in uniform invaded the beach opposite the opera house, and the movie *Gone with the Wind*, which their parents may have seen together.

She thought: not only the nursing home, but all the places and people and memories that filled her childhood stood between her and Arnon—and here, with a man she had met only six days ago but seemed to have known forever, how easily she connected her memories to his. She watched with pleasure as he lingered over one of the pictures, contemplative.

"What are you thinking about?" she asked.

"You won't believe it."

About Chicago, she thought to herself, and aloud said, "About the madman on Harav Kook Street."

"About the sea."

"Mermaids?"

"No."

"About the lifeguard who drowned his wife's lover."

"About Sheraton Beach," he said.

"Did I hear 'Sheraton Beach'?"

"Sheraton Beach."

"For me, too, the sea is Sheraton Beach," she said wistfully. "My mother used to take us there once a week, me and my cousin. My cousin would always get lost and I would find money in the sand." She burst out laughing at the recollection.

"Your cousin didn't find it funny."

"I have an idea," she said, standing up. "Let's go to Sheraton Beach."

"We'll go there in the summer."

"You won't be here in the summer."

"I'll come back specially."

"We're going now." She went looking for her boots.

"It's raining."

"It is not. They said on the radio that the last rain of the season was a few days ago." She was back in the kitchen with her boots on.

The sea snarled in the dark like a trapped animal, and the torn canvas of a forgotten beach umbrella thudded again and again, heaving itself suicidally, inflating like a ball trying to fly. The beach was deserted and ominous, the perfect set for a thriller.

"You're not planning to go out in this," he said when she opened the car door.

"You wanted Sheraton Beach," she shouted, trailing the picnic blanket she'd taken from the trunk and coming around to his side. She opened the door and dragged him into the uproar outside.

The wind knocked them off balance, thrashing their clothing. Saul halted every few steps like a balky horse, but Hamutal dragged him down the slope toward the empty beach, where she spread out the old blanket and dropped onto one end to keep it from flapping away.

"It's cold on Sheraton Beach. Hold me." She pulled him toward her.

When they were bundled together in the warmth of his jacket, he said into her ear, "You manage to hide the fact in those tailored suits of yours, but you are totally insane."

"My mother used to bring me here every week. This is where I'd sit and wait till she got herself organized."

"You didn't love your mother," he said, and she realized he had absorbed something she didn't know she had revealed.

"Where do you get that from?"

"Something in the way you talk about her. Or am I mistaken?"

"You're not mistaken," she said. "We were never close. That's why I don't understand this great effort I'm making to see her, why it's suddenly so important to me to get into her head. Five months after my father died I started my army service, and I never went back to her house again. I went to a kibbutz. Now, since she's been hospitalized, I think about her a lot, I keep remembering, I feel this pull to see her. It's become a kind of obsession, these visits. You don't think about your father when you're at work?"

"Sometimes I do. He used to bring me here every afternoon in the summer. He played paddle ball with women and I used to get bored because I couldn't read in peace. And I wasn't allowed to go in the water alone."

"Maybe I saw you then. I remember a few bored-looking kids."

"I was the most bored of all. But you couldn't have seen me because by the time you were born, I could go in by myself."

"But I do remember people playing paddle ball behind the lifeguard's hut."

"That's the spot, exactly."

"He didn't play with men?"

"Mainly with women."

"He thought they were easier to beat?"

"He loved women."

"Like you?" She was laughing.

"A lot more," he said seriously.

"My mother brought us here only once a week. If they'd taken me every day I would have made a fortune in no time. I was an expert at finding money."

"Yes, you told me."

"And I used to go in the water alone because my mother was usually busy looking for my cousin."

"I don't know why I relax when I think of the sea. I have pretty bad memories of it."

"I loved the sea, and not just because of the money."

"Because your cousin used to get lost?"

"No, we were actually okay together. We grew up like sisters. And besides, in the end she always got found."

A sudden recollection jolted her, a distant, forgotten movement impelling her limbs. She bent over and tucked her head between her knees as if ducking a whip. Afterward she would ask herself: what was so shocking?

Just a childhood memory. Described in the appropriate light tone, it could even be amusing. Hours later she would talk to herself about that movement secreted in the muscles of her body, about discovering just how deeply memory can be buried, about the accidental way it rose from its safe haven fathoms below, where it was sunk amid the detritus of dreams, the feeling she had when she sat alone in the sand, knees together, feet angled outward, with her right big toe pointing right, her left big toe pointing left, as she constructed a sand castle, dipping into a pool for a handful of dripping sand and coming up with an American quarter.

Then it came back to her: her birthday fell between the Passover and Shavuot vacations, between the spring evenings when her mother would do the cleaning after work, her hands exuding the odor of solvents—which was Tzippie's mother's smell all year round—and the summer Saturdays when they went to the beach and came home enveloped in the odor of seaweed and salt.

One day on the beach, maybe not far from where they were sitting now, she happened to sit next to a woman who was reading the newspaper. She didn't know why she had glanced at the date on the front page, but it looked familiar to her, and she focused on it for a long time before she remembered: it was her birthday. She ran to her mother, who was busy rubbing nut oil into her shoulders.

"What's the matter?" her mother asked at the sight of the flushed face, her hand still sliding over her glistening skin.

"Today's my birthday," Hamutal said.

Her mother suspended the motion for a moment, calculating, and said in surprise, "You're very right. How did you know?"

Hamutal's face grew even redder.

"What's wrong?" her mother asked, annoyed.

"You forgot my birthday!"

"But today's not over yet," her mother said reproachfully, as if she'd been falsely accused.

"You forgot."

"By the end of the day I would have remembered."

"And you didn't even get me a present."

"It's only morning now."

"But it's Saturday."

"So?"

"Everything's closed today."

"So we'll wait till tomorrow. Everything's open tomorrow."

"But my birthday is today!" By now she was snuffling with sobs.

"I'll tell you what." Her mother's eyes lit up after a short silence, as if she had finally arrived at the solution. She said in a low, enticing voice: "I'll give you a special present today."

"What?" Hope glinted in the eyes of a girl of nine.

"I'll give you something no child in the world has ever gotten."

"What, what?"

"I'll give you the sea as a present."

Sitting on the old baby blanket, wrapped in the American jacket, Hamutal could feel the piercing sting of that insult as if thirty years hadn't intervened.

"I don't want your present," she had told her mother, the sobs in her throat giving her hoarse voice a muffled echo. "You can give it to yourself." Then her head lurched to the side and she felt the saccharine taste of blood in her mouth and understood from the hand waving over her face that her mother had slapped her.

"Birthday or no birthday, you don't talk back to me!"

Now she whispered into Saul Inlander's ear, "I think we can go now," and he turned to her immediately: "You're crying."

"I am not," she said dryly, careful not to check all her baggage at his counter, but her heart went out to him for hearing that other weeping encoded in her voice.

At night, in Saul Inlander's bed, she thought about Arnon, about the great distance that had grown between them without their intending it and without their understanding what was happening in their lives. It had started as a narrow crack about a year earlier and they hadn't taken it seriously. How easy it would have been to mend it then, with talk, with a small gesture, with a few of Arnon's jokes, but neither of them had been in a hurry to mend it; maybe they had wanted to put themselves to the test, to see if things would develop and in what direction, and how quickly. And so, out of something like negligence, they had suddenly lost control. Hila's hostility and her mother's old age had also come between them, and the crack was now a rift difficult to patch. She looked around this room she now knew even in the dark and thought how irresponsibly she had put her peace of mind on the line, thought about her life now turned upside down, with a gaping void which, as if to prove some physical law, had filled with another man.

"I've been thinking about the question you asked on the beach," he said suddenly.

"What did I ask?"

"About your visits to your mother; you wondered why you're so obsessive."

"Why?"

"For the same reason I'm sorry my father isn't talking."

"And that is?"

"Your mother is the last remaining witness to your child hood."

"I have another witness: my cousin Tzippie."

"It's not the same. Tzippie can't remember what your mother remembers. The first word you said, the day you started to walk."

She drew herself up against him, lay her head on his shoulder, sank her face into his neck and kissed him, grateful that the question she'd asked on the beach had continued to perturb him until he found an answer.

"I'm sure my mother no longer remembers the day I started walking."

"Then maybe you go there to remind her."

She perused her memory and came up with photos she would have put before her mother if she hadn't been embarrassed to imitate the woman in black: "Look hard and you'll remember: Here's Daddy and you and me on Saturday morning at the café on the boulevard. The chocolate-and-vanilla ice cream dripped on my collar, and you started screaming and dragged me to the bathroom, and Nola Flederman and her parents, who were sitting there, laughed at us. In the bathroom you scrubbed my collar to get the stain off and your scolding sounded more like curses. You said it was a waste to take girls to a café who don't know how to keep their clothes neat and don't even care that chocolate leaves a stain that won't come out. When we got back to the table the ice cream was melting in the cone and with the lump in my throat I couldn't have swallowed anything anyway and the chocolate and vanilla got all runny and looked like soup. You sat with your head high and watched the people strolling down the boulevard, and responded to all of them because they knew you from the clinic and greeted you with exaggerated bows. I sat with my head hanging, the collar damp on my neck, and stole a glance at Nola Flederman and her parents. Daddy looked at me with pity and didn't say a word. Only when we got home did he dare speak, and must have thought he was making us both happy when he said, 'Look, the collar's dry and you can't see any stain at all!' and the lump in my throat exploded. Remember?"

She said into Saul Inlander's neck: "Most of the things I remember I would prefer to forget."

For five days she went to her house each morning, took the dog out for a walk, put food and water in his bowls, changed her clothes, listened to the phone messages— including a late-night inquiry from Noa the graphic artist, who must have wondered why she wasn't sleeping at home. Then she went to the office to do battle with the piles of paper rising on her desk, invented excuses to give Noa, spent many hours getting not much done. She visited her mother at the nursing home twice a day, glancing at the man staring into space in the room across the hall, and after work took the dog out again. Then she returned to Saul's apartment, where they spent all their evenings, storing up strength for what awaited them outside, talking a lot and sleeping little.

He never asked her explicitly to explain the disappearance of her husband and children, nor did she tell him about their trip, as if their circuit of shared responsibility was broken as soon as they left the building on Avniyahu Street. Then it was each to his own life.

One night at midnight she hauled him out for a walk, down Dizengoff Street and as far as the arts complex where, drowning in the intoxicating scent of Arab jasmine, they stood by one of the buildings and kissed as though they were alone in the city, ignoring passersby on the sidewalk, as immersed in the act as a boy and a girl on their way back from scouts.

They spent all day Saturday in the apartment, watching Scola films she'd borrowed from the video library, talking, and playing board games she'd brought from Michal's room, drawn to the bed, which remained unmade all day, making love and winding down and moving to the pillow-lair they'd set up on the living-room floor in front of the television. There they sat holding each other and watching *We All Loved Each Other So Much*, remembering bits of childhood, reconstructing snatches of things, goading each other on in their recollections, suddenly understanding why someone had done what he'd done, or the meaning of some event that had escaped them at the time. At night they made dinner together, poured themselves wine, and clinked glasses with arms high.

"What should we drink to?" she asked.

"To this honeymoon."

"*L'hayim*," she agreed.

He recalled one evening when his parents had clinked glasses and the glass in his mother's hand had shattered.

She flinched. "Was she hurt?"

"I don't remember. I just remember them fighting."

"About what?"

"She yelled that he had done it on purpose."

"She yelled? They used to raise their voices?"

"Horrendous shouting. In Hungarian. I used to race around closing the windows. Sometimes I'd run out of the

house or put a transistor radio in the window at full blast.
The neighbors' kids used to laugh at me afterward."

"In our house they used to fight with deathly silence."

But the hostility hung in the air, she well remembered—
piercing and overt in her mother, percolating unseen in her
father—almost as palpable as a smell. Added to the hostility was a sort of general resentment of Fate. Moments of
reconciliation were rare and always associated with food
served on the good china.

During this period she left three messages for Arnon and
spoke with his mother once, keeping it short, asking about
Michal's physics lessons and Hila's research in the library,
sending regards to the girls and to Arnon, and ignoring the
question about when she was coming to visit and where
she would spend the seder. When she hung up she realized
with surprise that she didn't miss any of them.

On the morning of the sixth day, before they went to their
respective offices—they had all the established routines of
a couple, with him taking out the cheeses in the morning
and her pouring the coffee—he put a book in front of her
and said: "I'll do the toast. You look at this meanwhile."

She started thumbing through a big book of photographs of Chicago, girding herself against the city, against
its beautiful boulevards and the superb color of the sky,
turning the pages and having to admit, in spite of herself,
that it would be easy to fall in love with all this—with the
street paved in colorful tiles patterned like a carpet, with
the breathtaking buildings, old and new, with the magnificent lakefront, with the tremendous metal loop that
unfurled the train above the roadways, with Michigan
Avenue crossing the river, with the rows of Kentucky cof-

fee trees and white birches along State Street, with the African elephant that is the largest terrestrial mammal in the Lincoln Park Zoo, which is one of the oldest zoos in the United States—and she slammed the book shut.

"How is it you wound up in Chicago?"

"The company I was working for sent me there for a year, and I decided to stay."

"And they agreed?"

"They had no choice. The head office is located in Chicago, and the manager made me an offer."

"Because you're talented?"

"Maybe," he said without a smile.

"Maybe because you didn't want to come back?"

"That's also true."

"You really didn't want to come back?"

"Really."

"Why?"

"There were all sorts of reasons."

"One of them was a call-up for reserve duty."

"No."

"What, then?"

"I couldn't live here anymore."

"Why not?" She tensed up, and they both heard the new aggressiveness and the hint of offense taken.

He looked at her. "It doesn't matter. Let's drop the subject."

"This subject actually interests me. Why couldn't you live here?"

"Because of the climate," he said reluctantly.

"And why else?" She wouldn't let him off the hook.

"Because of the people."

"You know all the people in this country?"

"This argument is starting to get ridiculous. Let's just drop it."

"The climate and the people." She ignored his protestations, determined to test the boundaries. "What else is wrong with this place?"

"It's not that it's wrong," he said. "It's just that I got to Chicago and felt comfortable there."

"And comfort is the most important thing, as everyone knows."

"I don't think we should get dragged into this argument," he said quietly.

"Why?"

"Because you won't understand."

"Why don't you just test my intelligence."

He said, after a long silence, "I feel that this place swallows me up."

"Swallows you up?"

"Yes. I feel stifled."

She wasn't in a hurry to respond. She was examining the gravity with which the statement was made and the tinge of sadness that accompanied it, until she finally said, "What a dishonorable excuse."

The sadness in his voice grew. "I knew you wouldn't understand."

"This place swallows you up," she said slowly, like a teacher trying to drive home to a student the stupidity of his answer.

"Yes. Like in one of the dreams in your journal: he tries to lift his head above the water, but can't. This is a place that doesn't give people enough room to breathe, because the division between private and public is practically non-existent."

She said, "What a slick rationalization."

"It happens to be the truth."

"And Chicago gives you enough room to breathe?"

"In Chicago things don't get me down as much because I'm not involved."

"What you said about climate and people was easier for me to take. This swallowing up is apparently beyond my intelligence."

"I imagined you wouldn't want to understand," he said, disappointed.

"You were right."

"I'm sorry."

"So am I."

"Let's get things back in proportion," he said moderately. "Most of my life was spent here. All my formative experiences—"

His attempts at appeasement provoked her anger and she was boiling, aware of the standard formulas she was spewing out, and unable to stop them: "I would have respected you more if you had said, 'I'm worn out. I'm sick of these wars, these problems, reserve duty. They offered me quiet and I couldn't resist. So what if my kids don't speak Hebrew? It's a price I'm willing to pay.'"

"I want to explain something to you—"

"Explain to yourself."

"I want—"

She was out of patience. Everything that had come into being between them from that first moment and been built up during this last week was gone. She got up suddenly, grabbed her bag and her jacket and walked out, leaving the door open, noting to herself with some wonder how easily she was giving him up. He came out after her, surprised by the speed of events, calling to the head disappearing around the turn in the stairs, "What happened?"

"I remembered I had a meeting."

"Don't run away from me again," he pleaded, but she

was already at the bottom of the stairs, convincing herself
that this argument was not just an excuse, promising herself that this time she wouldn't come back and that as soon
as she got to the office she would call her mother-in-law
and ask if the invitation still stood and if she could come
to the kibbutz for the seder.

Depression disrupted her work all morning, but she was
firm in her resolve: she would not see Saul Inlander again,
would compose herself and put an end to this maelstrom
that had sucked up her life. She would plan her visits to
the nursing home so they wouldn't coincide with his, and
if she bumped into him she would greet him politely and
not accept even an invitation to coffee. As soon as she
made that decision, she felt calmer, yet found herself
reconsidering every angle and mobilizing all her powers of
self-persuasion, as if this was not in fact the end of the
matter.

The more she incited herself against him the greater the
wave of warmth she felt toward Arnon, and she remembered the delight with which he closed his eyes, head
thrust forward, sitting shoulder to shoulder with childhood
friends during sing-alongs at the kibbutz: "From the slopes
of Lebanon to the Dead Sea, we will plow you and plant
you and build and beautify—"

She managed to maintain her resolve for two days, got
through a mountain of papers on her desk, and at home
tended the plants that hadn't been watered in a week and
aired out the spring clothes. Since he didn't dare call her
at home or at work, the nursing home remained the only
place where he could ambush her. Once a day she saw her
mother briefly at times other than her usual visiting hours,
steering clear of the room across the hall, suppressing

without difficulty the longing that rose within her from time to time for the son of the man her eyes couldn't help but notice, lying and staring at the doorway.

On the third day, in the afternoon, she found her mother asleep. Bertha saw her from a distance and toddled briskly toward her.

"I'm all right, but your mother's not all right."

"What is it?

"Not all right at all."

"Why, what happened?

"She was crying during the night. She wanted her mother. Then she wanted you."

"I'm here."

"She doesn't need you now. Now you may as well go home. She needed you at night. She was crying like a little girl. They gave her a pill so her eyes wouldn't dry up." Bertha turned around and walked out, bearing the offense to Hamutal's mother as if it were her own.

Hamutal sat down by her mother and looked at the face disheveled with weeping.

I know why I come, she said to herself. Not just because she's the last witness to my childhood. I come to get my own back for all the years she ran me down. Now I'm strong and she's weak—and that's what I come to celebrate. Also to plunder that tenderness toward me, which she could never give me then and can't withhold now. There's nothing noble about this, it's simply a matter of war: the loser waits for the winner to weaken. If you wait long enough, the moment always arrives, never too late to be savored.

She was just getting up to leave when Saul Inlander came into the room and stood by her mother's bed. Her legs failed her so that she couldn't even keep the soles of

her shoes steady on the floor, and remained in the posi-
tion of almost-rising, like in that game her daughters
called "Statues" and she and her friends used to call
something else, which now escaped her: frozen in
motion, her body tilted for liftoff, her knees still bent.
She felt the absurdity of her situation, and at the same
time, surprise that the body was weaker than the will. She
tried to lean back, overcome by the intensity of her muscles' response.

"May I speak with you?"

"What about?"

"May I invite you to the cafeteria?"

"No."

"May I know why?"

"Because I'm in a hurry."

"I just want to understand: are you angry with me
because I love Chicago?"

"You can love any city you want. It's none of my business."

"That's what I think, too, so I don't understand why you
ran away from me."

"You're a married man, I'm a married woman—" The
sentence was so untenable and childish that she couldn't
find the words to finish it, and if her body hadn't been
hurting so from the tension she would certainly have
laughed.

"I also love Tel Aviv," he said, ignoring what she said.

"Do me a favor. Don't treat me like a little girl." She was
surprised that the words had come to her.

"These days I even love my father's apartment."

"How nice for you."

"Since you started coming there. Before that I was going
to a hotel to sleep. I couldn't sleep in his bed."

She gave him a ferocious look.

"What's wrong?" he asked in the tone that had echoed after her down the stairwell.

"And how, in your opinion, am I supposed to respond to that statement?"

"I hope you'll want to come back there," he said without the trace of a smile.

"I find that infuriating, if you really want to know."

"Why is it infuriating?"

"Listen to what you're saying."

He said in a voice that filled the whole room: "I'm saying that I miss you."

She let out a small, crumpled sigh, aware that this was his first confession of feeling, sorry that it came about here, in this dreadful place, over her mother's bowed head, within range of Bertha, who hadn't taken her eyes off them. She knew that she'd been vanquished already, but acted as if the battle were still raging and her chances were good.

At that moment her mother opened her eyes and looked at her, and Hamutal froze before their piercing rebuke. Was she suddenly lucid, had she heard the entire conversation that took place across her bed and only pretended to be asleep?

"Where am I?" Her mother's voice sounded dazed with sleep.

For some reason the question made her suspicious. There was an alertness in her mother's eyes that didn't match the intonation of the question.

"You're in your bed. Everything's okay." It occurred to her that what looked like rebuke in her eyes was only a squint.

"Is that Arnon?" The narrowed eyes swung like a spotlight toward Saul Inlander.

Hamutal inclined her head to check if she had heard correctly, puzzled that Arnon's name had emerged from her mother's mouth instead of "your husband," the way she had referred to him since the night of their wedding.

"Who?"

"Arnon."

"Who's Arnon?"

"Arnon, your husband. Is that him?"

She was reminded of Master Eliahu, her amused question when he thought she was his wife, but this time her whole body was rigid and she said to her mother, looking at Saul Inlander: "It's not him."

Above her mother's expressionless face they looked at each other, examining whether they both understood what had been said.

Just before her mother turned toward her, he said, without lowering his voice, "I'll wait for you this evening. I'm asking you to come."

She remained seated after he'd left, her eyes trapped in her mother's, which were relentless, glittering under the trembling, half-closed lids, following her with an ornery satisfaction. Hamutal wondered what game her mother was playing now. Was she in fact having one of her rare moments of lucidity? Had she asked her bleary questions to mislead them, so they'd continue talking above her head?

Never in all her childhood had Hamutal managed to conceal anything from her mother's watchful eyes. From the most minimal of clues—wrinkles in a blouse, mud-stains on her socks, a note torn into a million pieces and tossed in the wastebasket, a lipstick butt concealed in a crevice of her book bag, aspirin hidden in the bottom of her pencil case—her mother had always succeeded in sleuthing out her secrets. Since her last year of elementary school Hamutal had known that her mother searched her closets in her absence, looked for things stashed in drawers, pulled out the thumbtacks and peered under shelving paper, turned her jacket pockets inside out, examined what she was reading, examined even what she was writing under the folded corners of her school diary.

Her mother vehemently denied all accusations and acted highly offended whenever Hamutal voiced her suspicions and detailed the evidence. And her father, his huge eyeballs practically leaping out of his face, would say, "You don't really believe your mother is capable of such a thing!" The intensity of shock in his voice testified to how little he knew either his wife or his daughter.

Now her mother opened her eyes and fixed her with a glazed look, and Hamutal saw that the spark she thought she detected there had gone out. Even if she understood something of what had transpired at her bedside, it had almost certainly been erased from her memory by now.

"It's me, Mother—Hamutal." She felt the bitter taste of victory over this woman who once controlled her life so cruelly and above whose bed a strange man could now say to her married daughter: "I miss you" and "I'll wait for you"; all secrets could now be discussed in her presence, without hiding anything and without fear that she would understand.

And yet, mistrustful of her easy victory and fearing that her mother's ears would conduct the words she'd heard to some living cell or other, Hamutal said before getting up to leave, as if she were obliged to promise her mother what she might have asked: "I'm going home."

Her mother tilted her head as she looked at her, a gesture that gave the look an air of derision.

"Word of honor." Hamutal's hand rose to her heart in the swearing gesture she used to make as a child, accompanying the childhood phrase. Her mother looked at Hamutal's clenched hand and closed her eyes.

Out of the corner of her eye Hamutal saw the nurse's aide striding into the room.

"Shifra's daughter," she said with serious mien, "I want to talk to you a minute." The aide looked right and left, then motioned her toward the end of the corridor, by the giant potted philodendrons. Hamutal, hurrying after her, now noticed to her surprise that their attractive leaves were made of plastic.

"What is it?"

With utmost gravity the aide drew from the pocket of her smock the gold bangle set with Eilat stones.

"Is this your mother's?"

"Yes."

"I thought so."

"Where did you find it?"

"Under someone else's mattress, I can't say whose. In the contract you signed it says it's forbidden to leave them jewelry, even trinkets like this. Maybe it's not worth much, but people here have things with such memories attached that the memories are worth more than the things."

"This is actually worth something. It's gold."

"Gold?" The aide dropped the bracelet into Hamutal's open hand, as if the metal had suddenly seared her fingers. "So do me a favor, don't bring in things that are made of gold. You wouldn't believe it, but a week ago, they even stole somebody's false teeth."

"Thank you very much." Hamutal slid the bracelet into a side pocket in her briefcase.

"I'd hate for things to be stolen here and I'd hate for the

department to get a bad name," the aide said. "And I
wanted to tell you something else: the nightgown you
brought her—it's better for them to have short ones,
because the long ones get in between, you know what I
mean, it's unpleasant, and it's not good for bed sores." She
took a deep breath and added, "And excuse me that I'm
saying this, but maybe you should go home and rest
because you look a little sick yourself."

She sentenced herself to work that night, battling the eyelids
that kept sliding shut, repelling again and again the recurrent image of Saul Inlander waiting for her in his father's
bed, and with that image a new longing for him arose. She
stayed in the office past midnight, reviewing the material
that had accumulated on her desk, and his words to her,
almost a confession of love, echoed over and over in her ears.

After midnight the phone suddenly rang and frightened
her, and she knew he was finding her without a ounce of
strength left, easy prey. If he implored her to come, she
would put down the article in the middle of a paragraph
and go. As she stretched her hand toward the phone she
examined the wrinkles in her sleeve, thinking she wouldn't
even go home to change.

"Hamutal?" Arnon asked, surprised to find her in the
office at such an hour.

"Arnon?" A quick switch in the name on the tip of her
tongue.

He regained his balance immediately: "I wanted to know
what prescription Michal got for her allergy last year." He
spoke quickly, without asking how she was, without asking
about work, without asking where she'd been all this past
week when he didn't find her home at night and left short,
matter-of-fact messages.

"Why, what happened?"

"She's just got a runny nose, nothing serious."

"Nosidex," she said.

"Thanks." He had concluded the conversation.

"How . . . " She started and stopped, not sure he was still on the other end.

"Yes?" His voice was wary.

"How are you all?"

"Just fine."

"How's Michal doing with the physics and Hila—"

"Everything's fine."

"I—"

"I hear you're coming for the seder."

"If you save me a place." She was trying to determine whether she was wanted.

"We'll save one, because you always know where the Afikoman is hidden." He hung up and she was unsure whether the sweet taste of the promise would overcome the sour taste of evasion.

She got home at two in the morning, glad that Arnon had found her at the office and that she'd resisted the temptation to go to Saul Inlander's; a moment later she regretted both and wondered how it was that Saul Inlander retreated from her life as soon as Arnon and the girls entered it, and how he came back and recaptured his place the moment they went away. As if her life had split at the root and each of them had a role in a different part of it.

Early the next morning the head nurse called her at home and asked her to come in immediately for a report from the department's chief physician. Hamutal asked to speak to her mother's doctor, and the nurse transferred her to the resident. A young voice explained that her mother's condition had worsened during the night: she was going from bed to bed, pulling blankets off people or rummaging under their pillows, claiming that someone had stolen her book. For now, the doctor said in a tranquil tone, it had been decided to tie her to her bed. "To what?" Hamutal shouted into the phone.

"Just until she calms down," the doctor explained. "By the Sabbath-eve celebration tomorrow she could be fine again, you'll see."

"Tomorrow's Wednesday. What Sabbath-eve celebration?"

"We'll explain when you get here."

The next day she went to the nursing home twice. On the first visit her mother was sleeping fitfully. A social-work student who was gathering data on Alzheimer patients explained to Hamutal at length the method she was trying out to revive patients' experiential memory. They would put on a sort of play re-creating important events from the patients' lives: the wedding, complete with bride and groom and blessings and presents, and each of the holidays with its traditional dishes and songs. The event they had chosen to start with was the Sabbath-eve celebration, with the blessing over the wine and the challah, which would be familiar from childhood. And in order to accommodate the families of religious patients, who wouldn't travel on the Sabbath, they had scheduled it for Wednesday.

On the second visit, in the evening, the patients were already in the dining room for the celebration. The first thing she took in was Saul Inlander's eyes seeking hers in the desperate appeal for a signal. She avoided his glance and turned to her mother, who was sitting in her wheelchair in a large circle of others. A man's belt around her belly was buckled behind the back of the chair to keep her from falling out. The tranquilizers she'd been stuffed with gave her eyes a drugged glare, which was directed the whole time at Saul Inlander's father and at Bertha, standing beside him. A thin, constant line of bubbly spittle trickled from the corner of her mouth, slanting across her chin with the tilt of her head. She had put the slice of cake she was given on her lap and apparently forgotten it.

At the other end of the room, next to Saul, who was still dispatching his inquiring glances, the elder Inlander sat in his wheelchair, upright, good-looking, clean-shaven, and impeccably dressed. His son stood to the right of the wheelchair and Bertha to the left, a proprietary hand on the old man's shoulder, her body leaning against the armrest. It was clearly difficult for her to stand, but she insisted on showing that she didn't need a wheelchair.

Hamutal followed her mother's hollow gaze toward Inlander and Bertha. Was it by chance that her look was fixed there? Did she understand what she was seeing? What was happening behind those empty eyes, that frighteningly pale face with all its features drawn into deep verticals? Was there any life rustling in that body, with its drooping limbs, the thick belt holding it in place? Was jealousy raging there? Was a soul hiding there, reaching out toward the pleasant-looking man ensconced in his chair like a doll? Would she—if she could—get up from her chair and swipe Bertha's hand away and take her place? Was this some kind of signal sent to her and Saul Inlander: two women and one man? The sight of them reminded her of the man who was jealous of his wife and had a nightmare in which one woman and two men sought shelter in Noah's ark.

Her mother's eyes were still fastened, unblinking, on the elder Inlander, who obviously had no idea what was happening around him. His eyes, which for weeks had accustomed themselves to looking at the rectangle of a doorway, were fixed there now, too, as if he were waiting for something to happen. He didn't see the big tray of sugar-dusted cookies that a young volunteer was holding in front of him with both hands, waiting patiently for the man to shift his gaze and notice her. Bertha suddenly shot out a hand and grabbed a cookie, clutching it in her fist the way the winner of a race holds the medallion. Saul Inlander also took a cookie, and thanked the girl. Old Inlander, his eyes visible above his son's lowered head, did not shift his gaze.

One of the nurses undertook to organize some singing and started with, "Go, beloved Israel, and greet your bride, welcome, welcome the Sabbath." The staff joined in with their strong voices and the old people with their breathy murmurs. Then the nurse tried to stir up some enthusiasm, walking the circuit of wheelchairs like an animal tamer at the circus, gesturing with both hands to draw out the singers.

A young actress set up a small table in the center of the room and placed two candlesticks on it. Then she wrapped her head and shoulders in a shawl, covered her face with her hands in the traditional fashion, and recited in a firm voice: "Blessed art Thou, O Lord, King of the Universe—"

Hamutal had the impression that a dim spark flickered in her mother's eyes when she thrust her head forward. Had her mother reverted to childhood, was she standing by her parents, among her brothers and sisters, listening to the words without understanding? "Blessed art Thou . . . "

Suddenly there was a sound of very soft weeping, and everyone fell silent. In the silence the weeping gathered force until it turned into sobbing, then into howling, and right away, as if someone were conducting a dreadful choir, the other old people joined in and out of their midst rose one horrific voice, like that of a maddened soloist, in a scream as lengthy as a lamentation. The social-work student seemed out of her depth: this was not the way she had envisioned her scientific experiment. And like some instrumental accompaniment to the chorus of horror came the clang of metal wheel rims, then a thud and a soaring screech of pain that amplified the other voices into a resounding echo. It was followed by a long, desperate wail, and Hamutal saw an empty wheelchair careering into the footrest of the chair across from it, and the woman who had been sitting in it sprawled on the bare floor. Like an echo again the others responded with a shriek of panic, even those who had seen nothing and only heard the wail. Those who were capable tried to direct their chairs to the place where the woman lay stretched out on the floor and immediately there was a chaos of wheelchairs wedged together, and in the midst of them the nurses and doctors trying to clear a path to the injured woman, who was now bawling like a baby, saliva and blood oozing out between her teeth.

Hamutal's mother hadn't budged. She was sitting in her chair, her neck outstretched, perhaps waiting for the prayer to continue, a trickle of drool that Hamutal hadn't caught creeping slantwise across her chin. The slice of cake was still on her lap, and her eyes traveled slowly from the elder Inlander to the middle of the room, flitting over the surface of the riot under way. Without stopping to think, Hamutal turned toward the door and ran out, leaving her mother in the mélée of shouting and weeping. At the end of the corridor, where the voices died down, she dropped onto a bench that was usually occupied but was now empty. There she covered her face with her hands and for the first time since she had set foot in this place—

three months and nine days ago that seemed forever—she
wept for her mother, and for the woman who had fallen
out of her wheelchair, and for herself, and for Arnon, and
for her daughters; wept over time, which mutilated people, over the hopelessness of life as lived in the room
down the hall, over the infamy of extinction and the
despair and the stupefying waste at the end of the road.
She didn't stop crying, not even when she felt Saul
Inlander's hand on her head, not even when he sat down
beside her and drew her into the familiar woolly odor of
his jacket.

Their lovemaking that night was different, as if their bodies, too, were aware of something new, distinct from the
pleasures of the flesh, an undefined commitment that
circumvented thought, communicating the new situation
as a physical command. They slept all night holding each
other, their legs entwined, feeling how, suddenly, the connection between them had deepened: a connection still
young, one that, seeming to sense that its days were num-
bered, incurred crises and climaxes. The scenes of horror
they had witnessed at the Sabbath-eve celebration
demonstrated again the fragility and temporality of peo-
ples' lives, including the fragility and temporality of their
own relationship, which was fated from the start to be
linked to the nursing home. Before he fell asleep, foggy
with fatigue and the wine they'd had with dinner, he told
her that for a few days now he'd been amusing himself
with thoughts about a woman who leaves her family and
a man who leaves his. People like that could start a new
life in another country—China, say, or New Zealand, or
some other place where the company he worked for had
a branch office.

She stroked his back after he fell asleep, trying to rein in her emotions, reconstructing word for word what it seemed to her he had said, knowing there was nothing explicit but enjoying the sudden thought that with this man, whom she didn't really know but who her heart said would never hurt her, she could live a new life in a strange place, as if they'd had no previous lives. Together they would buy a house, choose upholstery material, install a stove, put up light fixtures, hang pictures. And she would bear him a son—she already saw him in her mind's eye: a miniature version of his father, a boy who would be an outstanding builder of Lego bridges, which they would line up on a shelf in the living room. They would glow with pride when guests foresaw a great future for their son.

But in the morning, when he had showered and dressed and was looking clear-eyed and matter-of-fact and made no mention of his notions of the previous night, she was angry that he had dared to say the things he'd said and then ignore them. She decided she would not bring up what he'd murmured in her ear before he fell asleep, but would leave it to him to either contemplate or forget, and would by no means allow this to preoccupy her until he repeated his request explicitly. That morning, as they stood together on the sidewalk before getting into their respective cars, she said to him, knowing that the harder she was on herself now, the easier it would be for her later, "Let's take a break for three days."

"Why?" He was dumbfounded.

"To keep the right distance."

"What right distance?"

"Right for now: three days."

He gave her a puzzled look. "I don't understand."

"There's nothing to understand," she replied and to herself said, If it has to happen, better to separate gradually.

The more she tried to resist the idea he had planted in her mind the previous evening, the more vigorously it rebounded and ambushed her, like a cunning foe. And in the course of the day, despite the decision she had made in the morning, the idea evolved into a detailed plan: They would not go to China or to New Zealand. They would remain in Israel because it was right for people to live their lives where they had spent their childhood. The girls would remain with their father. She would not demand her share of the house, so that Arnon and Hila and Michal could all stay where they were. She would visit them every day, and the four of them would rebuild their relationships on a new foundation. Arnon would easily find himself a new wife, who would be affectionate with the girls and love taking care of the garden. Arnon and Saul would hit it off immediately. Saul's Israeli daughter would come back from America and they would welcome her warmly and everyone would celebrate the holidays at the kibbutz with Arnon's parents and live together as one big family. From time to time she rebelled at her own proposal for a three-day separation, then suppressed her longing and assured herself that the separation was necessary so they could put their thoughts in order.

That afternoon she paused for a moment in the hall and, out of habit, peered into his father's room. The old man was sleeping. It was unlike him to close his eyes. There was something disturbing about the way he was lying, very close to the edge of the bed, the blanket hanging off and trailing on the floor, his head on one end of the pillow, the other end sticking out beyond the edge of the bed. She lingered there looking, trying to overcome the agitation she felt at the sight of him. Then she walked around his bed, tugged the pillow, with his head still resting on it, to the middle of the bed, lifted the corner of the blanket off the floor and gently folded it under and laid it on the bed.

When she went into the room across the hall the first thing she noticed was the woman in black sitting by her mother, who had shrunk back against the wall. Then she saw her own mother standing at the window and looking outside, her forehead pressed against the glass. Hamutal, recalling stories she'd head about old people killing themselves by jumping out of windows, rushed over.

"Hello, Mother."

Her mother slowly turned her head and looked at her.

"It's me, Mother—Hamutal. Are you feeling sick?"

"Do you have a black car?"

"No. My car is white."

"I saw a black car."

"It's not mine."

"So whose is it?"

"I don't know. Mine is white. Come on back to your bed."

Her mother lay down on her back, closed her eyes, and remained motionless, her hands crossed on her chest like the hands of a Christian corpse in a casket.

In the silence, the voice of the woman in black grew louder. "Who's this?" she asked doggedly, holding a picture up to her mother's frightened eyes.

Like a talking-machine, as if her purpose in life were to sit and describe photographs, the woman in black was saying to her mother, "Look hard and you'll remember. This was on the trip to the Sea of Galilee, when we stayed at a hotel, and Haimke wet the bed. You washed out the sheets and turned the mattress over so they wouldn't know and wouldn't charge us for a new mattress, you remember that? Here we're eating breakfast in the hotel. They gave us a lot of eggs and you told Papa not to eat so many, but he finished everybody's omelet and in the afternoon he felt sick, so he stayed in the room while the rest of us went swimming. Here's Shoshana standing in the hotel garden, pointing to the window of our room. She's so proud, you'd think we had the deed to the place. And you remember the nuns we saw on the beach, and Haimke was so scared he dreamt that night that the nuns were chasing him and he started yelling and woke everybody up? You remember that? So you and Papa took him into your bed and that's where he peed."

The shrunken woman made no response, and Hamutal, upset by the stream of details filling her ears, said to her mother, who'd opened her eyes, "Let's take a little walk in the hall."

Halfway to the elevator, arm-in-arm with her mother and embarrassed by the unaccustomed proximity of their bodies—arms linked, fingers resting on fingers, shoulder rubbing shoulder, hip bumping hip—Hamutal heard a sudden thud, and knew at once: Saul Inlander's father had fallen out of bed.

She led her mother to the nearest bench, sat her down, and dashed back. Saul Inlander's father was lying on the floor, very pale, his blue eyes filled with fright and fixed on the doorway. His neighbor sat up among his blankets and looked, puzzled, at the empty bed beside him. She imagined she saw a flicker in old Inlander's eyes when she appeared.

She said to him, "I'm getting a doctor right now, Mr. Inlander. Lie down and don't move."

She ran from room to room, calling the male aide and the female aide and asking them to alert the doctor. She asked the girl in the office to call the son of the man who had fallen out of bed.

Meanwhile her mother had returned to the window by herself, again gazing outside intently, as if trying very hard to see something that insisted on hiding itself to the right of her field of vision. Hamutal went up to her and realized that her eyes were closed. She had fallen asleep like that, standing up, her forehead leaning against the pane.

"Come on, Mother." She pulled her gently by the elbow, and her mother, like a sleepwalker, allowed her to lead her to the bed and cover her up.

"Who are you?" her mother asked.

"I'm Hamutal."

With vacant eyes her mother followed Hamutal as she walked all around the bed, tucking the edges of the rumpled sheet under the mattress. A deepening furrow divided her mother's brow, as if she was trying to recall something.

"My little girl was also named Hamutal."

Hamutal froze in mid-tuck, one hand lifting the mattress, the other underneath it. There was a heartbreaking sweetness in the words "my little girl," a phrase she had never heard from her mother. She would usually introduce her by name, sometimes as "my daughter," but "my little girl" carried with it a promise of love that had never been fulfilled.

Without knowing why, Hamutal gathered up her hair with both hands, pulling it back from her forehead and cheeks, and holding it at the nape. Then she leaned over toward her mother, bringing her exposed face close, and whispered, "Who's Hamutal?"

Her mother looked closely at her. The furrow cut her forehead from the bridge of her nose to the roots of her hair.

"My little girl," she said softly, and Hamutal's eyes filled with tears.

Three and a half months earlier, when they had just brought her mother to this nursing home, she and Arnon had stood in the doorway, shocked by the sight: three beds practically side by side, three small metal cupboards, a closet with three narrow doors, bare walls. On the window sill was a small planter with a fiddle-leaf fig in it, its base still wrapped in cellophane.

Her mother had had a room to herself in the assisted-living center she had left. A large bookcase had stood by the window, and lined up on the top shelf had been all the old family pictures and a few of Hamutal with Arnon and the children, almost always with a dog standing by them or in the arms of one of the girls. And here—they hesitated at the door, surveying the bare room.

"Hello, Shifra." The aide glanced at the paper in her hand bearing the new name, then slipped it into a large clipboard at the foot of the bed. "Welcome. Would you like something to eat?"

"She ate not long ago," Hamutal said.

"This is your bed." The aide pointed to the one nearest the door. "Get yourselves organized and I'll come back in a little while. I'll take you to the activity room. Her room-mates are working on crafts."

Arnon, seeing Hamutal's gray face, said, "It reminds me of the children's house at the kibbutz."

"Look, there isn't even any place to put the photos."

"You don't put out photos in this place, what's the matter with you? The ones who can stand on their own two feet get up at night and steal their roommates' grandchildren."

"Cut it out, Arnon."

"I know that from the old-age home at the kibbutz. I worked there for a few days when I got out of the army."

"Do me a favor." She pulled from his hand the plaid travel bag in which she'd packed her mother's things.

"I'm not kidding. Once one of the heroes of the Hashomer guards stole me. I was actually pretty proud of that."

"Arnon," she said, pulling at the zipper, "I understand what you're trying to do, but it doesn't help, so quit it."

When the three of them went into the activity room, the aide pointed to an old woman gaping into space and pulling at a few strands of wool wound around a broom handle. A young girl as round-faced as her grandmother sat beside her, tucking back between her grandmother's fingers the strands that escaped. The aide introduced the old woman with an air of celebration: "This is Rivka." Then she bent over toward Rivka, pointing at Hamutal's mother, and confided into her ear, as if the news would gladden her heart, "This is your new roommate, Shifra." But Rivka said nothing and didn't look at the new arrivals standing before her.

At the other end of the table sat a sprightly old woman whose hands were playing with wooden spindles and whose wide eyes followed Hamutal. The aide pointed to her and said affably, "This is Rosa, your other roommate. Everyone say hello to Rosa. Rosa—this is your new roommate. Her name is Shifra. Say hello."

"I still haven't eaten," said Rosa, without detaching her wide-eyed, curious gaze from Hamutal.

"Of course you ate," the aide said patiently. "You had yogurt and bread and tea. You ate very nicely."

"I still haven't eaten," Rosa insisted.

The aide tried to interest Shifra in various handicrafts, placing before her baskets filled with spools of thread, knots of rope, wooden spindles, rubber balls, and bottle caps. Shifra gave the objects a weary glance and asked to lie down. Arnon left, and Hamutal led her mother to her new bed. Rivka and Rosa were also led in and put in their beds, and the granddaughter sat by her grandmother and stroked her hand. From the moment she came into the room, Rosa did not take her eyes off Hamutal.

"Do you want to get washed, Mother?"

"No."

Hamutal drew the curtain that hung from a rail above the bed and helped her mother put on her nightgown, take off her shoes, and get into bed. Then she opened the curtain to Rosa's wide eyes and covered her mother up to the neck.

"Do you want anything, Mother?"

"Sleep."

Her mother sank into her bed, exhausted by the move and by the new sights, and Hamutal sat by her, remembering the moments of terror that used to come over her at bedtime when she was a child, when she would lie there in the dark, knowing she was not allowed to call her parents or open the door and let a little light in, pulling the blanket over her head to stifle the trembling or the chattering of her teeth, afraid to cry and annoy her parents.

All that time Rosa was tracking them with her hungry eyes, following Hamutal's every move, until Hamutal, discomfited, said to her, "Do you need anything?"

The old woman's eyes lit up. Hamutal went around her mother's bed and stood next to the roommate's.

"Do you want something to drink, Rosa?"

"*Mein kind*," said Rosa, trembling, and sat up in her bed. Shifra, who had already been half asleep, opened her eyes all at once.

"What does she want?" she asked with a snort.

"*Mein kind*." Rosa stretched out her arms to Hamutal, who was bending over her.

Hamutal was standing between the two beds, and out of the corner of her eye saw her mother, now wide awake, suspicious, not sure her ears had heard correctly. And Rosa, pulling herself up straighter in her bed, her eyes tender with happiness, her face aglow with love, said, "*Mein kind, mein kind.*"

"What?" Shifra leaned toward her.

"*Mein kind,*" Rosa gushed.

"*Mein kind?*" her mother screamed, thrusting her head menacingly toward Rosa. "*Das ist* mein *kind!*"

Hamutal recoiled. The girl stopped stroking the back of her grandmother's hand.

The aide was immediately at the door, and at the sight of the two old women quarreling and Hamutal pale, drew Hamutal backward and stepped into the space between the two beds. With experienced hands she gently nudged the women back onto their pillows and said, "Let's have some quiet now. Go to sleep." And to Hamutal, "You'll get used to it. Every time there's a daughter here who takes good care of her mother, they all want to adopt her."

"She doesn't have any children?" Hamutal looked at Rosa, who had still not taken her wistful eyes off her.

"She doesn't have anyone. They found her wandering the streets a week ago, chilled to the bone. So far no one has come looking for her. It took us two days to thaw her out. She latches onto all the children, not just you."

Late that night, long after her mother had fallen asleep,

Hamutal left the nursing home. Before she walked out of the room she glanced at Rosa, who was finally asleep.

From the elevator to her car she took huge strides, almost galloping, as if she were running for her life. She turned on the ignition and sped away. When she got to her house she turned off the engine and sat, confused by what had happened and by the compassion she suddenly felt for her mother, a compassion she had never had for her before. Was it the words *"Das ist mein kind,"* said with such vehemence, that stirred her like this and silenced the grievances of many years? She sat motionless for a long time, remembering how her mother's hands had clutched her as she was dressing her, the bony toes she discovered when she took off her mother's sock, the determined *"Das ist mein kind."* If she had heard that *"Das ist mein kind"* years ago, everything would have been different between them.

"So what happened?" said Arnon. "Did they try to kidnap you?"

"No." She was full of hostility toward him for amusing himself, oblivious of the shock she'd undergone. She remembered Rosa's outstretched arms and thought to herself that, as if by some law of conservation, nothing was being lost here: what was given to her mother had been taken away from Arnon.

Now she was looking at the bed by the door. Rosa had been the first to disappear, and in her place came a woman whose name she couldn't remember, who also used to look at her longingly, and that woman, too, had disappeared, and Bertha had inherited her bed. Rivka slept most of the time. Her children, as quiet as she was, used to put her in a wheelchair and take her into the garden. On windy days they sat with her in the lobby near the

glass wall, and from there she would look out into the garden. Sometimes one of her daughters would undo her
hair, letting it down to its full length, silky and thin, then
comb it gently, making a slim braid that could wind
around the crown of her head four times. Each evening
another grandchild would arrive, feed her, and stroke her
hand until she fell asleep. When Rivka died, her bed went
to the woman whose sight was threatened by a tumor in
her brain and whose daughter's intensive attempts to
revive her memory came to naught.

Getting up to leave, Hamutal wondered what had become
of Rosa and remembered her desperate, nightmare-inducing
*"Mein kind, mein kind."*

Approaching his father's room she leaned against the door
frame and watched Saul Inlander from the back as he
tended his father. His left hand held his father's hand, and
his right stroked his forehead, the fingers trailing gently
back and forth. The old man, as lost as a little boy, gave
him a plaintive look, a look Hamutal had seen in the eyes
of the dog when he was sick, when Michal had walked
around the house carrying him like a baby. As he stroked
his father's forehead Saul Inlander was talking to him,
seemed to be promising him things, trying to persuade him
that the promises would be fulfilled.

His father threw her an inquiring glance that deepened
the creases of his forehead for a moment, the same expression her mother had when she was straining to remember
something. Saul turned his head in the direction of his
father's gaze and saw her standing behind them.

"Hello," he said.

"Hello."

"Two days left."

"Yes." She wondered if he also remembered what he had said to her the previous night.

"How's your mother?"

"Asleep."

"How long have you been standing here?"

"A few minutes. How is he doing?"

"He broke his ankle and he has some bruised ribs. The doctor is supposed to be here any minute."

"Is he in pain?"

"Yes. Do you think you could change your mind about the three days?"

"I'll wait for you in the car," she said.

She sat in the dark for some time before he arrived. As soon as he sat down he grasped her head with both hands and covered her face with kisses.

"I'm not good at talking," he said. "I didn't understand your attack of patriotism before and I don't understand these three days now. Your escapes paralyze me, because I don't understand why you run away. I simply can't tell you how much I miss you and how important you are to me."

"Like Chicago?" she joked.

"More," he said seriously.

"Really?"

"Yes. Chicago doesn't take any interest in my father's pain."

"That's true."

"So maybe you'll forget about those two days?"

She looked at his hand resting on the steering wheel of her car and decided that what had seemed to her a proposal was apparently said under the influence of the wine. She didn't take her eyes off his fingers, remembering how those fingers had stroked his father's forehead. She was incredulous at the stupid suggestion that they separate for three days, and glad that the coming night, and maybe, after all, the rest of her life, would be spent with this man, under this hand so adept at reassurance.

"The doctor wanted to talk to me," she said. "I have to go back."

"I'll wait for you at home."

He didn't repeat what he'd said to her in his drunken state and she didn't ask, but there was new excitement in their lovemaking that night, as if their bodies wanted to express what speech held back, what life outside Ya'akov Inlander's bedroom promised but could not deliver.

# CHAPTER THREE

"Then give me some proof of love."

On the way to her mother's bed the next day Hamutal spent some time beside Ya'akov Inlander's. The blue eyes accustomed to staring at the doorway, unblinking, had been closed these last few days, as if the muscles controlling his lids were terminally exhausted. She found him lying alone in the room and came in quietly, standing in front of his bed. For the first time she could observe him at close range, linger undisturbed over his features, bend down and examine the degree of resemblance between father and son.

The old man's face was relaxed, the flesh shrunken under the excess of skin, wrinkles dense under the eyes and around the neck. His hair was combed to the side, with a part straight as a ruler: hair that might have been a boarding-school boy's if not for the white, almost snowy color. The lines of the mouth were sharp, unlike most old people's, and retained a surprising sensuality, also present in the way the lips were drawn in, petulant. A thin ray of light slanted in from the space between the curtains, traversing the room and lying across his eyes like a white-hot blade.

One recent night, lying beside his son in bed, she had studied his face like this, and now she was astonished by the resemblance between them: this was how Saul Inlander would look in another thirty years. And maybe then his son's lover would stand over him, comparing the son to him, whose hair for now was only lightly touched with gray and whose skin was still young, though already it had been stamped with that expression of disaffection and impatience, which would intensify with the years.

Saul Inlander's father was not sleeping. The whole time she stood there watching him, he lay with eyelids crinkled shut. She was sure that he sensed her presence but did not want to see or know or understand or allow anyone to disturb his peace, because he had decided to take leave of the world.

Behind her she suddenly heard a woman's loud, singsong voice: "Excuse me, is there anything I can help you with?"

Hamutal turned her head and saw, blocking the doorway, a woman whose cheeks were painted deep orange, like the faces of peasants burnished by the sun.

"I see you standing there like that," the woman said, looking her over. Her polite tone barely masked her suspicion. "Do you know this man?"

"No."

"I'm his sister and I don't know you, so that's why I'm asking." Saul Inlander's aunt followed Hamutal with her eyes until she was out of the room.

She found her mother asleep. Sitting down beside her, she remembered the article she'd been editing that morning, "Conversations with the Unconscious," which described a Canadian researcher's experiment in penetrating people's unconscious as they slept. Twenty students had volunteered for the month-long project. People with a proven ability to penetrate the unconscious of others had sat by them each night and managed to implant detailed information on subjects the students knew nothing about.

Hamutal decided to address her sleeping mother, directing her thoughts to her mother's unconscious.

"I want to talk to you, but there's no one to talk to," said
the voice within her. And not because of your condition.
It was always that way between us. In fact, I don't really
know how to talk to you. We never did it, not the way Dorit
used to talk to her mother. They had a 'talking corner'
between the refrigerator and the wall, where there were
two stools, and when there was something important to
talk about, the two of them would move the stools away
and bring in two small rugs from the bedroom and sit huddled between the refrigerator and the wall, ear to mouth,
and talk. Once when I arrived in the middle of a conversation they didn't stop, just asked me to wait. I sat in the living room and saw their feet sticking out from behind the
refrigerator. I couldn't hear words, but I could hear whispering. My throat hurt from trying so hard to stop the sobs.
In all my life I've never wanted anything the way I wanted
just then to have a mother with a talking corner. And once,
when I was feeling particularly bold, I asked the teacher if
I could go home before the last lesson, and she said okay.
I went to Dorit's house."

The voice addressing her mother fell silent, and
Hamutal remembered the moment when she had knocked
at the door of Dorit's house and Dorit's mother had opened
it, glancing worriedly over Hamutal's head, looking for her
daughter.

"Did something happen to Dorit, honey?"

"No, Dorit's okay."

"So you didn't go to school today?"

"I asked to get out early."

"But Dorit isn't home yet."

"I know. I wanted to talk to you."

"To me?" She still hadn't extended her arm to open the door wide. "What happened, honey, did you have another quarrel with Dorit?"

"No. Could I sit in the talking corner?"

"Sit where?"

"In the talking corner."

Dorit's mother looked at her and burst out laughing. "You mean put the rugs down and all that?"

"Yes."

"Who do you want to sit with?"

"With you."

"Me and you?"

"If it's okay."

Dorit's mother looked at her for a moment, perhaps wondering at this determination she hadn't seen before in her daughter's quiet friend. She frowned in pursuit of some evasive thought, and then, as if she had suddenly understood, stretched out her arm to open the door wider and said with extravagant politeness, "Do come in."

She went to the bedroom and came back with a scatter rug in each hand, wearing a forced smile that was somewhere between embarrassment and jest. Hamutal hurriedly moved the stools aside, and Dorit's mother spread out the rugs in the empty space.

"Like that?"

"Yes."

"So come, sit down." She held out her hand and gestured to the space between herself and the wall.

Hamutal squeezed into that narrow space, feeling right away how the warmth of Dorit's mother's body infiltrated the pores of her skin, enveloping all of her and warming her to the tips of her ever-cold toes. Then Dorit's mother put a hand on her shoulder and a new wave of warmth burst from there, as if an oven had been turned on. She closed her eyes and rubbed her knees with her hands, her face lifted toward the ceiling like some half-frozen person warming up and thawing out in the winter sun, surrendering to the pleasant sensation. They sat like that for a few minutes, side by side, in complete silence, listening to the monotonous hum of the refrigerator.

"Did you want us to talk about something?"

"No. I just wanted to sit for a while."

"Fine," said Dorit's mother, her eyes round with amazement.

Hamutal continued to sit like that with her eyes closed, squeezed against the huge, soft bosom, breathing in the fragrance of Assouta soap diluted with the smell of frying, giving in to the bliss that was reviving cell after cell, grateful to Dorit's mother for not moving and not getting anxious and not even wanting to know the meaning of this strange request, just sitting there quietly, letting Hamutal store up the warmth of her body and relax.

"That's it?" Dorit's mother asked when Hamutal stood up and shook herself. Hamutal wasn't sure if there was relief in her voice.

"Yes, I just wanted to sit here with you for a little while."

"That's just fine," said Dorit's mother, her voice struggling to sound natural, as if what had happened here was a routine occurrence.

"I'll put the stools back—"

"You don't have to, honey. I'll put them back," she said, apparently eager to get this peculiar business over with.

Hamutal picked up her schoolbag and went to the door. Before going out she turned around, saw the strain in Dorit's mother's eyes, as if she was wondering what else awaited her, and said politely, "Goodbye."

"Bye-bye, honey."

That afternoon, as the sweet memory of radiant warmth began to mingle with the growing fear of a reaction from Dorit, who might come looking for her at home, Hamutal escaped to Tzippie's house, and from there, since Tzippie's mother was busy washing the floor, she escaped to the clinic. Sheltered among the people there, she could pretend to be busy with some task she'd been given, and that would make it easier to explain what had happened without having to look Dorit in the eye. Maybe she could even laugh the matter off, she told herself.

But Dorit didn't come looking for her at the clinic, and the next day at school she behaved perfectly normally. After a few days Hamutal realized that Dorit's mother hadn't told her daughter about the puzzling incident, perhaps because she herself was concerned about how it would be interpreted. Dorit's mother continued to welcome Hamutal cheerfully, but Hamutal thought she detected some worry—as if she were keeping an eye on her from a distance—as well as acknowledgment that they shared a secret pact. For the next few years, whenever their eyes met—when she came to Dorit's to study for exams or to go with her to class parties, and even on chance meetings at the shopping center—Hamutal thought she saw a question mark in Dorit's mother's eyes, a hint that the riddle of that incident had come to mind again. But these intuitions were conveyed only through a quick exchange of glances, and nothing was ever said.

Only at high-school graduation, when Hamutal stepped down from the stage with her diploma pressed to her heart, did she make her way over to Dorit's mother and give her a bold hug and whisper in her ear, "I want to thank you for that business, back then." Dorit's mother knew immediately what she was talking about, as if she'd been waiting all those years for an explanation; she didn't pretend not to remember. She hugged Hamutal, and the sizeable, motherly chest was squeezed between them.

"You're welcome, honey."

"I think I just needed warmth," Hamutal said a bit apologetically, like an old man understanding some youthful folly.

"If you need more, just say the word," Dorit's mother said as she released her, spreading her arms wide, her huge breasts expanding to the full width of her body. Hamutal thought she sounded relieved, as if only now was she convinced there was no madness in what had happened.

And Hamutal gave her a wan smile: "Thanks, but I wouldn't fit into that space anymore."

Just at that moment—with the memory of Dorit's mother standing before her, arms wide—her mother opened her eyes and gave Hamutal a piercing look, her pupils glittering between motionless lids.

"It's me, Mother—Hamutal."

"Where's Dorit?"

"Who?" she cried out.

"Dorit."

"Which Dorit?" She was panicking.

"Dorit, you know which Dorit. You only had one Dorit."

"There's no one here, just me." Hamutal could feel her heart pounding in her throat.

"Her mother steals my food." Hamutal's mother clenched her fists and Hamutal looked at her, thunderstruck.

"Dorit's mother?"

"She thinks I don't know how she got to be a kapo. Everbody knows."

"What are you talking about?" Hamutal sputtered, absorbing one shock after another, feeling increasingly helpless. Her mother suddenly sat up straight, attentive, listening to sounds outside.

"You hear that?" She was turning her head left and right, then cocked her ear toward the window as if she had a radar implant.

"It's a bus."

"Is that what they say?"

"It's pulling in to the number-twenty-five stop."

"They say it's a bus. Don't believe them. Never believe them. It's a train. Can you hear a train?"

"No."

"I'm not getting on a train. Let the Germans finish me off on the spot. That would be the best thing for me. I won't get on that for anything. I want to get out of here, but there's nobody waiting for me at home."

"I'll wait for you."

"Where will you wait for me?"

"Wherever you want."

"No one's waiting for me. I wake up and there's nobody waiting for me."

"I'll wait for you, Mother." She found herself compassionate and tender toward this woman who was by now more foreign than familiar. The word "Mother" linked the new feeling with ancient habits that were not about to change.

"Here?"

"Wherever you want."

"Until I wake up?"

"Yes."

"And you're not going anywhere?"

"No. I'll wait for you."

"I like to be where there are people waiting for me."

"So I'll wait."

"And you have time? Have you finished your home-work?"

"Yes."

Her mother closed her eyes. A moment later the confusion in her face was replaced by a focused expression, and she peered at Hamutal from between her eyelids, as if to check whether she was still sitting in her chair. There was something weird in her mother's look, scrutinizing, suspicious, contentious.

"You little whore," her mother whispered, her eyeballs simmering in their slits. There was no doubt about the word she had used. The mumbling was intelligible enough, and this time Hamutal decided she wasn't going to fool herself and say she'd misheard. Her heart stood still, as if it had become immune in recent days and its walls had grown tougher, protecting the soft interior from the horrors yet to come. Hamutal looked around to see if anyone had overheard the profanity that had been uttered without enmity, without indignation, almost dryly, indifferently, like a statement of fact. Bertha wasn't there, and the woman who had lost her memory was sitting on her bed and looking at her fingernails. Hamutal crossed her legs again, making herself comfortable until her mother fell asleep.

As a child she often used to wait for her. Twice a week her father would travel to the north and sleep over in Nahariya, at the home of people from his town in Europe, and on those days Hamutal would be alone all afternoon, until it got dark and the clinic closed. Sometimes, especially in the winter, when she was afraid to stay by herself in the dark, she would run to the clinic, into the bubble of her mother's private, white world, with its special, stifling reek of medicines and cleaning agents so dominant that it seemed to stick to her mother's clothing and skin.

Her mother suddenly thrust her head up to Hamutal's face.

"What is it, Mother?"

Her mother gave her a hostile look.

"It's me, Mother—Hamutal."

Her mother gestured for her to come closer, and Hamutal hesitated a moment, then bent her head down until she could hear the whisper: "They're not letting her in. She's banging on the door, and they can hear, but they're not opening the door for her."

"For who?"

"Rayzele." Her mother was flushed, and her cheeks rose, pushing the eyes back into her skull.

"Who's Rayzele?"

"Rayzele. She's sitting in the rain and waiting, but they won't open."

"Why?"

"They're afraid of the Nazis." Her mother waved her hand as if to dispel the sight, and a new spark of deep and unfamiliar horror flashed in her eyes.

"And now he wants me to come to him."

"Who?" Hamutal was thinking about the people who refused to open the door for Rayzele.

"With a stick," her mother said, and Hamutal thought of the Nazis.

"Who wants you to come?"

"At night," her mother said fearfully, and Hamutal's thoughts shifted to the male aide.

"Who is he?"

"He wants me to come now. He says he's waiting for me."

"Where is he waiting for you?"

"In heaven."

"Who is waiting for you there?"

"Him."

"Menachem?" She pronounced her father's name, and it sounded strange to her.

"*Gott,*" her mother said. "*Ehr vart.*"

"What are you talking about, Mother?" Hamutal was shocked by the sudden Yiddish, aware that she was witness to a mind slipping gears.

"*Yo, yo. Ehr vart.*"

"So he'll wait for you a little longer." She strained her throat to produce a neutral sentence.

"I'm scared of him." Her mother closed her eyes, and tears glistened in the corners, as if the juices of the eye were being squeezed out under pressure.

"Why are you scared?"

"Tell him not to do anything to me."

"What would he do to you?"

"It said in the paper: beating and acid. Acid on the face and in the eyes. That's what he'll do to me."

She's talking about my father, Hamutal thought to herself and chuckled bitterly, remembering the short, emaciated man, always fearful, who coughed summer and winter and only in his dreams dared to express the savagery that was bottled up inside him. He spent most of his days trying to suppress the violence, diminish himself, speak sparingly, shrink into corners, creep quietly into the house, tiptoe so as not to make noise, listen to his wife's complaints with the submissiveness of a servant, head bowed, boiling with anger inside but not giving vent. And in the end, when he left this world, his absence went unnoticed except for the decided relief at night.

"He won't do anything to you, Mother. He never used to hit."

"Now he does. He's been waiting for me with this for a long time. Read the paper. And in the end there'll be the crematorium, too. You'll see."

What Hamutal wanted now more than anything was to see Tzippie, to entrust her mother to Tzippie, who had long been acquainted with the norms of behavior in this area where hazardous memories ran rampant and tremendous caution was needed to step among them, a region that Tzippie had entered voluntarily as a child, and where Hamutal had refused to set foot.

When she came back from the nursing home that evening, Hamutal called Tzippie and told her: "It's what we were afraid would happen, Tzippie. Today she started talking about the Holocaust. I need you now."

And Tzippie, immediately volunteering for the cause that had been her responsibility since childhood, said, "Okay, I'm coming."

There was silence at both ends of the line, and Hamutal wondered if Tzippie was remembering, as she was, the shouts that year after year used to burst from the living room, which served as her parents' bedroom at night.

"Why does my father scream like that?" Hamutal had once asked her on the way to school, her body still clenched.

"Because of the war."

"How do you know?"

"He told me."

"Did you ask him?"

"Yes. Last year."

"What happened in the war?"

"The Germans killed his two little sisters in the ghetto. They rammed their heads into a wall. He saw it through a crack in the closet. He had climbed into an armoire to hide. That's what he dreams about at night. He—"

"Don't tell me!" Hamutal slammed her with her school bag. "I can't listen to this."

Now, recognizing the old quaver in Hamutal's voice when she said, "She started talking about the Holocaust," Tzippie responded immediately, as if in fulfillment of an agreement they'd had since childhood. "I'm coming. But not tomorrow. I don't have anyone to take over here. I'll come the day after tomorrow. We'll talk. This isn't for the phone."

That night Hamutal dreamt about Tzippie's father. When she woke up at three a.m., the details had blurred, but the man's face, with its mix of wonder, fear, and evil intent, haunted her as she got out of bed, careful not to wake Saul, and continued to haunt her as she went into the kitchen and poured herself some Coke. There was a familiar sensation in that moment of thirst, that sitting in an empty kitchen in the middle of the night, and she knew that if she continued to sit quietly for a while and let the memory come nearer, she would identify it.

The old kitchen reminded her of the one in her parents' house. She could still remember the unusual bustle that sometimes arose there, the way the house would be thrown into a frenzy of activity that broke the routine: a guest was about to arrive. The adults' faces would cloud over and they would whisper a lot, her father and mother and Tzippie's parents, staying up later than usual. The women would labor over chopped liver and all sorts of pastries, and the smell of herring would fill the refrigerator. Hamutal gradually learned that all these signs heralded the arrival of someone "from there"—a distant relative, an acquaintance, a neighbor, a friend, someone who erupted out of the past and had some connection with her mother or with Tzippie's mother, someone from the town where their fathers had lived before the war, who had never forgotten the taste of Sabbath challahs fresh from their grandfather's oven. Sometimes her father would go to meet the guest at the bus stop, showing uncharacteristic emotion, and come back brimming with excitement, carrying the man's battered suitcase for him. Sometimes the guest would turn up on his own. The encounters were always impassioned, accompanied by weeping, whispering, choked voices, long and desperate embraces, as if they were all about to be parted again and sent to their separate fates.

The children would peek in at them from the hall, giggling to each other to cover up the chill that went through them, until one of the adults would recall their existence and present them to the guest. He would open his arms wide as if he were about to fly, and hug them to his heart as if they were very dear to him and close his eyes as if he were praying, and suddenly remember something and rummage in his suitcase and present them with a bar of chocolate or other sweets, and again kiss them lovingly. Then Marek would take off and Hamutal and Tzippie would sit together in one chair, practically choking on the chocolate crammed into their mouths.

The grownups would sit huddled together late into the

night, arms around each other, knee against knee, speaking Polish or Yiddish, emitting hushed sobs or sudden wails and falling silent while one of them groped for the words that wouldn't come. From her bed Hannutal would hear their murmuring, their weeping, and from time to time their rare, brief laughter. In the morning she would find the guest sleeping on the folding cot near the kitchen door, exhausted from talking and crying. Something very powerful linked him to her father and mother and to Tzippie's parents, something courageous and mysterious and very terrible, bound up with the secret they never discussed: the howls her father would let out from the midst of his troubled sleep, rupturing the quiet of the night, when he would rush out of bed with a demented look in his eyes, dash to the door, burst out of the apartment and thrust himself down the stairs as if he were being hounded; grunt like an animal, spewing out the fury he'd stifled all day long, all the way down to the very last step, the one before the bomb shelter, then turn around and climb slowly back up the stairs, as if he had suddenly aged twenty years.

On their way to school Tzippie would tell her about the guests. One, leaving his parents and younger brothers behind, had jumped from the train that was on its way to a death camp and escaped into the woods; one had been in charge of gathering the corpses of Jews after they'd been gassed; one had been the subject of experiments on her uterus and arteries; one had been buried an entire night under a pile of corpses, thinking he was dead himself, until at dawn a peasant who had come for plunder dragged him out from under the mound; one had been on the death march with his brother and forty-eight other survivors out of hundreds when, eight hours before the Americans caught up with them, his brother had slipped out of his grasp and a

German soldier had shot him in the head. Hamutal would slap her schoolbag against Tzippie's thigh with revulsion and say, "I already told you once, I don't want to hear it."

Sitting now in the kitchen of Saul Inlander's home, sipping a second glass of cola, remembering those days and the dream she'd just had about Tzippie's father, she realized where she'd seen Tzippie's father's worried, malicious face, and it came as a blow. One night, when she was eight or nine, she woke up thirsty, got out of bed, and went toward the kitchen in the dark. Passing the living room, where the sofa was opened into a double bed each night, she thought she heard whispering. A stripe of light fell across the raised blanket, and Hamutal, still a bit groggy, was surprised to find that someone else was awake, too. In the morning her mother said to her, "Daddy's sick. Stay away from him today, so you won't catch whatever it is." And on her way out the front door—she could hear Tzippie saying goodbye to her mother as she left—she called over her shoulder, "Feel better, Daddy." When she got home that day her father wasn't there, and when her mother arrived she dismissed her question with: "Daddy felt better, so he went to Nahariya."

In the evening, as he came in the door with the suitcase he always took when he spent the night in Nahariya, Hamutal ran up to him, but her mother was already addressing him in a rush of urgent Polish, and when Hamutal asked him, "Are you better already, Daddy?" he just said, "I'm okay now."

In the dark kitchen, with the empty glass in front of her, Hamutal turned back the wheels of memory and knew beyond a doubt that it had been Tzippie's father lying under the blanket with her mother the night her father stayed over in Nahariya. Now she dared to contemplate what she'd made her eyes not see all these years: fragments of scenes in which her mother and Tzippie's father were sitting side by side at the cinema, side by side in the family group—were their hands clasped under the jackets folded on their laps?—or huddling in the kitchen—were they trying to set up a rendezvous somewhere, maybe in the clinic storeroom, where she had once found a pillow in a pillowcase she recognized from home? Now she suddenly remembered the cigarette butts she used to find in the trash or in the toilet, and the tension in her mother's face when Tzippie's father would suddenly show up at the clinic.

Tzippie's father and my mother—she said it to herself in astonishment, seeing all the evidence and still finding it hard to believe, astonished also by her success in deceiving herself, overlooking what she'd seen with her own eyes, stashing the memory in a safe place for thirty years, until she could grow up and understand and brace herself to confront the knowledge face to face. Her eyes on the glass of cola, she knew very well why the distant memory had chosen to return on this particular night.

Two days later, in the nursing-home parking lot, when Hamutal raised her eyes to the fifth floor, she saw her mother standing at the window. There was something strange about her face, and only when Hamutal got to the room did she realize what it was: it was slathered in reddish makeup, her lips highlighted with a crooked line that widened almost to the middle of the chin and extended to the cheeks. Hamutal stood in amazement before the painted face: "Who did that to you?"

"I did it."

"Why?"

"Because today they decide who's going and who stays."

"The nurse's aide didn't say anything to me. I just saw her."

"There's no aide there."

"So who decides?

"They do," her mother said in a whisper, her eyes blinking as if she'd lost control of them.

"Who? The doctors?"

"The doctors, yes. I had to put on some color, so they'd see I was okay."

Only then did she understand, and she immediately felt the need to escape. She glanced at her watch: Tzippie was supposed to be there any minute.

"I'll be right back." She dashed out of the room and went down to the lobby. Through the glass door she saw her cousin battling the wind, holding two small children by the hand. Hamutal went out to meet her and they hugged.

"Are you producing another client for day care?" asked Hamutal, putting her hand on Tzippie's belly.

"Nah, just getting fat," said Tzippie, pulling her into the building. "How is she doing?"

"Today she put on makeup like a diva, so they won't send her to the gas chambers. I didn't understand at first. For two days now she's been talking only about that."

"What exactly is she saying?" Tzippie was drawing her toward the elevator.

Hamutal answered weakly: "She talks about trains, about the crematorium, about some Rayzele waiting by the door and they won't let her in."

Tzippie went pale.

"She said 'Rayzele'?"

"Yes."

"Then you have to listen to this." After warning her son not to go too far into the garden with his friend and not to get lost like last time, she hauled Hamutal off into a corner of the lobby where they could be alone, between a huge *Monstera* plant and a pay phone.

"You have to listen to this now, so you'll know how to respond if she talks about her again," Tzippie whispered. "Your mother was twelve and was hiding in the home of a Polish family. Her parents had given them jewelry and money, and they promised to take care of her until the war was over. She didn't know why they hid her but kept her younger sister at home. Maybe they had plans for her but couldn't manage in time. She had a six-year-old sister—that was Rayzele. One day Rayzele came home in the ghetto and didn't find her parents, but she knew where her sister—that is, your mother—was staying. She went to the home of the Poles. She knocked on the door, but they didn't let her in. She sat down outside and after a while went away. Your mother saw her from a small window upstairs. She couldn't do anything."

"She told you all that?" Hamutal whispered.

"Yes. For years she had nightmares because she hadn't saved her, her little sister. She never managed to find out exactly what happened to her after she left the home of the Polish family. One of the neighbors told her after the war that dogs had once bitten a Jewish girl to death, but she didn't know if that was her sister, or what really happened to her."

"And she stayed with those Poles until the end of the war?"

"No. They handed her over to the Germans a year before it ended."

The old urge arose, to swat Tzippie with something and stop the stream of words coming out of her mouth, but she restrained herself, thinking feverishly: can't, can't in any way understand these things now. Have to set this horror story aside, pull myself together. Meanwhile, maybe to reduce the nightmare impact, she said to Tzippie, "But she also says totally ridiculous things."

"Like what?"

"Like this week she said about the mother of a friend of mine from school that she was a kapo."

"Dorit's mother?"

"Dorit's mother," Hamutal repeated after her, astounded. "How do you know?"

"She really was a kapo."

"What are you talking about?"

"It's true."

"How do you know?"

"Your father told me. Your mother's cousin was in the same barracks as her, until she was taken to the hospital with typhus and never came back. Your mother recognized Dorit's mother at a parents' meeting for your class. She could have let that cousin stay in the barracks, some kapos did that. But she sent her to the hospital instead, and from there it was straight to the gas."

"When did he tell you all this?"

"One of those times he seemed in the mood to talk, so I asked him. It was usually after he had a coughing fit because of his lungs. I asked your mother, too, and my parents." Tzippie pulled her away from the *Monstera* and steered her into the jaws of the elevator.

"Dorit's mother was a kapo?" Back came the memory of the motherly breast, soft as dough, crushed against her cheek as they sat on the kitchen floor in the talking corner.

"Yes. You never wanted to know about what happened during the war. Whenever I started to tell you anything on the way to school, you'd put your hands over your ears. I always asked them."

Hamutal thought she heard a tinge of rebuke in Tzippie's voice. The elevator stopped and they got out and walked toward her mother's room.

"My father and mother were in the same camp?"

"No. Your mother was sent to a camp in Germany. Your father was in Mauthausen."

"And your parents?" Hamutal was wondering how to find out what Tzippie knew about the illicit relationship between their parents.

Tzippie opened her mouth to answer, but there was a shout in the hall, then a startled silence, and then a disturbance of the silence and tumult broke out. A male aide went running into the room at the end, old men and women toddled and limped in that direction and a few wheelchairs, too, rolled toward the doorway. At the other end of the corridor a young doctor burst into view with a decisive stride and pushed his way through the people and the wheelchairs, saying impatiently to the female aide, "Would you please get them out of here?"

Through the doorway, above the white heads, Hamutal could see the ceiling and the metal curtain rail, with the curtain gathered in the corner. She didn't glance around when Tzippie turned toward her mother's room, just stood there, her eyes on the curtain rings that collided and tangled as the curtain was jerked shut, hiding the bed near the door. Then she suddenly grasped that it was Saul Inlander's father, and her heart raced.

"What happened?" she asked over the heads of the people.

"A guy fainted," one old woman replied without turning her head.

"Died, died," someone said, and turned to go.

Amid the voices came the tinkling of the Indian bells, and Tzippie asked, "What's going on, Hamutal?"

Hamutal opened her mouth but was afraid to speak, as if speech would dictate reality.

"Someone died, apparently." Hamutal yielded, whispering.

"It's terrible like this, in front of everyone," Tzippie said to the back of her neck.

"He's dead," Hamutal informed herself, knowing she hadn't quite absorbed how much this death touched her life, too. In a fog, she followed Tzippie into the other room.

Her mother recognized Tzippie immediately and asked after her father, who had died years ago, inquiring whether he was still allergic to cream cheese and if he was still smoking so much, and Tzippie answered her in her normal voice, as if she'd been asked an ordinary question, and promised to see that he quit smoking. Hamutal sat down, her head spinning, still listening to her mother talk about Tzippie's father, aware that this was the time to verify her suspicions of the previous night, but unable to distract herself from the sentence pounding inside her like a mantra, "He's dead, he's dead," expecting the sounds to shed some light on the situation, knowing that she had to do something, but not knowing what. Meanwhile she was pretending to take great interest in Tzippie's news about her youngest son, Uriel, now that the conversation had gotten around to him, and all the while wondered how she would get herself out of the room to the phone by the elevator to let Saul know what had happened.

She was consoling herself with the hope that his father

had only fainted, and surrendering to a peculiar weakness
spreading through her limbs when she suddenly saw Saul
Inlander in the doorway, pale and agitated. For a moment
he seemed to her a mirage born of her desire, but she
pulled herself together right away and understood that
they had called him. He glanced into the room and his eyes
lit up when he saw her, but at the sight of her face he withdrew immediately. Tzippie meanwhile had finished her
story about Uriel.

"Aren't you feeling well, Hamutal?"

"I'm a little dizzy."

"So why don't you go home? I'll stay with her for a
while."

"I wanted to ask you something about your father . . . "

"I promised her he'd quit smoking," Tzippie giggled.

"Not that." Hamutal couldn't join in. "I suddenly
remembered him and my mother . . . "

"What about him and your mother?"

"They were . . . what were they like together? What do
you remember?"

"They couldn't stand each other."

"Really?" Hamutal again saw the face in the stripe of
light across her parents' bed.

"I didn't want to tell you: he cursed her nonstop the last
week of his life."

"Why did he curse her?"

"I didn't understand exactly. Maybe it had to do with the
war. With them everything had to do with the war." Tzippie
was peering at her worriedly. "Go home, Hamutal. I can
stay with her for a while."

"It'll pass in a minute."

"What if she keeps talking about it?" Tzippie was looking at her closely.

"About Uriel?"

"About the Holocaust."

"Can I call you in to help?" Hamutal was sticking close to reality.

"Of course, as often as you need to. In an emergency Dovik can take over for me at home."

"Thank you, Tzippie."

"Have I been any help?" Tzippie put her arm around Hamutal's shoulder.

"You have no idea how much." Hamutal stroked Tzippie's hand.

"Call me if you want to talk, if something new comes up."

"It's too bad she didn't forget those things, too." Her eyes were still on the empty doorway, and she was amazed that she was focusing on her mother.

"She still might."

Tzippie hesitated a moment and then, as if she couldn't resist, put her mouth to Hamutal's ear and asked, "Do you know him?"

"Who?"

"The tall guy that came and looked in."

"Uh . . . I think he's the son of the man who died."

"What did he want in here?"

"I didn't notice that he wanted to come in."

"He was looking at you. I had the feeling he wanted to talk to you."

"I don't know the guy."

Hamutal walked Tzippie to the parking lot and, after watching her drive off, returned to the cafeteria and sat down beside Saul Inlander at a table near the window, by a window box of pansies in full bloom. Starting to grasp the immensity of the change this death would make in her life, she tried to describe to him blow by blow what she had seen: how she suddenly heard someone cry out, how the nurses had rushed in, how the old people had crowded around in the hall, how the doctor had arrived and yanked the curtain shut, how he'd emerged after a few minutes, conferred with the male aide, and left. The whole time she wanted to say: How strange that I was there right at that moment. I hadn't been planning to visit my mother then. Tzippie was coming, and I had to talk to her. I was there only by chance.

He put his hand over hers, both hands hidden under a fold of her sweater, and said, "I'm glad at least you were there, that he didn't die among complete strangers."

His face colored suddenly and a childish, lost look came into his eyes that she hadn't ever seen there. He covered his mouth with his hand, a new gesture that reminded her what strangers they were and how little she really knew him. In this trancelike state one definitive thought came into her mind: He no longer had any reason to be here. His father would never again lie in the first bed from the door and stare vacantly at the doorway as if waiting for someone to come, for something to happen, or squeeze his eyes shut, weary of the world. She stretched out her free hand toward his face and with her fingertip gently traced an arc under his lower lid, the same gesture she used to wipe her daughters' tears, and said, "Enough, enough," knowing those were not the right words, but those were the ones she was used to saying in situations like this. He calmed down and sat there, very sad, until the lost look was replaced by a steady gaze and his hand cupping hers under her sweater blazed with warmth.

"I'm sure he would have liked you. It's too bad you had to see him this way, at the end. He was an impressive-looking man even three or four years ago . . . "

"Yes. . . . They called you right away."

"I was in the car, on the way back from Carmiel."

"I wanted to call you myself, but I couldn't leave my cousin. When was the last time you saw him?"

"Early in the morning."

"Was he awake?"

"He was sleeping. I sat by him for a while, and he woke up."

"Did you talk?"

"Two sentences. It was hard for him to speak. I gave him something to drink, and he fell asleep."

"What did he say?"

"The last sentence was, 'You have to take care.' He was thinking about the children. Maybe I should have brought them."

"Stop," she said. "Don't get into that now. You did much more than others do. Even the nurse's aide said what a good boy you were."

"I'm so happy I met you." There was pressure on her fingers.

"You should thank her."

"Who?"

"The nurse's aide."

"I'll do that."

"What's going to happen now?" she asked, recalling his peculiar proposal of marriage.

"I have to arrange the funeral."

"I want to ask you something," she suddenly ventured, knowing that if she didn't ask explicitly now she'd be forced to live with the doubt forever. "On Wednesday, after the Sabbath celebration, before we fell asleep, do you remember that you proposed something to me?"

"What?" he asked.

"You had some idea about the two of us."

"I don't remember."

"I guess I didn't understand."

"I guess," he said. "I also have to notify a few relatives about the funeral."

So. That was that. She forced herself to relinquish the last obsession.

"There's something I have to consult with you about."

"What?" Hope was so easily rekindled.

"They asked me if I wanted funeral notices posted."

Those notices, posted in the streets, hugging utility poles, stretched across billboards beside theater and movie posters, announcing: *There was a man by the name of such-and-such. He died.* Sometimes she would stop in front of one of them, reading the name, trying to remember whether she knew the man, thinking how odd it was to study details of the identity—including the names of a wife and children and sons-in-law and grandchildren—of a person whose existence she had never detected and who would, she was hereby informed, no longer be seen in these parts.

"Maybe it's a good idea. There were neighbors who knew him. Maybe they'll want to come to the funeral."

"I doubt it. He didn't really have much of a connection to anybody." There was annoyance in his voice, as if he felt something was being imposed upon him, and he seemed to her distant and detached, preoccupied now with his own affairs.

Like you? she wanted to ask. Are you also not connected to anybody? Can what was between us be called a connection?

"You might regret it later if you don't do it."

"We'll see, maybe," he said, evasive.

"Do you want me to come to the funeral?"

"Would you want to come?" He was surprised.

"If you want me to."

"Maybe you shouldn't. People could ask questions. If there's some neighbor, maybe they saw you. And my aunt would certainly recognize you. I don't think you should."

Here he goes, shaking me off already, she thought, the hurt starting to bubble up. I performed a function in his life, and now it's finished, and I'm sitting here like some diligent worker who just got pink-slipped. She pulled her hand out from under his fingers and he didn't react.

And that's how it ended.

They sat facing each other with the two cups of coffee between them and the tray with the watermelon pattern drawn in such splendid detail, the seeds glistening in the flesh of a fruit cut in neat wedges.

Saul suddenly fixed his eyes on her scarf, which was draped over the back of the chair.

"Why are you staring like that?"

"Because of the color. That purple . . . "

He's no longer here, she said to herself. His father's not even buried yet, and he's no longer here. The purple of the flowers is the less mysterious excuse.

"Are you going to the apartment now?"

"Yes. I've got to get organized, call relatives."

"Do you want me to come with you?"

"No, that's okay," he said, looking extremely preoccupied. "I'm most efficient when I'm alone."

In the car on the way home, nearly blind with rage, humiliation, the speed of a change in her life that she neither initiated nor agreed to, she tried to rein in the emotion, addressing herself in the second person, calling upon reason. It was clear from the beginning, you connected with each other at a particular time, you were companions on a particular journey, like businessmen signing a contract of a single clause. The journey is over, the contract has expired. If your mother had died first you would have rejected his request to come to the funeral and been preoccupied with your own affairs.

But all of her arguments, apt as they were, collapsed before her memories: the strong, protective embrace that buried her face in the warmth and pulse of his neck and stifled her breathing, as if he were swallowing her up inside him; the mouth that was responsive from the first moment, as though they'd had a thousand rehearsals for that first wild kiss in the dark; the sweetness of the hungry, frenzied touch that beckoned to her to save him because only she could assuage his need; his life that opened so powerfully to her life. How could she give all that up now?

All the next morning she was split, one half of her sitting in the printer's office intently examining the final galleys, the other half following Saul Inlander from a distance and observing his father's funeral, step by step. Here are the relatives and maybe a neighbor or two gathering at the cemetery. A few of them walk closer, hesitant, recognizing him by the relatives already present. They steal glances at his face, noting his good looks or telling themselves that age had crept up on him since they last saw him. They apologize for not managing to visit his father in the nursing home. They hadn't realized his condition was so grave. They were actually planning to visit and about to call the number he'd left them, but then it was apparently too late. They ask about his father with exaggerated interest, guilt evident in the tone of their voices, and he repeats the story again and again, struggling to maintain his composure. Twenty minutes have passed.

Now they're moving over to the roofed area where his father's body is brought, wrapped in a shroud and a prayer shawl. A few curious types, as always, elbow their way close to the corpse, their eyes sweeping up and down the body parts configured under the cloth. Saul Inlander's eye will linger, for some reason, at the toes. He will repeat the cantor's words in a steady voice: "Merciful One who dwells on high, cause his soul to find rest . . . " Another fifteen minutes gone by.

Now they're walking in slow and stately fashion to the grave, an entourage mostly lame, white-haired, and gray-haired; even the youngest of them, Inlander's neighbor, is over forty. They pass by an open grave with a large crowd gathered beside it. The wailing of children there draws the gazes of passersby, but Saul Inlander keeps his step firm and doesn't bat an eye. Another ten minutes.

Now the cantor is performing the graveside ceremony. The voices of the weeping children reverberate with his voice. The people bow their heads. Saul Inlander seems focused on the words of the mourner's *kaddish*: ". . . His great name. In the world that He has created as He sees fit and may He establish his kingdom . . . " Fifteen more minutes.

After the ceremony they linger around the grave. A cousin from Kfar Saba puts down a bouquet of orange carnations. A few of the old people bend down to pick up small stones and lay them somberly on the grave. Droplets begin to dot people's hair, heralding rain. Saul Inlander doesn't feel them right away, perhaps because of the big skullcap on his head, but no one will leave the grave until he gives the signal. His aunt takes a kerchief out of her bag, shakes it out energetically; he lifts his eyes to the sky and turns back toward the entrance gate. Another ten minutes.

Near the gate they wash their hands at the tap. Now that the interment has been completed there are some who venture to ask him about his children and his wife. Saul Inlander comes back to life when they mention Chicago. Maybe he tells them about the purple flowers his wife planted in the garden. Despite the quickening drops they stay with him awhile, drawing out the good-byes. For the first time today he gives them genuine attention, regretting perhaps that they haven't had an opportunity for real conversation, and now the rain is getting worse. He sends regards to the relatives who couldn't make it, knowing, certainly, that he will never see most of them again. Suddenly he remembers the furniture and pots and pans and linens and the many pictures and knickknacks in the apartment. He asks if anyone is interested in the contents of his father's apartment. Three people volunteer to accept a memento. They agree to meet in the apartment and hurry to their cars as it begins to pour. Another twenty-five minutes.

Last scene: Saul Inlander in his car, perhaps giving a ride to one of the neighbors. The neighbor, ill at ease in the company of this unfamiliar, silent man who is making no effort to be amiable, tries to dispel his awkwardness with words of praise for the deceased, telling stories that demonstrate old Inlander's goodness and refinement: how he opens his wallet to the many solicitors of donations who come knocking, how he always picks up laundry that blows off the line and returns it to its owners. Saul Inlander refrains from correcting the neighbor, who is speaking in the present tense, and the neighbor, disappointed by the chilly response to his narrative of good deeds, assumes the man is preoccupied with the usual concerns of those who have buried their fathers and stops talking. For the rest of the trip, until they pull into the parking area near the apartment, silence prevails: thirty-five minutes.

Three hours after he should have gotten to the apartment according to her calculations, Hamutal's patience ran out and she called him. His voice was even and unfamiliar, with a new busyness about it.

"I thought you'd call when you got back. I gave you the phone number at the printer's. I'm home now."

"Yes, I was planning to call."

"How are you?"

"Fine, fine."

"How was the funeral?"

"Fine."

"I was thinking of you."

"I . . . There are people here, and it's a little inconvenient. Maybe you could call in another, say . . . it's now six . . . let's say in another two hours?"

Without answering she dropped the receiver onto the cradle and decided on the spot to wipe him out of her life, as he had undoubtedly done with her. If he had decided to end their relationship like that, she was not going to protest or plead. Maybe, if she was sufficiently determined, she would not even regret it. Defeated and unable to stop the gears now grinding in her stomach, she defrosted two wedges of pizza and ate them standing up near the stove, holding them in her hand without a napkin, the way the girls sometimes did and for which she scolded them. As the grinder in her stomach increased its speed, the feeling of defeat gave way to a burning desire to say things to him that would make his trip back to Chicago a misery. Hours later she was still pacing back and forth in the living room, relieving her irritation by yanking leaves off the farn. Then she was overcome by the need to see the look on his face when she hurled at him all those sentences that had accumulated inside her like poison, and on an impulse she got into the car and drove to the apartment.

He hugged her when she came in as if she were a lost child the searchers had given up on. He opened the whole breadth of his chest to her, drew her to him, and kissed her forehead and her hair, and she was surprised by the intensity of the emotion.

"Thank God you got here. I've been going crazy, didn't know what to think."

Her ear pressed against the base of his throat, she listened to the fierce pulse and wondered about his choice of the phrase "going crazy" which wasn't consistent with anything he had done or said.

"Why didn't you call?"

"You were sounding so removed, I really didn't feel like it."

"Because my aunt was here, the one you met. She was standing right there and I was afraid she'd hear you. Why didn't you come sooner?"

"I was debating whether to come at all." She broke away from him.

"My hand was on the phone a million times, but I know I can't call you at home. My plane is leaving at midnight. I've already ordered a cab. What would I have done if you hadn't come?" He gathered her hands between his, enclosed them the way sepals hold a bud, and brought them to his lips.

"You would have taken off on your merry way." She forced her voice to sound matter-of-fact, so as not to betray her tailspin.

One suitcase was waiting by the door and the other was open on the bed. Among the clothes piled beside it was the green jacket, and those in the suitcase included an embroidered blue velvet Bedouin dress they had bought together at the flea market in Jaffa. He led her to the bed, sat her down next to the suitcase, and continued his skillful packing.

"So then." Her voice sounded too thin to her, like the voice of a young girl who's been slighted. "Then I won't ever see you again?"

"Listen," he said, as if he hadn't heard what she said and hadn't noticed the slender scream in her voice, and she noted to herself: goodbye, heightened emotion; hello, pragmatism. "I've left you a key here. I wrote down the number of the real-estate agent by the phone. He has a key, too. I thought you might want to come here because what happened was so sudden." He lifted his face from the suitcase. "Would you want to come here after I'm gone?"

"I'm not sure."

"Sometimes people want to say goodbye to a place," he said, as if he weren't talking about either himself or her. Since she was silent, he went on, "So that's it. When you've decided you're not coming back anymore, call him and he'll rent out the apartment."

"How long am I allowed to keep it?"

"As long as you want."

At that moment the reality of his leaving hit her. He had returned the car and she would never again watch him park in the lot of the nursing home. Tomorrow he would be in Chicago, having left the empty apartment at her disposal and his father's empty bed in the nursing home.

She came up behind him and embraced him, burying her face in his back, her chin pressing against the vertebrae through his shirt, and linked her fingers over the buckle of his belt, trying to ground him to this place and to herself, finding it so hard to give him up now, when he had just shown such a surprising storm of emotion. He froze, imprisoned in her arms.

"I have a request." She turned her head so her mouth was by his ear.

"What?" She heard a note of worry in his voice.

"Don't go today."

"I beg you, don't ask that of me."

"Why?"

"Because I have obligations."

"What?"

"You know what."

"Tell me."

"The family, the job—I don't have to explain," he said, and she translated to herself, without sparing herself and without tempering the cruelty: This is about places in my life that have nothing to do with you; if I gave you the mistaken impression that you connect with every part of my life, I'm sorry; we had a finite amount of time together for a particular mission, the mission is over and our time is up, we're grownup people and let's not complicate matters; I've given you the apartment, I've been nice to you, I've shown you a lot of emotion, it's not routine with me, take it as a compliment, make do with that, let's get through this goodbye with good will, I find theatrics repulsive, don't test me like this—. She kept trying to stop the flow, until she found a sentence to say to him: "I would have waited with you until your father died."

"I'm sorry," he said.

"You won't even remember me." The remaining firmness in her voice dissolved all at once and she let out a wail, more tremulous than she'd intended, and she dropped her arms from around his hips and backed away, like someone realizing too late that she's been the victim of fraud.

He turned around and tried to take her in his arms the way he had when he opened the door, but she, for whom offense had been intensified by humiliation stemming from her own behavior, shriveled in his embrace.

"I will never forget you. But you yourself said that our being together is something out of another life and our acquaintance is a double exercise in separation."

"Well, for me the exercise apparently hasn't succeeded."

"You said you're developing a talent for goodbyes."

"I'm not that gifted."

"I really have to go." He stopped her in her tracks.

"So we say goodbye, just like that?" She was attacking from another angle.

"Yes."

She panicked at the answer, its finality. But the sense of insult and embarrassment were nothing compared with the awareness that the hardest part of her mother's illness was yet to come and she would have to deal with it alone.

"I wish your father had lived forever," she said, pulling in her arms in a gesture of surrender, watching him put the other suitcase by the door.

"I don't know how to say goodbye," he said. "There are things I want to say, but I don't know how. I'll write to you."

"Don't you dare."

"I'll write and I won't send the letters."

"So what was it, this thing between us?" she asked in despair, as if its nature would be determined by words and not by what had happened.

"It was a relationship between two adults with no illusions"—he emphasized each word, like a teacher addressing a slow student—"who came together on a journey where the end was known from the start: he was accompanying his father, and she was accompanying her mother. At the end of the road they have to part."

"That's all?" Tears came to her eyes at the finality so explicitly stated and the dryness in his voice and the sudden realization that this was how he had seen the situation all along. It might also have been put this way: This was a relationship, with nothing naïve about it, between two people the sea spewed out, and briefly, until each went his own way, they helped each other struggle to their feet.

"That's a lot. And if one of them also falls in love, the way I did with you, then the journey is much more enjoyable and the parting more difficult."

"If one of them what?" She was wondering if her ears had distorted his words.

"The way I did with you," he repeated.

"Then give me some proof of love." The sentence burst out of her, and it occurred to her that only now, a moment before leaving, had he used the word explicitly for the first time, apparently suspecting that if he'd entrusted the word to her any earlier she would quickly have used it against him.

"How?"

"You proposed marriage to me on the night of the Sabbath-eve celebration, are you aware of that?"

"It was temporary insanity," he said. "Let's say it was temporary insanity."

"Let's say the whole thing was insanity." She remembered how she had aimed her car toward the museum in that violent rain.

"I think it really was."

"You hinted that night that you would leave your family."

"I don't remember."

"You do remember. So why do you suddenly have to get on a plane?"

"You don't understand why?"

"Explain it to me." That was all that remained: to make it hard for him.

"Because I'm an orphan, and you're not yet." He was apparently trying to amuse her with this clumsy joke, not knowing how the words slashed her, suddenly bringing Arnon between them. When she didn't respond to his joke, he pulled himself together and said, "I simply have to go."

Out of despair she did something she had never done before; she had never imagined it would come to this. Even though she was now used to discovering in herself urges she didn't know existed, this moment was a surprise to her also, as if she was way beyond her own boundaries. Her two hands reached for the zipper of his pants. One gripped the belt and the other pulled on the tongue of the zipper and thrust itself, gluttonous, into the gap that was revealed, spreading all its fingers to grasp the large, flexible bulge it found there, which in an instant swelled in her hand.

"No, Hamutal." He gripped her wrists with both hands.

"Once more," said the woman who was new to both of them, putting her left hand, too, inside his pants, wrapping all her fingers around his penis.

"It won't work, Hamutal." There was sorrow in his voice at the depths she had descended to, and he slipped out of her greedy grasp and struggled to zip up his pants. "The taxi will be here any minute."

"Wait with me at least until my mother dies." The insult, while wreaking havoc, also cleared away the sobs that until now had constricted her voice, creating the new, open tone that was coming, incredibly, from her own throat: steady, insistent, neither embarrassed nor apologetic, matching itself to the decisive action her hands had taken until they were stopped. She looked him straight in the eye but didn't know how to read his features and was again aware of how little she knew him.

"I would wait with you a lot longer than that," he said. His voice was cautious, wary of the woman who had just burst forth from her unannounced.

"She's starting to talk about the Holocaust. I don't have the strength to be alone with her and the Holocaust."

A car horn honked in the street.

"She'll stop talking about it."

"No. She's only getting started. Please, don't leave me alone now."

"I wouldn't leave you at all, but I must go."

"It won't take very long." She was negotiating.

"I can't." There was impatience in his voice.

The horn sounded again.

"Chicago is calling you." She leaned against the wall, yielding.

He kissed her on the forehead and didn't wait for a response, afraid perhaps that her arms would surprise again, seizing him. A moment later she could hear him going down the stairs, fading into the distance with his two suitcases. She watched him from the window until he came out at the end of the walk, passing under the pruned arch of the hedge, and followed his movements as he tossed the suitcases into the open mouth of the trunk and as he slammed the trunk lid down hard and as he climbed into the taxi and looked up and gave her a small, cautious wave that wrung her heart because she knew he was trying to discourage any false hope that at the first bend in the road he'd change his mind and come back to her. Even before the car had moved out of sight she turned away from the window and sat down on the edge of the bed, sat like that for a long time, not knowing what she was supposed to do, like a survivor she saw once on the news broadcast, sitting amid the ruins of his house, which had been destroyed in some earthquake in South America. Then she got up and walked around the apartment alone, from room to room, looking at the few pictures that remained on the walls, unwanted leftovers of life. Empty squares were visible where he had removed family photos and apparently taken them to Chicago.

"I wish I'd never met you," she said out loud, her heart inert inside her, so heavy that it hurt, and she guessed that by now the taxi had turned off the highway and into the airport.

In the kitchen she washed three dirty cups left on the table and two teaspoons forgotten in the sink and laid them on the ancient counter. Then she opened all the wooden cupboards and the refrigerator, took out the remaining bits of food and put them into the garbage bag.

"I wish your father had died before my mother ever got to the nursing home," she said, again out loud, hearing the distant echo of the curses children used to exchange when she was a child, and assumed that he was now going through security and that a young girl in uniform was rummaging among the articles in his suitcase, fingering his toiletry bag, the little bottle of mouthwash, the blue razor, the clipper for ear-hair, flipping through the black jeans and the green jacket and the thin flannel shirts and the brightly colored American underwear, and the family photos he'd taken with him.

On her most recent visit to the nursing home, when she was sitting with her mother in the dining room and watching her, feeling removed, allowing a strangeness to come between them and flood her with a sensation she knew from childhood, she silently addressed the woman licking a teaspoon. I'm Hamutal, Mother. How could you have forgotten my name? Was I a fleeting detail in your life, one of thousands of other details whose medical files you used to pull with an expertise that filled me with awe, someone you gave birth to by chance, who grew up at your side while you were busy with other things, whose coughing disturbed your sleep, or maybe didn't disturb it in the least, since you never bothered to help her get rid of the coughing fits that wracked her body for entire winters, a girl whose habit of getting her clean clothes all stained used to drive you crazy, a girl who, you apparently discovered, just didn't arouse the anticipated maternal feelings, so that you didn't want another child—

Her mother lifted her head and said suddenly, in the old, intelligent voice, "They really go overboard, pampering us with this chocolate pudding."

"It's about time you got pampered."

Her mother gave her a clear-eyed look. "Pampering ruins people."

"Is that why you didn't pamper me?"

"That's right. I brought you up to be strong."

"Why is that so important?"

"Because the pampered ones are the first to fall. I've seen it again and again in my life."

Hamutal took in a deep draft of air and said quietly, "A child needs love, Mother."

"You had as much love as you wanted. It was pampering you didn't get."

"I didn't want to be pampered. That wasn't it at all."

Her mother, as if choosing the convenient moment to escape lucidity, looked at the teaspoon and said dreamily, "So everything's fine."

In Inlander's kitchen now, after cleaning the counter and the tiles, Hamutal was standing at the sink, briskly shining the faucet, fogging it with her breath and polishing it with a dry cloth, enjoying the way it began to gleam under her touch, aware of the absurdity of the act, not knowing what she would do and where she would go when she finished. Still rubbing the nickel pipe that curved as if it had a crick in its neck, she remembered with a pang that first meeting in the parking lot, thinking who could have guessed then that this was the way the matter would end, with her standing and rubbing away so determinedly at a faucet in an old apartment. And underlying it all was the persistent awareness, throbbing like a tom-tom, that a new chapter was about to begin, terrifying and inevitable.

The telephone rang and, violating the agreed-upon rule of caution—an admission that the rules no longer applied—she picked up immediately.

"I was afraid you'd gone already," he said.

"I'm still here because I'm completely confused."

"Me, too."

"And sad."

"Me, too."

They were quiet for a moment and then she asked, "Where are you now?"

"In the passenger terminal, upstairs. I thought we might not be able to talk again, because there's probably no way of calling you at home."

"No, don't call."

"Are you still angry with me?"

"I don't know what I feel. I told myself I wish I'd never met you."

"I'm happy that I met you," he said.

"We met and we parted. What's there to be happy about?" She could feel anger coming on and didn't know about what.

"I don't feel that we've parted. You've become an important part of my life, you don't have any idea how much." She understood what the anger was about: that he was daring to tell her things that were untrue now because of the safe distance between them.

"How much?" She was provoking him.

"Someday I'll tell you."

"When?"

"We'll find our time. I'll be back."

"Yes," she chuckled. "In another forty years. In the nursing home."

"I promise you before then."

"I don't know." Her strength gave out all at once. The tears came easily, and with them, the vision of the South American survivor. "I'm just so miserable now. I don't know why I got into this with you. I wish my mother had died before your father."

"I wish I could come back and hold you. I don't know how to explain to you how important you are to me. I wouldn't have found the right way to say goodbye to my father without you."

She wiped the tears with her fingers and again could smell his neck.

"What have you been doing in the apartment?" Embarrassed by the show of emotion, he was returning to safe ground.

"Cleaning the kitchen."

He let out one of his rare laughs. "Really?"

"What did you think I would do?" she said, getting back some clarity of voice. "Sit and cry?"

"If I wasn't ashamed of the practice, I would cry myself."

"Why exactly did you call?" She was not going to be dragged into emotionalism.

"To explain to you why I took the first plane, why I ran away like that—"

"The family, the job—you don't have to explain." She was quoting the affront precisely.

"No. If I hadn't escaped right away, I would have stayed. It wasn't right for me to stay, not for you either."

Her heart ran amok with pain. "Why did you ask me to have coffee that day?" she asked in despair.

"I wouldn't have asked you if the nurse's aide hadn't told me you were looking for me."

"When?"

"The same day. I don't invite women wearing wedding bands to have coffee. The phone card is about to run out. Come on, say goodbye to me."

"I wish the nurse's aide hadn't been such a blabbermouth."

"I want—"

The receiver emitted an aggressive dial tone, and she returned it to the cradle. Then she put the apartment key on her key ring and said out loud, again hearing the echo of a childhood phrase, the kind always followed by vows impossible to keep: "I wish I could forget you right now, forever, this second."

Before going into her mother's room, she went into Inlander's and looked at the bed, which stood empty, made up, with a fresh sheet tucked neatly under the mattress and a blanket spread over it. Hamutal stood by the bed for a long time, ignoring inquiring glances from the old man who, as he watched her, was holding onto the rail below the window with both hands, like a coachman holding the reins. She thought how innocent this bed looked, as if it had just come off the carpenter's workbench and had no past whatsoever, as if it weren't a trap waiting for the next old man to fall into it and lie there until the final throes redeemed him from staring at the doorway, from waiting for some visitor to breach his loneliness for a few minutes. When his strength failed, he, too, would close his eyes for days at a time, continuing to lie here and welter in the pain of body and soul, a victim of his own mocking memory, which would fly out of whatever cells remained, until the body gave out and he departed this world, ceding his place to the masses of old men waiting to come and die in this bed that had been his for some apportioned time.

Saul Inlander would not come here anymore. Again she grasped her incidental place in his life during these last three weeks in which his father had declined, and she felt hurt and furious with his father for dying before her mother. She walked out of the room and across the hall, where she found her mother sleeping and panicked at the thought that from now on she would be alone with her.

A young doctor passing in the hall paused when he saw her. He introduced himself, asked what her relationship was to the patient, and told her there was no point in waking her mother, since the injection she'd been given an hour earlier, on the previous shift, was intended to make her sleep until morning.

"Why did they give her a shot like that?"

"She was in a lot of pain, and the results of the blood work were not good."

"Her condition is that bad?" She was frightened that her secret wish was about to be fulfilled, that the department chief and this young resident seemed to have read her thoughts and were teaming up to make them a reality.

"Better for her to sleep and not suffer." He was already turning away, denying the collusion she had begun to invent in his name.

She sat down by her mother's bed, as if declaring that she would carry out her duties no matter what, and remained there for some time, glancing out of habit toward the empty bed in the room across the hall. She thought about how deeply Saul Inlander had managed to penetrate her life, remembered his asking her once in surprise, "How did this happen between us? Women like cheerful men, and I'm so gloomy."

She had replied, "I'm attracted to gloomy people. I was born to them. They gave me a role: I have to make gloomy people happy. All my life I was supposed to make my parents happy."

He said, quite serious, "You really do make me very happy."

She laughed, "I'll relay that to my superiors."

By this time, she thought, he's reached home. Maybe his gloom has been dispelled there. His wife and children were waiting for him at the airport, waved to him from afar, ran to meet him, and they stood bundled together in a big hug, with his arms around all of them, and he kept telling them how he hadn't stopped missing them for a moment. Then they drove down Michigan Avenue in the big car and he looked up at the Kentucky coffee trees and the white birches and told them how excited he'd been to see the twin towers and the Sears building in *The Fugitive*. On the front door of the house he found a sign that said WELCOME

HOME, with drawings all around it, and in the middle of the laid table was a vase of purple flowers from the garden, and his wife told him about the teacher's high praise for their son, and about the Chicago Bulls' latest win, and he took out the presents he'd bought them, and his wife especially loved the blue velvet dress with Bedouin embroidery, and they ate and laughed and realized how the separation had weighed on them and how good their life together was.

And then in the king-size bed, as wide as it was long, her back to his belly, he would draw her closer, his hand making its way from the top of her head to her knees, lighting fires all along the way, and then he would turn her to him and let his tongue meander over her body, and his wise fingers, which could find their way even in the dark, would ease inside her and elicit the familiar whispers of pleasure and he would take her with his addictive ruthlessness, until she cried out, and he would breathe heavily in her ear and whisper how much he'd missed this moment. Then she would fall asleep, relaxed and smiling in the tight circle of his arms, a bit bewildered by the violence alternating instantly with tenderness, and he, too, would sink into sleep among the folds of an American down comforter.

She would stand there watching them for a moment, as he had stood and watched once in her bedroom, and then she would go to the foot of the bed and lift the edge of the blanket and squeeze in between the two of them, crawling up the length of his body, gently removing his arms from around his wife and putting them around her own body, sinking her head into that familiar niche between his neck and his chin, sniffing him like a dog seeking the scent of its previous master—and would hear him mumble some English word in his sleep and realize that even in his dreams he was back in Chicago, not for a moment musing on the woman he'd left in Israel, to whom he'd sort of proposed marriage one day and retracted the next, not thinking the thoughts that plagued her endlessly, about tyrannical Chance, which hurls people together and lets them stick before it pulls them apart either on a cruel whim or out of indifference, causing the same pain either way.

It occurred to her that she was so preoccupied with the separation from Saul Inlander that she was unprepared for a second parting within such a short time. Despite the malicious voice that kept whispering inside her that it would be better for both of them if her mother were to sink into death right now, as she lay there with eyes closed and that strained expression on her face, Hamutal leaned over the sleeping body and said, "My birthday is in another five weeks, Mother, exactly on Lag b'Omer. Hold on until then." She stood up, hesitated a moment, then leaned over again: "Please."

Seventeen days after his father's death, sitting in her office and looking at her diary to schedule an appointment with a journalist about the forthcoming issue, she suddenly discovered that her period was six days late and for a moment was totally flustered.

From the tangle of thoughts the memory of a taxi ride emerged: the taxi that picked her up at the clinic where she'd had an abortion in the third month of pregnancy, two days after her release from the army and a month before her twentieth birthday. The gynecologist, the only person besides herself who knew about the pregnancy, was surprised when she arrived unaccompanied, and suggested that she call someone to come and take her home, but Hamutal had insisted on ordering a taxi.

"I have a request," she said to the driver when the taxi turned in to her street. He'd been absorbed in his own thoughts during the whole ride, picking his teeth with a short piece of wire.

"What?" he said, jarred from his reverie.

"Look at me and tell me if I'm pale."

He threw her a glance. "You look fine to me."

"Not pale?"

"Not pale and not not-pale. You look normal, just fine."

"Because an hour and a half ago I had an abortion."

The wire fell out of his hand with a *ping* as thin as a scream, but the driver made no attempt to pick it up. She could see his astonishment, the new look he gave her, as if to say, "I can spot the weirdos anywhere. This one didn't look weird when she got in, but who knows?"

"Perfectly normal," he said and stopped the car at the address she'd given him. "Not pale, nothing."

"Thanks," she said, and struggled with the door handle.

He quickly got out, walked around the car, and opened the door for her, reaching out a hand.

"Maybe you need help? Should I grab the bag for you?"

"Thank you very much. If you could just put it by the stairs."

"I'll take you and the bag right to the door," he said with exaggerated gallantry, to cover his embarrassment.

"Then maybe you could put the bag by the door on the third floor, apartment eleven. I'll go up slowly. I really appreciate it."

Half an hour later, in the empty house, lying on her bed with pain sawing through her where the gynecologist had dug around, she thought about the driver she had startled out of his dreams, almost regretting the shock she'd caused him, and consoled herself with the thought that taxi drivers were used to having passengers share their secrets. Anyway, she'd had to talk to someone, preferably a stranger, so that one day, when she'd forgotten the abortion and the smell of the clinic, she could call to mind the sound of the words, which was no less real than the act itself. Even if she were to doubt the truth of what had happened, she would certainly remember the sentence she had uttered so indifferently into the air of the taxi, as if it were something routine: "An hour and a half ago I had an abortion."

She thought now of that moment, but there wasn't even a taxi driver around to talk to. This pregnancy would put her among the small percentage of women impregnated despite the use of an intrauterine device. She tried to calculate which of the two it was from. The last time she'd slept with Arnon—she paged through the diary, frightened by the new information and the fact that this hadn't occurred to her earlier—when they waited until after midnight because of the missing bedroom door was two months ago, exactly the same day she met Saul Inlander for the first time, four hours after she had relayed to him the aide's request. Sitting in her desk chair she stroked her belly and said to herself: This is the child of the man from Chicago.

She remained in the office into the night, delaying her return home, afraid to run into Arnon or the girls before she'd calmed down, occupying herself with busy-work and thumbing through the new issue. Around midnight she felt that she'd grown used to the idea, and a tingling from the depths of her body, a kind of greeting, came as confirmation.

She stole into the house after midnight, went straight to the kitchen, and fried herself some spicy eggs, over easy, till the edges were black—persisting in the whims of her earlier pregnancies. Then she carried the tray she'd prepared into the dark living room, sat down in an armchair with the tray on her belly, and tried to calculate the due date.

"A son," she promised herself, and in her mind's eye could already see the boy sitting in his room, hunched intently before the computer screen, his eyes serious, every bit the junior version of Saul Inlander.

"*Bon appétit*," said Arnon from the head of the stairs. She looked up in panic and saw his shadow outlined on the illuminated wall, like a serial killer in some movie she'd seen.

"Thank you." The charred white got stuck in her throat.

"Too bad your current issue is already in print. I could have contributed a nightmare." She stifled a cry.

"What nightmare?"

"Maybe you can put in an addendum," he suggested soberly, and she summoned up all her energy to feel out whether this was a joke or a threat.

"What's the dream?"

"I dreamt that I was in basic training," he said. "We had a unit commander whose favorite punishment was to make us go hungry and then fry up a big omelet for himself and stand near the flap of the tent eating it."

Suddenly relieved, she burst into overly hearty laughter, and right away, as if triggered by some mechanism that coupled laughter and crying, the tears started to flow. Through them she saw him come slowly down the stairs to her, the darkness swallowing his legs and the light lingering on his head.

"Are you crying, Hamutal?"

"No."

"Why are you crying?" He bent over her.

"I'm not crying."

"Why, Hamutal?"

"I don't know."

"Is it because of me?"

"No."

"Because of your mother?"

"Maybe." She was quick to adopt the idea.

"So cry," he said. "They say it's good for you." And to off-set his seriousness, as if he realized that they could still not fall into each other's arms, as the circumstances might so generously suggest, he reached into the plate, tore off a piece of the white with his fingers and put it in his mouth, while wiping her wet cheek with his other hand. "I'd cry, too, if my over-easy got burned like this."

For two days she felt her pregnancy ripening and her uterus expanding. At home the four of them were cautious, each in his own way. Arnon and the girls, she now found out, had met with a psychologist at the kibbutz. They refused to tell Hamutal what they'd talked about or what the pscyhologist had said to them, but she sensed that their changed behavior, particularly Hila's, showed the influence of those conversations. At home that hesitation suited her: the girls measured their words when addressing her, trying to reconstruct the way they'd talked a few months earlier, and she responded accordingly and made them meals. Arnon asked her a few questions about the gas heating, and she gave him the requisite answers and went out to shop and came back, her heart attentive the whole time to her swelling womb. She was already planning how she would teach this little boy to love trees, especially Kentucky coffee and white birch, and how she would take him to Chicago on a bar-mitzvah trip, and show up in his father's office, and how Saul Inlander would look at the boy and recognize himself from his own bar-mitzvah pictures at the Great Synagogue on Allenby Road.

The next day, in the bathroom at the office, she discovered bloodstains, and sat a long while on the edge of the toilet, staring at the smear of blood there was no mistaking. She suddenly remembered the nurse in seventh grade and wept with grief for the child who had come into being in her imagination and lived for forty-eight hours.

"No more appetite?" Arnon asked her that evening.

"No."

"Too bad," he said. "I was just getting into over-easy."

The phone rang and Arnon went to answer. He didn't say a word, and his face grew suddenly serious as he held the receiver out to her: "It's the doctor. Your mother's unconscious."

For eight days Shifra Baum lay unconscious but kept her heart beating. She died on the twenty-ninth of April, eight days before her daughter's thirty-ninth birthday.

At the funeral Hamutal saw every detail she had imagined for Inlander's funeral. All the way to the open pit she had the feeling she was in a play for which there had been a rehearsal a few weeks earlier. Only after the corpse had slid into the grave could she look at it with a sense of relief that the torment of the body had ended and the nightmares of the soul had let up. For the last time the words came to her with tenderness and compassion: "I'm here, Mother—Hamutal," as if she wanted to reassure the body wound in shrouds that she would stand there until the grave was filled and the prayer came to an end, and would wait until the few mourners found bits of stone and put them on the fresh sand that gave off a sharp scent of seashore, and would not leave before scattering over the grave the flowers that came from the same store where her bridal bouquet had been bought.

On the way back she wanted to go alone in her own car, and although she had no plan in mind when she said that, the car was drawn automatically to Avniyahu Street, where it stopped in front of Inlander's house. A woman in the building, wearing a man's faded plaid robe, opened her door a crack and peered out into the stairwell, and Hamutal was afraid she was going to talk to her or would recognize her, but the woman just followed her with a suspicious look until she disappeared from view at the top of the stairs, then slammed her door with a jangling of many keys.

There was a suffocating odor in the kitchen, and Hamutal calculated that it was almost a month since she had been in the place. She opened the windows, then went into the bedroom and lay down on the hard mattress, wondering about the scenes this room had witnessed over several decades, about Saul Inlander's parents, about his father's lovers, about his father in his loneliness, about the short, tempestuous love story between her and Saul, about the mattress that had absorbed the sweat and vitality of bodies, and now the tears. She closed her eyes and found herself talking to him silently, assuming he must be sleeping in his part of the world, and directing her words to his unconscious, crossing the ocean in her mind: How are you, there in Chicago, where rain may be falling—even now, in the middle of summer, you said—on the trees and on your wife's purple flowers? What are you doing with your sadness in that rainy city? Do you sometimes stand at the window and think about Sheraton Beach? Does having room to breathe in your foreign place sometimes assuage that sadness? You must be sleeping now, embracing your wife as you embraced me here. Are you, too, failing this exercise in separation? I still have a few questions, because our parting was so sudden. You remember that we argued about what remains when memory fades? Pain is what lasts the longest. I understood that only after you left. Are you still mourning your father? Do you know that I've been mourning our little boy for a week now? Maybe you also occasionally entertain yourself, the way I do, with that notion of taking off for New Zealand? Do you ask yourself, the way I do, if we could actually be company for each other on a road where no one was dying? Do you think of me sometimes? Do you miss me? What do you remember of all the hours we spent together? I hope you won't curse me in your final days, the way Tzippie's father cursed my mother. Issue number thirteen is ready, maybe that will interest you, my birthday is in another eight days, I'm sure you won't remember, I'll be thirty-nine, which is how old Cleopatra was when she died, I missed you so much that I read about her in the encyclopedia. The woman with the photographs went blind a few days after you left, and my mother died yesterday—that you couldn't know—and now I'm an orphan like you.

She couldn't estimate how long she had lain there. When she got up she went to the phone, dialed the number of the agent and responded to the recorded message, summoning up a decisive, official voice: "Hello, sir, I'm calling with regard to the apartment at Sixteen Avniyahu Street. The apartment is now available for rent. I understand that you have a key. Thank you."

She had second thoughts after she put the phone down, and she called again and left the phone number in Chicago, which she herself would never dare to dial. Then she walked to the door and stopped in front of it, turning

around for a parting look at the old kitchen cupboards visible through the doorway; at the living room, dark and
mysterious; at the bedroom with its door closed, preserving
what it had seen and what it had heard, soon to be entered
by new people, who would bring to it their weeping and
their sweat and their secrets.

On the last day of the week of mourning she had a call
from the old-age home her mother had been in previously.
The secretary, with fatigue and rebuke in her voice,
reminded Hamutal of her mother's possessions that had
been stored there until she got settled in the new place.
And that was almost four months ago, and if no one came
this very day to pick them up, everything in the closet
would be given to charity.

Hamutal said, "Okay, give away whatever's there," but
then thought she'd better take a look at the stored items,
that she might find a letter or some valuable document
among them. She went to a great deal of trouble to locate
the person responsible for storage and promised she would
come within the hour.

When she got there, the woman took her to the base-
ment and, dragging a large carton behind her, led her past
rows of metal cabinets until she opened one of them and
said, "See what you want to take, and put the rest in the
carton, and we'll give it to someone who needs it."

Alone in front of the open metal closet, amid dozens of
locked metal closets that looked like a morgue she'd seen
in some movie, where corpses were kept in metal drawers,
she stood and looked at dresses, most of which she didn't
recognize. At the bottom of the closet she found four pair
of shoes that had been worn, one pair that was new, and
three handbags. There was no letter or document there,

only a small zippered compartment in one of the bags that was stuffed with bus tickets and with coins no longer in use. As if paging through a book, she flipped through the dresses and blouses on hangers, some of them covered in clear plastic just as they'd come from the store. Many of them were completely new, apparently bought for some special occasion that never arrived, the way some of her own clothes had been bought when she was a child, too light in color and too fancy for everyday wear. There was never a right time to wear them, and when they were finally too small on her, her mother would go back to the store and argue with the saleswoman or the owner, who would refuse to take back a blouse that had been purchased two years earlier, even if it had never been worn, until they finally gave in to pressure—the head nurse of the local health clinic, after all—and exchanged it for another white blouse, no less elaborate, for which a sufficiently festive occasion would perhaps be found sometime in the next few years. All this time Hamutal would be standing there with downcast eyes, in the end nodding her head when the store owner, apparently taking pity on the girl, asked if she liked the blouse.

Hamutal looked at the dresses her mother had bought and never worn—the chiffon dress with the plunging neckline, the yellow dress with the train, the black dress with transparent sleeves and a slit all the way up the thigh—and thought about the woman who had bought herself dresses designed for another life, about the life she had lived in waiting. That was the way she had brought up her daughter, to feel there was no pleasure in the life lived now, because the moment of the real thing had not yet arrived. These dresses—Hamutal could not guess when her mother was intending to wear them—were heart-wrenching evidence of a spark that had remained alive in her mother, of her hope that one day the proper occasion would be found for this green chiffon or that blue one, and until that day of redemption, the dress would wait in the closet. Hamutal thought how little she had known her mother and continued to survey the dresses as if reviewing a litany of illusions.

Sudddenly her hands stopped at a dark red suit, a color her mother used to call "bordeaux." This bordeaux suit with the little sparkling buttons, like polished diamonds, she remembered immediately: her mother used to wear it sometimes when they went to the café. When people greeted her she would lean forward politely in acknowl-edgment, and the V-shaped collar would slide down, revealing some cleavage. The full skirt was nice for danc-ing, and Hamutal remembered that her mother had worn it at one of the rare parties they'd held in their home. Lots of people had been invited, many she didn't know, and after dinner the furniture was moved against the wall and the rug rolled up, and the floor bared to the dancers' feet. Her father and her mother in the bordeaux suit were the first out on the improvised dance floor, with Hamutal and Tzippie watching from a corner and giggling. Others paired off and joined the dancing couple, moving across the floor in measured tango steps, gliding here and there with grace-fully matched movements. Only her mother and her father hardly budged from their single floor tile, their back-and-forth minute and imperceptible. Now, as if viewing an old movie, Hamutal saw Tzippie's father sitting in an armchair in the corner, just a step away from them, smoking intently, sucking at the cigarette with a sensuous languor, watching her parents dance. His legs were stretched out provoca-tively in front of him, one foot riding the other, and her

mother's calves and the hem of the bordeaux skirt—
Hamutal could see it clearly—secretly brushed his feet
behind her. Fascinated by the sight, as if peeping through
a keyhole, Hamutal struggled with herself until she won
out, obliterating all memory of that dance.

She ran her hand down the weave of the bordeaux fabric, feeling a blast of warmth from it as though she were
stroking a live body, and this gave rise to a new sensation
that had apparently been repressed in the depths of her
memory. When they had come home from her father's
funeral, as soon as the door closed behind them, her
mother had gathered her up in her arms, enveloping her in
the warmth of her body, and said, "Now I have to take care
of you." She had felt a wave of resentment toward her
mother, who hadn't made much of an effort to take care of
her until then, when she was already seventeen. The feel of
the fabric had suddenly brought home to her the strength
of her tie to this woman, who even before giving birth to her
had been part of her flesh. Everything Hamutal had done
was the result of this bond that had held her life in its grip
and continued to hold it even now, after her mother's death.

She slipped the bordeaux suit off the hanger. She had no
idea what she would do with it but was not inclined to make
things difficult for herself by wondering why she had chosen this, of all the items of clothing. Folding it over her arm,
she told the woman in charge of storage, "I've left everything
in the closet, since in any case it won't fit in the carton. You
can give it all away," and heard inside her the rising echo of
Arnon's laughter: "Try the Queen of England."

Early the next morning she woke up to the faint sound of
singing, close to her ear, accompanied by embarrassed
laughter. Arnon, Hila, and Michal were standing there and

leaning over her, their heads together, singing "Happy Birthday." She tried to raise herself onto her elbows and noticed a gift they'd placed on her belly.

As she did every year, she tried to guess what it was before opening it, moving practiced fingers over the surface of the rustling wrapping paper. She enumerated her guesses one by one: a harmonica, a makeup bag, sunglasses. Only afterward was she allowed to rip the paper and discover a black leather handbag from which, to the accompaniment of laughter from the girls, she extracted a clear plastic box containing a pacifier. The image of Arnon lying on the floor and demonstrating the movements of a baby before his diaper change came to mind.

The girls left the bedroom, and before she got up for the traditional festive breakfast, she asked Arnon, "Are you all still in touch with the kibbutz pyschologist?"

"Why do you ask?" he said warily.

"I get the impression you're behaving according to instructions."

"Is that bad?"

"It's not bad."

"That's what I think."

"Did she talk to you about my mother?"

"We promised her we wouldn't talk to you about it for now."

"Why, did she scold you?"

"What for?"

"For deserting me. You left me to take care . . . "

He looked her in the eye suddenly and said, "We deserted you?"

". . . to take care of her alone."

"She didn't tell us we deserted you," he said sharply.

"But you talked about my mother?"

"Maybe."

"About what exactly?"

"I promised—"

"About the connection between her mothering and my mothering?"

He hesitated a moment. "The truth is," he began, and the hesitation in his voice testified to his seriousness, but Michal was already calling them from downstairs, inviting them to the table, and he stopped.

"What is the truth?" she said, agitated, knowing she was close to the root of it all.

"Uh . . . " The expression in his eyes had changed, and she knew that what he had intended would never be said. "The truth is that in third grade I locked her in the tractor shed for a whole night, and now I'm a little suspicious of all of her advice because I figure she must be taking revenge."

And then, as she did every year—she, too, pretending that nothing had occurred between her last birthday and this one—she put on her robe and went down and joined them in the dimmed breakfast nook, where they were already sitting around a table beautifully set with flowers and wine and lighted candles and cloth napkins rolled up in little silver rings.

After she had remarked on the beauty of the table, the four of them ate breakfast by candlelight, and Hila asked for a note to her teacher in case she got drunk, the way she had at last year's seder, and they reminisced about how Hamutal had gotten up at that seder and joined the kibbutz choir in a medley of spring songs, and out of the corner of her eye she caught Hila's face in profile, its doll-like features suddenly gone, and regretted that she'd missed out on the growth of her daughter from a child not long ago to almost a young woman now, and her heart went out to her: *mein kind.*

The girls joked about the advanced age of the guest of honor, and Hila mentioned the nursing home and then immediately apologized, and Michal said that at her age she could still have a child: look at Limor's mother, who was even more ancient and had just had twins. Only then did Hamutal say that this was her first birthday without her mother, and there was general silence until Arnon asked if he could express a wish: now that the issue was finally printed and there were no more visits to the nursing home, maybe they could usher in a "nightmare-free" era. He raised his wine glass and the girls clinked theirs against it with gusto, and Hamutal recalled Saul Inlander's parents, who had launched into a noisy quarrel over a glass that broke that way.

And all the while, doing and saying exactly what she had done and said in past years, repeating the ceremony as if it were a ritual, aware of the belabored rhythm of things, as if they had decided to force reality back on its abandoned track, she knew that this time there was a kind of heaviness inside her that a psychologist would define as mild, prolonged depression. Arnon, too, suspected its existence—if she could judge by his sidelong glances, examining her responses.

Then she saw each of them off at the door with a cursory kiss, as if they were all wary of too bold a kiss or too committed a hug. Michal called from outside, "I'll be gathering wood for the Lag b'Omer bonfire after school, so don't worry about me!" and just by her ear she thought she heard Arnon whispering, "My present is on the way. You'll get it when you're ready." And he ran out, joking: "By order of the vengeful psychologist!" Still puzzling over his words, she heard them shouting goodbyes to the dog and slamming the car doors, and their voices echoed even after they were gone.

She lingered in the house after they'd left, enjoying the quiet after their riotous departure, thinking about the hint the girls had delivered in the clear plastic box and "My present is on the way. You'll get it when you're ready." She wondered what Arnon knew about these weeks in which she had split off from him, remembered his burning eyes when he had said, just now, "We abandoned you?" and suspected that he had known everything from the first moment. Meanwhile she showered and dressed and put on makeup, astonished to see in the mirror that her faced looked the same, revealing nothing of the tribulations that had recently turned her life upside down. All the while her ears were alert. When she was finally ready to leave the house, a bit disappointed, the phone rang and her heart bounded.

"Congratulations," said a cheery voice. "I wanted to know if someone will be home in the next hour or so."

"Who's calling?"

"It's Springer, the florist. We have a bouquet ordered from abroad."

"I'm home." She dropped her briefcase.

She sat for a long time in front of the breathtaking bouquet of lilies, big as a bush, its bulbs fixed in a copper bowl, and cried, reading again and again the note that had no sender's name on it, only her name and address, and on the back a message: "Seas will not extinguish etc., and certainly not on Lag b'Omer." She was overcome by a longing that was painful to the point of suffocation, pushing up inside her chest and under her ribs. She longed for her mother, to whom she'd found a few important sentences to say only after her death, and for this man who had been a guest in her life for a brief time, like a migrating bird, and had flown away, leaving behind him memories she could share with no one else. He had hauled her to the far ends of her being, places she had no idea existed within her, where she experienced such profound sadness, such quiet joy, such bodily arousal as she had never known before him and would perhaps never know again. And now she also missed him because he was part of her last memory of her mother, and all the memories that arose during that period. Until he went away she hadn't understood how precious he was to her and how right it was for him to have come into her life. She felt compassion for both of them when she remembered that sliver of time—like the split-second of a near-accident—when the paths of their lives had intersected and they had come together for eighteen stolen days, making their way through them like two blind people crossing a busy street, believing their success depended on how firmly they grasped each other's hand. Her need to sniff his neck and touch him or see him or talk to him and let him know how grateful she was to have met him was suddenly urgent, and she was stricken with sorrow that this was the way of the world, that people understood their lives only in retrospect.

For a while she just couldn't get up and call the office to say she'd be in late; one half of her was standing beside her and mocking the other half, pointing out what a ridiculous picture she made, this thirty-nine-year-old woman sitting and clutching a note to her chest and bawling in front of a bunch of flowers.

Then she remembered how he'd chosen to take his leave, and her hands slipping inside his pants, and how she had begged him, "Stay with me until my mother dies. I don't want to be alone when she dies," as if she didn't have a husband and daughters and a cousin. She remembered the "My present is on the way. You'll get it when you're ready" and knew she had to cleave to reality, because memories brought nothing but pain. The yearning immediately turned into anger at him, for pulling her hands away from his groin, for not staying with her until her mother died the way she had stayed with him until the death of his father. At that moment she didn't want to live with a bouquet that would assault her with memories until it wilted.

With resolute hands she divided the bouquet in two, peeling the dry husks off the stems, tore the rustling sheet of cellophane and wrapped the two halves individually. Then she found two glass jars, put it all in the car, and drove to the nursing home.

Midway there she changed her mind and turned toward Avniyahu Street. Apartment five at number sixteen already—she found herself marveling—had new tenants. From the car she could see that the window frames had been painted white and mint was growing in a window box on the kitchen sill. She wondered if they had kept the bed with the hard mattress and what they had done with the copper plaque engraved with the name of Ya'akov Inlander. She pulled a flower out of one of the bouquets, greetings to the new tenants from the previous ones, got out of the car and stuck the end of the stem through the slit in the mail box, a little embarrassed at the sentimental gesture. On the mailbox it said EMMANUELA AND GAL YA'AKOBI, and she felt a flood of unexpected joy at the thought that a married couple was living here, making love with great serenity—the way it ought to be, not troubled by the kind of thoughts that rattled around in her head in the midst of the act—and then sitting together, Emmanuela and Gal Ya'akobi, in the cramped breakfast nook in a kitchen that must be the most old-fashioned in the city, drinking their mint tea and planning a trip for the fall or researching names for their baby. From the car she took another look at the bedroom window, like someone perusing a childhood photo.

Then she drove to the parking lot of the nursing home and pulled into the exact space she had parked in that first evening, and with her feet tracing the route on their own, she made her way to the fifth floor, past all the wheelchairs lined up along the walls. For a moment she imagined she saw Bertha shuffling toward her but discovered it was a woman she didn't know. When she got to the room she found in her mother's bed, like a recurrent nightmare, the woman who had lost her memory, sitting up and staring into the air with sightless eyes. The other two beds also had new occupants, white-haired women who resembled each other like sisters, and when they lifted their heads toward her she saw in their eyes the familiar spark of hope. She greeted them, went to the sink, and filled the jars with water, her every movement followed by two pair of groping eyes. She put half the flowers in one jar and took it to the window facing east, near the bed that had been occupied until recently by the woman who was stroked in shifts by her grandchildren. She put it on the sill next to the fiddle-leaf fig plant, which she had known in its infancy and which was already putting out strong, dark leaves. Then, taking another look at the woman in her mother's bed, she went across the hall and into the room where his father had lain, and where light now kindled in the eyes of two old men awake in their beds. She said hello to them, went to the window facing west, and put down the jar with the other half of the bouquet, which had retained its splendor even after being split.

Sensing someone looking at her from behind, she spun around, afraid she would see the image of her past self, sitting on that chair at the foot of her mother's bed, regarding her future self with curiosity.

The nurse's aide was standing in the doorway, beaming.

"Look who's here!" she exulted. "Too bad I wasn't thinking of a million dollars! I never in my life saw such beautiful flowers. As soon as I saw them in your mother's room, I thought about you first thing, and right away I knew you were here, in his father's room!"

Hamutal stood frozen in place, as if caught in the act.

"How are you?" she asked, for lack of anything else to say, wondering if this hearty welcome was put on, and if so, why there was any need for that now.

"I'm the same: up, down, all around. Isn't that the way it is?"

"And how did you know... that is, that I would be in this room ... "

"Oh," said the nurse's aide, and her face fell, worried. "I'm sorry if I said something I shouldn't of said."

"But how did you know?"

"Know what?" The aide was feeling her way, searching Hamutal's eyes, careful this time not to say the wrong thing, but added in any case, "How did I know that you and his son—?"

"Yes."

"I see everything that goes on here. And besides, I started it, didn't I?"

"Yes." It struck Hamutal that the nurse's aide was the only witness to what had occurred in her life during that period, and she immediately felt an attachment to her: "I have a request."

Out of the corner of her eye she noticed Bertha standing in the doorway, leaning on a walker. The top half of her body tilted forward, her neck outstretched, her eyes narrowed.

"Hello, Bertha," said Hamutal, glad to see her as if she were a favorite friend.

Bertha beckoned impatiently for her to come closer, then said in her flat voice, "No him and no her."

"Who?"

"No him and no her," she flung at her, angry at what she took to be a pretense of ignorance. "No nothing!"

"How are you doing, Bertha?" Hamutal was overcome with compassion for the lonely woman who had now given up on her and turned to go, shifting the walker along with difficulty.

"What did you want?" the aide asked Hamutal.

"Excuse me?" Hamutal's eyes were still following Bertha as she moved slowly off. Her ears echoed with "No him and no her," exactly as the words been pronounced, with neither sadness nor sympathy, defiance nor acceptance, but to register a fact—the tone of a merchant counting his inventory, of someone who has become adept at the business of parting.

"You said you had a request."

"What request?" Hamutal watched Bertha disappear from view.

"I don't know. You said before you had a request."

"Yes." Hamutal got hold of herself. "I have a request. Will you join me for coffee and cake?"

"Why not?" The aide shrugged with relief, and it was clear that she had been bracing herself for something more troubling. "Another ten minutes and I'm free as a bird, like they say."

In the cafeteria Hamutal headed straight for the table where she and Saul Inlander had sat the first time.

"So he left, hmmm?" The aide didn't lift her gaze from her fingers, which were tearing open a packet of sweetener.

"Yes."

"It started when I yelled to you to tell him to bring the diapers for his father, right?"

"Yes." It was becoming clear to Hamutal why she had been drawn back to the nursing home.

"With the Super Maxi everything was leaking out, poor guy."

"Yes."

"So are you sorry I told you to tell him about the diapers?"

"I don't think so."

"I didn't feel like going out, there was an awful wind, and I saw you leaving, so—"

"You don't have to apologize, really you don't."

"Well, if I didn't say that back then, maybe nothing would have happened."

"That's right. But I'm not sorry at all. Just that it's a little . . . you know . . . when it ended . . . "

"In this life you eat a little honey and you drink a little vinegar." The aide had understood immediately. "But a hurting heart is better than a dead heart, don't you think? Sadness comes and sadness goes, but the memories— that's what stays with you in the end."

"Right." Hamutal was impressed by the lyricism in the crude formulation, aware that this was the last place in the world to talk about the virtues of memory.

"But because your mother was here and his father was

here, maybe it was easier for you . . . You know, sometimes my sister comes to visit me and I start telling her about this place, and she doesn't understand a thing. From the questions she asks, she doesn't know which end is up. This place is another planet. If you don't set foot in here, you can't understand. The most normal people, as soon as they get here, something cuckoo comes over them."

"What, for instance?" Hamutal asked, eager to learn something about herself and what had happened to her in this place.

"All of a sudden their lives take a thousand-degree turn to the right, a thousand-degree turn to the left. And they do things they didn't dream of doing before. You and him, because you were both here, understood each other right away. Just that it's not such a good place to meet someone."

"No?"

"Of course not. It's a place where people come to die, your mother, his father, the wheelchairs, the diapers—it's not the place to make a relationship. In the whole five floors here, you can go looking from room to room with a flashlight and you won't find half an ounce of love. So now it's over, and maybe that's the way it had to end. That's what I say: whatever has to happen, happens. God is smarter than people, don't you think? And besides, no use resisting here, Mr. Universe and his muscles couldn't do a thing for you."

Hamutal, intrigued, said, "I think you're very right."

"Exactly. And you don't have to be so sorry. The tide comes in, the tide goes out. You have something to go back to. I saw your husband and your daughters. Nice family."

"Yes, I have something to go back to."

"Good-looking guy, your husband, and nice. He was joking with me about something, I can't remember what."

"Yes, he likes to laugh."

"So go back to him, he'll make you laugh, take away the sorryness."

Hamutal looked at the aide, who was studying the filling in the apple cake. "You're very nice," she said, crooning as she would to a beloved child.

"Thank you very much," said the other, biting into the cake. "Full of pieces of the whatsit in the apple. You're nice, too."

Hamutal suddenly felt an urgent need to touch her, to hug her, but since she couldn't do that, she quickly opened the zippered pocket of her briefcase, took out the bracelet of hammered gold, and put it in front of the plate of cake.

"Excuse me for not wrapping it. I want to give you this. From me, and on behalf of my mother, as a memento."

Her mouth open for the last bit of cake, the aide looked at the bracelet.

"Isn't that the one that was your mother's, that they almost stole from her?"

"Yes."

"It's made of real gold, isn't that what you told me?"

"Yes. But I'm not going to wear it. And you said it was beautiful."

"Oh my God!" The aide was beside herself, looking at the bracelet but not touching it. "A gold bracelet! Nobody here ever gave me a present like that."

Hamutal picked up the bracelet and slipped it onto the aide's wrist. The aide rotated it slowly, holding her forearm out, then moving it up to her eyes.

"No." She suddenly slid it off, and the bracelet rocked, clanking on the Formica, then lay still. "My husband will be thinking I did who-knows-what to get this. He already heard stories. Next thing he'll think I stole it. No, I can't."

"I'll write you a letter." Hamutal was already opening

her briefcase and taking out a notebook. "And I'll put down my phone number, in case he wants to ask anything." She put pen to paper and lifted her head.

"I don't know your name." She suddenly remembered "Seems I should be allowed to know your name at this point."

"Dina," the aide laughed. "But here they call me Nurse, they don't rack their brains remembering."

"To Dina," Hamutal wrote, sticking with the usual formula, "the nicest nurse's aide in the department. Thank you for your devoted care of my mother. Hamutal Naor."

"I really don't know what to tell you." The aide's eyes let go of the bracelet and made their way over to Hamutal. "You're so sad and all, and I'm happy because of your bracelet."

Hamutal returned the notebook to her briefcase. "That's how it is in life, no? Now it's your turn for honey."

"I'll share the honey with you. You had enough vinegar with him."

Hamutal gave her an affectionate look, and probed to see if that sentence reflected her good sense. "Why? Did he look sour to you?"

"Sour isn't the word for it. Two hours with him and you need something for heartburn."

Hamutal laughed, and the aide looked at her in a new way.

"You're prettier when you laugh, believe me. People don't laugh enough. If you laugh a lot in your lifetime you don't end up in a nursing home so fast."

"We never got a chance to talk, and now I'm almost sorry that I won't be coming back here and won't see you again."

"It's a good thing you have no more reason to come here, believe me." She turned serious suddenly and there were lines at the sides of her mouth that made her look older. "It's not nice to say, but they'd be better off dead, every one of them."

"You see a lot here, hmmm?"

"Millions of stories." The aide lifted her chin toward the ceiling and rolled her eyes; the momentary melancholy had left her. "I told my husband, 'I don't need television and I don't need trips abroad and I don't need newspapers. All the stories in the world come to my department.'" She smiled and gave Hamutal a sidelong glance. "You know what he said to me?"

"I have no idea."

"Yes you do. Men are all the same, right away they think of themselves. He said to me: 'Maybe you don't need me either?'"

Hamutal laughed. "What did you tell him?"

"Me," she said, stroking the bracelet with her fingers, "if I say one wrong word, that's the end of me, he won't let me work the night shift. I said: 'You're what I need most in the world. You're my sun, you're my light.'"

"And it's not true?"

"Of course not. If it was true, you think I'd be running over here to wipe old people's backsides? I'd sit tight in his house, shining, polishing, looking at him all day long."

She was forthright in a childlike way, with no attempt to prettify her words or fool herself: the whole sad story of her life was contained in that one sentence, and that moved Hamutal and saddened her more than she might have expected. If there weren't other people around, she thought, she would just put her head on that sturdy shoulder and cry like a baby.

"Wow, I have to get home now. I've already missed a few buses." Dina the nurse's aide got up, cake crumbs raining down around her. "Right away he looks at his watch and thinks who knows what. We'll see what he says about the

bracelet. Really, thanks such a million for the bracelet."
Then she fell silent and looked at Hamutal, who was still
sitting, her arms loosely encircling the tray with the watermelon pattern.

"Come on, come on, everything's okay." Her voice took
on the tone she used in the department as she gently but
firmly reached under Hamutal's arm and pulled her up.
"Let's get out of here. And don't come back. You have to
pick up your life, forget what you don't have to remember.
And you, too, they must be waiting for you at home. Come
on, we all like to go where someone's waiting for us."

**The dream of Hamutal Naor, editor of a psychology journal, married
and the mother of two, on the night of her thirty-ninth birthday,
eight days after her own mother died.**

The woman dreams that she is entering a busy playground. Most of
the children are accompanied by a grandfather or grandmother. In a corner of the playground is a colorful ice-cream truck playing the sweet
melody of a street organ. The woman walks around among the people
and the play equipment and wants to get on the roundabout, but it
already has a tight circle of children on it. She stops the roundabout with
a touch of her finger, and the children quickly slide off it. She gets on
the empty roundabout and lots of children and adults volunteer to spin
her. They all run at the same pace and she's very happy.

Suddenly the playground empties: adults, children, the ice-cream
man, and even the flowers and trees and birds all disappear. The roundabout stops. She wants to get off, but she's quickly getting smaller and
can't release the safety latch with her fingers. She shouts, "Mommy,
Mommy," and the echo of a man's voice answers her.

She feels that her limbs are growing and she's getting taller and
stronger, and can now get off easily. She reaches for the safety latch and
sees that her hands are wrinkled and full of dark age spots and realizes
that now she has turned into an old woman. She can't get off anymore
without help. She sits down on the wooden bench of the roundabout to
wait until she becomes a child again and then a strong young woman,

so that she will be able to get off. Meanwhile she's not frightened at all, just sits patiently, looking around and waiting for the right time. On a nearby swing sits a skeleton peering at her with curiosity. He seems to be rummaging in his memory, and she says to him right away. "It's me, Hamutal."

He looks at her for a long time and says, "When are you going to quit that 'I'm Hamutal,' 'It's me, Hamutal' business? People are sick of hearing 'It's me, Hamutal,' 'It's me, Hamutal'. As soon as you came in here, everybody ran away. Even the trees ran away. Everybody knows you're Hamutal. Now let's have some peace and quiet for a change."